Lancaster bomber pilot Wally Mann and his six crew members undertake what they hope will be their final bomb run – a risky air raid on Berlin. Meanwhile, in Germany, a young Messerschmitt fighter pilot grieves for his parents, killed beneath a shower of Allied bombs in Cologne. And he wants revenge . . .

"A screamingly taut narrative that carries a burden of sensitive reflection." – *The New York Times*

"Dunmore has, with extraordinary skill, woven technical details of the opposing aircraft, their tactics, the words, fighting skills and the hidden thoughts of ten human beings hurtling toward their destinies in the dark." – *Calgary Herald*

"Taut, nerve-plucking story." – *Los Angeles Herald-Examiner*

"I will buy **Bomb Run**." – Len Deighton

ALSO BY SPENCER DUNMORE

SPENCER DUNMORE

Bomb Run

An M&S Paperback from
McClelland & Stewart Inc.
The Canadian Publishers

To my Parents

An M&S Paperback from McClelland & Stewart Inc.

First printing January 1991
Cloth edition printed 1971

Canadian Cataloguing in Publication Data

Dunmore, Spencer, 1928-
Bomb run

"An M&S paperback".
ISBN 0-7710-2925-X

1. World War, 1939-1945 – Fiction. I. Title.

PS8557.U54B6 1991 C813'.54 C90-095160-5
PR9199.3.D8B6 1991

Cover design by K.T. Njo
Cover illustration by Wes Lowe

Printed and bound in Canada

McClelland & Stewart Inc.
The Canadian Publishers
481 University Avenue
Toronto, Ontario
M5G 2E9

THE CREW

Pilot: Walter Mann,
Flying Officer, RAF

Navigator: Paul J. Taylor,
Flying Officer RCAF

Bomb-aimer: Douglas Griffith,
Sergeant, RAF

Flight engineer: Harold R. Whittaker,
Sergeant, RAAF

Wireless operator: Charles D. Newton,
Warrant Officer, RAF

Mid-upper gunner: Philip A. Ross,
Sergeant, RAF

Rear gunner: Leonard Green,
Sergeant, RAF

1

They scrubbed it.

But, being them, they waited until the aircraft had been bombed up, until the crews had been briefed and bundled into kapok and fleece and transported through the rain to the dispersals, until the engines had been run up and the let's-bloody-well-get-it-over-with vibrations were drumming through networks of alloy transverse members and longitudinal stringers, until the aircraft had waddled out on slender oleo legs, bellies heavy with high explosive and incendiary, along the perimeters ...

Then, a queue. A queue of Lancasters at the end of the runway, all awaiting take-off permission that didn't come. Why? Definitely something up. But what? Eyes studied the darkness. Had someone pranged? If so, it was the most discreet prang imaginable. Nothing to be seen of it. Rum do.

An Austin van splashed along the peri-track. Stopped by the control hut. Out bustled someone in peaked cap plus scrambled eggs. Wearing a mac. Scores of eyes watched him through water-beaded perspex. He vanished into the hut. The black-and-white striped door slammed behind him. Importantly.

More waiting.

Then: it was off. Scrubbed. Just like that. Pack up shop. Go and find some other way of spending the evening, chaps; you aren't required to bomb Berlin after all. Frustration mingled with relief. Pleasant knowing you would definitely be alive tomorrow morning, unpleasant knowing that all the pre-op agonies were for naught and that you would have to go through it all again, the next night perhaps. A slightly sour feeling. Some men said it was the same feeling you got when you'd made love so badly that you wished you hadn't made love at all.

He woke suddenly. Alert, startled out of his sleep, he peered into the darkness, listening. No sound. Nothing. The whole place was dead. He closed his eyes and lay still for a minute. No use; he was thoroughly awake. Irritably he twisted on to his back and looked at the ceiling he couldn't see. Blast! What was the time? He groped for his watch and squinted, trying to interpret the luminous glow of the hands. Ten past four or twenty past two? In either case, hell's bells!

Furiously awake now—it would be the very devil of a job to drop off again—he threw back the blankets and grimaced as his feet touched the linoleum floor. Better to get up, move around, look outside. He tugged his red-and-white striped gown off the chair and padded across to the window. Holding the blackout curtain aside, he could discern between the protective strips of adhesive tape the corner of the main mess building and the path leading from the station's main road. Still damp. Hardly surprising that They had cancelled the op. Stupid of Them to call for one in the first place. Ah—someone moving! Clump of boots. Regular, very military. Probably the SPs doing their stuff, guarding against the fearful possibility of an airman consorting with a WAAF beneath an HM Government roof.

He sat on George Tompkins's bed and lit a cigarette. George Tompkins hadn't slept in the bed for several nights, nor would he ever sleep in it again; for George had taken a Lanc for an air-test last week and something had gone wrong with the power just as he came unstuck. One wing hit the ground, the aircraft cartwheeled and blew up. There was little left of it or the air crew or the four ground crew who had gone along for the ride. No one had had a chance. But wait—that wasn't correct; there was always a chance. Remember the famous story of the rear gunner who discovered that his turret wasn't working; neither was the intercom—and what had happened to the engine noise? Besides which the aircraft seemed to be behaving in an alarmingly erratic manner. The gunner's escape door was jammed; he could do nothing but sit it out. Which is what he did. After a while there was a gentle bump. Silence. He looked out. A German soldier appeared; he seemed astonished. A moment later the gunner saw why. Helped out of his turret, he found that there was no aeroplane. The tail unit, including the turret, had been blown off and had glided down to a gentle landing all by itself.

It was a well-worn story; possibly it had some root in truth. In any event, it was the sort of story airmen remembered and repeated; proof that there was always a chance. Always. All you needed was lots and lots of lovely luck. Hadn't there once been a Spitfire pilot who baled out only to discover his parachute was full of holes and hadn't he tumbled down, down, down to certain death only to land in a huge snow-drift? And hadn't he lived? Hadn't he? Everyone said he had.

Poor old George. A cheerful type. A fellow Londoner. Good room-mate except for an occasional groan in his sleep.

'Groan? Me? Don't believe a word of it. You're making it up, Wally old son. Why should I groan in my sleep? I have lovely dreams. Lovely and dirty. Lots of fun.'

Before George there had been Jim Lowe in this bed. A quiet Kentish man, Jim had completed his tour of ops and had gone to a training job. Thankfully. 'The first dozen ops are the worst,' Jim Lowe had, said. 'After that, they go surprisingly quickly.'

One more trip. Say it loudly but silently. One more trip.

Perhaps in twenty-four hours it would be over and done with. Perhaps that was the reason he had woken so abruptly. Perhaps at that very moment Bomber Harris was planning a big show and perhaps Bomber Harris's brain and Flying Officer Walter Mann's brain were on the same wave-length and perhaps the Air Marshal's thoughts had hurtled across the ether to jar Flying Officer Mann from his sleep in far-off Brocklington, East Yorkshire ...

The cigarette tasted awful. Why did he light it? Hadn't he learnt from past experience that cigarettes tasted absolutely bloody until one had had breakfast or at least a cup of tea? He stumbled around in the darkness looking for an ash-tray.

One more trip.

They'd scrubbed two in a row. The bastards. Once they'd scrubbed an op after everyone had taken off. Bastards.

One more trip, then a deliciously long end-of-tour leave. With Ann. It had to be with Ann. She had to get her leave at the same time. It was imperative.

His feet were becoming chilled.

An engine started. Not an aircraft engine; MT of some description. Who was driving anywhere at this hour? A clandestine trip, perhaps: someone nipping down to the hangars to steal hundred-octane for sale on the black market. Profitable but dangerous. A corporal had been nabbed mixing the stuff with paraffin; he was said to have received ten years' hard labour for his trouble. The sentencing officer said the corporal was lucky not to have been shot, considering that merchant seamen died bringing fuel to Britain. All very true, of course, but what airman hadn't seen hundred-octane being used to wash the oil from hangar floors in preparation for visits by AOCs?

He considered putting on the light and reading. But after some thought he decided he didn't want to read. Soon he would be cold and longing for the warmth of his bed.

Possibly the driver of the jeep or lorry was speeding towards a passionate encounter with one of the local village belles. But did Brocklington have any belles? If so, they were kept out of sight. The Brocklingtonians were a pink-cheeked, stocky, sturdy lot. Healthy but cheerless, the sort of folk one would expect to see inhabiting a village of no-nonsense houses and two funereal pubs, clustered around

4

a cobbled square, everything in grey stone—righteous look-ing stuff. Rumour had it that one of the councillors was run-ning a brothel in a house behind the Methodist church. Doubt-ful ... brothels were few and far between in Yorkshire in 1944; this wasn't France in 1917. No lines of shamefaced Tommies waiting to spend their francs on a couple of minutes of assembly-line sex with some over-worked French whore. (Rest assured, madam, that no effort is being spared to make this a Hygienic War; your son/husband/father/brother/uncle/nephew will be in a Sanitary Condition when he is re-turned to you, or buried, whichever is applicable.)

Wally was not fond of Brocklington, though sometimes he walked its streets simply to be among civilians and to look into shops. On warm days he sat in the grass by the canal. Once, an eight-year-old girl had sat beside him and demanded to know what he was doing. Just watching the water go by, he told her. She accepted this; then she wanted to know if he flew a Spitfire. He said no, sorry, he did nothing so glamorous. Abruptly she grinned and told him it was all right. He chuckled; she burst into laughter. For the first time in his life Wally wanted to hold a child in his arms. Instead, he took her hand—it was sticky and not very clean—and solemnly shook it and she laughed again and ran a dozen yards and stopped and waved before disappearing around a corner.

How would it be to have a child of one's own? He thought of Ann. Would she ever bear his child? He smiled; it sounded as though she might bring it in on a silver charger. Back to bed.

The first thing to do was to get out of this particular line of work. Right? He snuggled down between the sheets. Bloody right. He considered the coming day. It might turn out to be a day of pottering, if the weather was bad enough. More like-ly, however, was a spot of Military Activity. The powers that be were bursting to send everyone out to bomb things.

One more trip.

The crew of G-George had survived thirty-two operational sorties. A minor miracle. What made it even more miraculous was the fact that the original crew was still intact. No one had missed a single trip. The same seven: Wally, Paul, Douglas, Harry, Charlie, Phil, Len. Not a scratch between them after thirty-two trips. Small wonder the new bods regarded them with awe. They'd been lucky. But what was luck? Attempting to calculate your chances mathematically was a sure way to drive yourself around the bend. You could take the squadron losses for, say, a year. Easy enough. Then you could work out the average per sortie. Then you could apply this to the number of sorties you had to do to complete your tour. According to your calculations you would go for a Burton after about a dozen ops. Not too encouraging. But weren't there other considerations? The efficiency of one crew compared with another, for instance? A sprog crew was surely much more likely to buy it than a crew who'd been around awhile. True enough. The statistics proved it. The loss ratios were lower for crews with twenty to thirty ops. The 'professional attitude' counted, according to the Wingco. He presumably regarded G-George's crew as professionals. Professionalism *was* one of the reasons they kept coming back; the other reason was that they had been bloody lucky. No matter how professional you were you couldn't do anything about flak clobbering your fuel tank and blowing you to kingdom come. Or a motor conking out on take-off. George Tompkins probably considered himself pretty professional.

Wally was fond of flying but he recognized that it was dangerous at the best of times, downright suicidal at others. Although G-George was a terrific kite it was subject to an incredible number of ailments and frighteningly vulnerable to attack. Its hide was paper-thin; it carried hundreds of gallons of highly inflammable fuel and tons of explo-

6

sive in the form of bombs and ammunition. The tiniest of wounds could destroy it; the smallest of errors could kill its crew. Norman Livesey had put it well: 'We're all quite mad to go up in those things,' he had declared one evening in the Mess. 'When I'm dashing down the runway full of petrol and bombs my brain tells me, "Of course you will soar into the air. It's all worked out in advance. The velocities of the airflow over the upper and lower surfaces of the wing are unequal because of the wing's shape, faster over the upper surface than over the lower surface. Low static pressure accompanies high velocity pressure. Thus the fluid pressure acting on the upper surface is lower than the pressure acting on the lower surface. This lower static pressure results in a net force acting upwards." Lift, gentlemen! We all know that perfectly well. Good heavens, we are civilized, technical individuals. I know the aircraft will fly! I know it from past experience; I've seen it fly; I've flown it myself. And yet every instinct handed down to me from every one of my miserable ancestors screams at me and tells me I'm absolutely round the bend to think that a great big chunk of metal is actually going to fly off the ground and go soaring into the air. No, it's going to go smack into those trees at the end of the runway and serve me bloody well right for thinking it's going to do anything else!'

Make it a milk-run, thought Wally. We deserve a milk-run: quick jaunt over the French coast, drop the bombs on anything reasonably military and beetle back. Modest beat-up of the field (nothing dangerous, of course) then a copybook three-pointer. Taxi to dispersal, to pats on the back from the ground wallahs and the lads from the other crews. Rude remarks and envious glances. And considerable relief from Squadron Leader Owen Pinkerton, DSO, DFC. Poor Owen; he'll finally be getting rid of the One Who Thinks Wrong Things.

He closed his eyes.

He wanted to stop killing people.

2

The weather reports were encouraging. The high-pressure system was finally on the move again; and this time it looked as though it might be good enough to keep moving. Already temperatures were dropping; soon the mist and drizzle of the past weeks should begin to clear.

At Bomber Command they considered the targets and weighed the priorities. Everyone from Churchill down wanted places bombed. There were military targets, morale targets, tactical targets, strategic targets. The mixture was important and it all had to be co-ordinated with the Americans' efforts. The Americans by day, the British by night: round-the-clock bombing to soften and sap the enemy for the invasion that was only a matter of weeks away.

The Commander-in-Chief of Bomber Command had a formidable weapon at his disposal: some sixteen hundred heavy bombers, principally Lancasters and Halifaxes plus some outdated Stirlings and even more outdated Wellingtons. An aerial army, his command consisted of several divisions, called 'groups'. Each group was responsible for about three hundred and fifty aircraft divided among squadrons, eighteen to a squadron. Each squadron consisted of two 'flights', nine aircraft to a flight. Each Lancaster and Halifax was flown by a crew of seven airmen. The Lancasters carried up to twenty-two thousand pounds of bombs; the Halifaxes carried up to thirteen thousand pounds.

For a variety of reasons, Berlin was to be on the evening's programme. Poor weather had restricted attacks on the German capital for too long. The place had to be hit,

hit hard; a sizable effort; at least one group.

Subordinates began working out the details.

Starched tablecloths, marmalade in glass platters, tea-cups and saucers and a room full of thoroughly nice people, male and female, mostly very young, many beautiful: pleasant people who did unpleasant things. Admirable people, courageous people, splendid people, blue-clad people: a club of some exclusiveness, dedicated to the unsavoury business of dropping high explosive and incendiaries from great heights on to shops and houses and factories and people ...

Wally drank his tea. Belt up, he told himself. He listened as Paul argued with Fred Sanderson about the delicacy of the situation that would be created when the Russians and British-American armies met—if the latter ever got around to invading the Continent. Fred Sanderson said the Russians wouldn't stop marching west once they had started. Paul didn't agree; the Russians had had enough of war; besides, they were our friends; they could be trusted. Good old Paul. Paul liked people. And trusted them. Even Russians. Even mad old artists. Wally lit a cigarette and sighed the smoke away towards the ceiling. Of all the pleasant people, Paul was surely one of the pleasantest. Before joining the RCAF, he had been in advertising art in Toronto; now he was G-George's navigator. A good navigator, Paul. A good artist too; a gentle fellow; fate should have found him something better to do for his country. Paul dreamt of being a fine artist; he spent his spare time with a surly old blighter in the village, apparently the greatest thing since Rembrandt ...

Wally saw Ann. She came in with her friend Lillibeth Armstrong (Lillibeth of the horsy chin). She saw him the moment she entered the Mess but she didn't nod or wave or even smile. Ann knew what was done and what wasn't.

WAAF officers were definitely brother officers in spite of being sisters. WAAF officers were to be treated with all the respect and courtesy due any brother officer. But no more. Warmer feelings simply didn't exist, officially. You exchanged good mornings with all the fervour of one undertaker greeting another. Cool, casual, positively antiseptic. But eyes met and spoke and said private things. A delicious game: An I'd-love-to-make-obscene-advances-to-you tossed across the sugar and salt and porridge. An I-might-not-object-too-violently-if-you-did in return. She sat two tables away and she talked to Lillibeth Armstrong; still, somehow, she managed to communicate with him and transmit joy to him. He smiled to himself. A girl in God knows how many million, was Ann. Not incredibly beautiful: mouth a trifle large, forehead a mite too broad, yet marvellously feminine. Indeed her femininity seemed accentuated by the battledress she wore. The sheer contrast did it: Ann's face had no business emerging from a uniform of any description, certainly not one with a collar and tie. Hair light-brown, eyes a soft blue-green, delightful ear lobes. Wally had known her three months; now it was hard to imagine life without her. Love? Possibly, disturbing as the notion was. In any event it was important to keep such things to oneself. If officialdom discovered that Flying Officer Mann and Section Officer Strickland were having more than a passing fancy for one another it was absolutely certain that Flying Officer Mann or Section Officer Strickland or both would be posted elsewhere. Post haste.

He finished his cigarette. Eyes met and said '*Au revoir*', in an instant. Interlude concluded. He touched Paul's shoulder and said 'See-you-later' to which Paul winked a North American acknowledgement without interrupting his argument with Fred Sanderson.

From the window the Lancasters looked cold and damp, squatting back on their haunches, shivering under their tarpaulins. Frightful weather—and yet there was a lightness in the grey to the west. Perhaps, perhaps ...

'We're on tonight,' said Pinkerton, thumping himself down behind his desk. 'Briefing at fifteen hundred.'

'Where to this time?' Wally asked, knowing full well what the answer would be.

'You'll find out at briefing.' The standard answer.

Pinkerton picked up his telephone and banged the cradle: a monotonously impatient movement that sounded like morse. Pinkerton was twenty-eight years old; he looked forty. Now, mid-way through his third tour of operations, he had a DSO and a DFC. He was a first-class bomber pilot and flight leader. Wally respected him. Too bad it was so much harder to respect what Pinkerton had done in his two and a half tours.

In the distance a Merlin exploded into life. It roared for a moment then relaxed to a steady rumble. Ops. The day would follow a familiar pattern. Assemble the crew. Check on the kite. Do a thorough night-flying test—no matter that the kite had been tested the night before; repeat it; the CO liked his crews to leave the ground as frequently as possible. Briefing. Waiting. Then, away ... if They didn't scrub it. Pinkerton kept bellowing into his phone. Something about serviceability. Duquette came into the Flight Office. A French Canadian, Duquette had done six ops. He said the weather was supposed to clear. Then he said that his kite had gone U/S the day before.

'Port inner. Revs all balled up. Wouldn't synchronize. I don't know whether they've got it fixed yet.'

Did he hope the ground crew would have his port inner fixed in time or did he hope they wouldn't? Wally conjectured that Duquette probably wasn't sure himself.

'Weren't you George Tompkins's room-mate? I saw him prang, you know. He damn nearly hit a couple of houses.

Thank God he just missed them. Anyway, he was blown to hell. He lost an engine just after coming unstuck.'

'It doesn't happen very often,' Wally observed.

'Once is enough,' said Duquette with a sad smile. 'Say, isn't this your last op?'

Wally nodded. 'When we get around to flying it.'

'Great,' said Duquette, 'really great. I hope it's a milk-run. Gee, it's nice to know guys really do go thirty ops.'

'You'll soon be doing your last one.'

'My kite won't hold together for thirty ops,' said Duquette. 'It's been around a hell of a time, you know. Tim Reilly's crew finished their tour in her. She's due for the scrap-heap.'

'Tell Owen about it,' said Wally. 'He doesn't want you to fly a kite you don't have confidence in.'

'I sure as hell don't have confidence in that bucket.'

Duquette's nerves were in bad shape and he was finding fault with his aircraft. It often happened that way. The kite just wasn't handling properly ... difficult to put one's finger on the precise problem but something definitely amiss ... too many creaks ... sounds of imminent structural failure ... well, damn it, tails and wings had been known to part company with aircraft, hadn't they?

Wally thought them the bravest of all, the pilots who coped with such fears yet still went on, op after op. The tragedy was, in so many cases they were a menace to their own crews. Sometimes, mercifully, the MO would step in and there would be a discreet posting. But too often it was a case of continuing to fly until something irreparable happened. Example: the Lancaster that returned from Bremen had made a good landing—but on the canal to the east of the village instead of on the runway. The aircraft flipped over and exploded; everyone died. It might have been written off as an unfortunate error but for the fact that, during the landing approach, the pilot told the tower that his navigator and bomb-aimer were telling him not to land but he didn't trust them; he knew better ...

'I'll talk to Owen when he gets off the phone,' said Duquette.

'Good man,' said Wally. He went outside. Yes, the weather was clearing. He made his way along the path towards the hangars. Soon he would have to collect the crew. For the last time. He hoped. The little bubble of excitement pranced around in his stomach. A familiar pre-op friend, companion for all day, the bubble would vanish during take-off to be replaced by boredom, anxiety, fright, sometimes stark terror.

A-Apple stood forlornly near No. 1 hangar. The wreckers (nasty little men with beady eyes and mean mouths) were dismembering her. They had ripped out her engines; now they pecked at her instruments. Soon they would tear her wings and tail off, leaving only the shell of her. Shame! A-Apple had brought her crew back on three engines—two and a half, according to the skipper. Clanking like an ancient railway engine, emitting alarming puffs of black smoke, one undercarriage leg dangling uselessly, one rudder almost totally gone, A-Apple kept flying; stout-hearted lady, she kept going until there was no need for her to go any more. Harsh, for the technical bods to examine her and declare that she must be struck off charge. Now she was submitting to the final indignity.

Wally looked out across the airfield. Acres of flat, windy, miserable countryside; bleak, unlovely buildings—and still the peculiar magic of flight and flyers kept working. There was delight in the settling of a Lanc, flaps down, main wheels and tail wheel in perfect geometry, all twenty tons ready to kiss the tarmac in a Landing As It Should Be Done. Aeroplanes were fascinating things, metal clad, fabric clad; they had beautiful parts: propellers and wings and canopies, formed by function. The audacity of the whole business never ceased to fascinate: the little man-made worlds rattling bravely into the air, kept aloft by precarious balancing of forces, a waggling of surfaces to direct streams of air, blind faith in flimsy structures ...

Don't scrub this one, he thought. Let me get it over and done with. Please. And afterwards? Afterwards, everyone would get blotto. A party of heroic proportions. Even Douglas would get paralysed. Innocent Douglas. Had he ever been drunk? It was about time. Another question: should he invite Ann? Or should it be restricted to crew members? He wondered; he would ask her about it. She would know; she had a fine sensitivity for such matters. Dear Ann. Am I going to marry you, Ann? Are we going to live together? Share the same bathroom? Use the same towels? Ah, but this was no time to think of it. After-wards was the time. After the trip ...

He watched as an Oxford banked and slid down to a neat landing.

And then he knew he was going to die.

Like a cold wind, the realization simply enveloped him.

Numbed, he stood still; at once, in awful clarity, the scene burst upon him, the elements springing into position like props in a fiendish play: left stage, the aircraft, a blazing skeleton of ribs and struts; the pilot, centre stage, lying on blackened grass, a charred gargoyle staring unseeingly at the sky, pipe-like stubs of arms reaching out for help that would never ever come ...

He stepped back, hands instinctively rising to shield his face from the heat.

But there was no heat. No burning aircraft. No cremated pilot—just the Oxford turning noisily off the runway.

'Oh God,' he said aloud. He felt weak, sick, as though someone had struck him unexpectedly. Sweat broke on his forehead and chilled in the winter air. He wanted to run and hide. The desire was almost irresistible; he had to force

14

himself to stand still and pretend to watch the Oxford. An erk walked by and glanced at him curiously. Someone laughed a short distance away: an explosive, generous laugh.

He looked down at the loose gravel at his feet. There—there was reality: the gravel existed; he could feel it, touch it. He swallowed. God, what a hell of a thing. Scared to death ... *I saw myself dead. That was me, done to a turn.* God ... He kept on saying, God.

Now there was a short compact figure at his side, a figure in dark Australian air-force blue: Harry Whittaker, G-George's flight engineer.

'Hello there, skipper. We're on tonight, aren't we?'

He wanted to know what time briefing was, whether Wally had any idea of the target, when the air-test would take place. Wally found himself answering the questions carefully, thoughtfully. He thought it rather admirable of himself to answer the questions so carefully and thoughtfully. And when he had answered them, he wanted Harry to go away. But Harry lingered, hands in pockets, toeing the gravel, curiously ill at ease. He seemed to be thinking of the best way to say whatever it was he had to say. Then, abruptly, aggressively, he kicked a small stone at the WAAF lavatory and said: 'Skipper, I want to ask you something. Do you know Greening? The MO?'

Yes, Wally knew Greening, the MO.

'I mean, *personally*. Do you know him personally?'

Yes, Wally knew Greening personally, personally enough to say good morning, personally enough to consider him a sanctimonious twerp.

For God's sake, Harry, just because I'm not saying it out loud doesn't mean I don't want you to go away somewhere. Anywhere.

'I've got a sort of a ... problem, skipper.'

15

You too, eh, Harry?

'You see ...' He scratched his left eyebrow; fair hair
tumbled over his forehead; he was handsome in a boyishly
robust way. 'You remember that seventy-two-hour pass we
had a couple of weekends ago? I went to London. I met a
girl at the Palais. We danced a bit ... you know. She was
nice. And, well, I took her home. To Leytonstone. From
Hammersmith. Cost me five bloody pounds.'

Five bloody pounds. Wally nodded but none of it made
any sense. Why wouldn't Harry go away? Why didn't
Harry realize that his problem was a minor event compared
with his skipper's? A chap didn't *really* have a problem
until he had been informed in no uncertain terms that he
would get the chop.

But Harry kept mumbling on. Something about getting
to Leytonstone and being invited in for a cup of cocoa and
realizing that there was no way to get back to town, and
then being offered a night's rest on the Put-U-Up in the
front room.

'Well, she went away and got sheets and blankets,' Harry
said, 'and then she came back and I got put up all right. But
I didn't enjoy it,' he hastened to add.

Wally wondered dimly what that had to do with it.

'Anyway, she's in trouble now,' said Harry.

'Oh dear,' said Wally inadequately. He thought, If you
go for a Burton with me you won't have a thing to worry
about.

Harry said, 'I was going to see Greening. Then I got
talking to one of the orderlies. He said Greening was a
bit sticky about things like that; he'd suggest things for
officers but not for sergeants. You see, we've got to do
something now; it's important to do it early on, isn't it?'

Wally looked at him. 'I really don't know,' he said. 'I'm
lucky, I suppose. I've never been faced with the problem.'

And never will be.

16

'I thought you might speak to him, skipper.'

To Greening? Oh God, Harry. Is that what you mean? Yes, that obviously is precisely what you mean. Pleading eyes.

'Well, you know him personally, skipper. You see him all the time in the Officers' Mess. So I thought you wouldn't mind asking him over a beer or something. Would you, skipper?'

Harry. Blast your eyes, Harry. A shrug. 'All right.' He supposed it was the least one could do for one's flight engineer on one's last day. A thought: 'But aren't you married, Harry?'

Harry nodded. 'That's what makes it so bloody lousy.' It was as though he was talking about something over which he had never had the smallest degree of control. He patted his pocket. 'I got a letter from Dorothy this morning. I can't read it. I can't even ruddy open it.' He shook his head. 'I've written to her. Twice. It wasn't hard at all. But I just can't read her letter. Funny, isn't it?'

Funny as hell. Wally wished Harry would go away. Why did Harry persist in thanking him for the miracles of persuasion he was going to perform on Greening? Mental memo: Better talk to Greening today because there may not be a tomorrow for you, chum.

Christ, Wally Mann, you don't *believe* that?

Don't I? No, I suppose I don't. No. I definitely don't. And yet ... it was something terribly real, frighteningly urgent ...

Suddenly more people: the crew, gathering around him: Phil, the mid-upper gunner, Len, the rear gunner, Doug, the bomb-aimer, Charlie, the wireless op, assembling in their casually efficient way, knowing what was to be done, wanting only to be told when.

Christ, Wally Mann, are you going to kill them all?

3

RAF Brocklington geared itself for action. All outside telephone calls were cancelled; only a privileged few persons were permitted to pass through the main gate. Everyone on the station reacted to the ops-on signal. This was, after all, everyone's reason for being here. A man or woman might have a job far removed from piloting or navigating a Lanc but every job contributed in its own way. Clerks, cooks, fitters, guards, drivers, service police: on ops days they sensed a new purpose in what they did. This was what it was all about. Everyone helped a bit to send the Lancs lumbering away to clobber Jerry.

Almost everyone said 'clobber', few said 'bomb'. 'Clobber' suggested a clean-cut, athletic young hero dashing through the gauntlet of enemy fire and personally delivering an upper-cut to Adolf's jaw. 'Bomb' was what the enemy did: destroyed homes, killed women and children. Rotterdam, Coventry, London. Bombing was savage; clobbering was sporting.

Air-force personnel were practised euphemists. Flying Officer Blake 'bought it' over Cologne. Bert Phillips 'went for a Burton' near Aachen. Harry Andrews 'bent the kite a bit' on landing. The fact that these men died unpleasant deaths was better avoided. Useless to ponder; didn't help a bit. Often, gently, the blame was shifted to the victims. They turned to starboard when they should have turned to port and the searchlights boxed them in and they didn't have a chance. A bit slow with their evasive. Night fighter gave them a couple of squirts and that was that. They tried to make it home when they should have baled out. Poor show. Good types but not too bright.

He felt exuberant.

Cramped in the back of an Austin van, bulky in flying gear, jammed in on all sides by his crew, squashed by parachutes and satchels, he had never felt better.

He had beaten it; he had faced it and he had fought it and he had won. A triumph of reason over unreasoning fear. He had been frightened—hell, he had almost panicked, had longed to surrender to panic—but he had resisted. And now he knew what had scared him: his imagination. Shadows on a tired, vulnerable mind. Nothing more. He had told the vision to go to blazes and it had gone.

Now he felt marvellous. Nothing could possibly go wrong. G-George was the best Lanc Messrs A. V. Roe had ever constructed; his crew comprised the finest, noblest, cleverest men ever to don air-force blue; the ground wallahs were craftsmen beyond compare, faithful to the last locknut.

He knew the mood. It wouldn't last. Soon everything would find its level. He would calm down. He had tried hard not to reveal his feelings to the crew. Thank the Lord he seemed to have succeeded.

The WAAF driver had clutch trouble. There was a snarling of metal as she attempted to change from first to second. The van slowed and almost stopped. Gritting her teeth, she kept pushing the lever until, finally, with an exasperated heave, the van leapt forward.

In the rear, the seven airmen disentangled themselves and their gear.

Paul said, 'Jeez, skipper, she's a crummier driver than you!'

Wally sniffed in mock disdain.

'She may be a crummy driver,' said Len, 'but she's got big tits.' He nudged Douglas, the nineteen-year-old virgin from Penrhyn Bay. 'Did you notice them, Doug? Eh?

Yeah, I thought so; you noticed 'em all right. Old Doug doesn't miss much. If there are big tits anywhere in the target area, old Doug's going to spot 'em.'

Douglas's face turned throbbing pink. Wally smiled; it was hard not to. Douglas was so incredibly innocent; if there were medals for innocence, Douglas would get the VC.

'You can't beat big tits,' said Len with relish.

'You've got tits on the brain,' said Charlie Newton. Almost thirty, balding rapidly, Charlie was the old man of the crew. Father of three, he hailed from Bethnal Green. He had seen hard times; now, as a warrant officer wireless operator, he was far better off than he had ever been in civvy street.

Phil declared loudly and enthusiastically that he liked Elsie Trimball from the Parachute Section. 'They say your only problem is trying to keep up with her!' He leered at Douglas. 'She likes it ... *too* much! Some sort of female imbalance or something. Marvellous! Like to try a bit of that, Doug?'

Face aglow, Douglas mumbled that he really didn't know what Phil was talking about.

'Not bloody much.'

The van stopped for a Lancaster emerging from its dispersal. Tyres squealing, it turned on to the peri-track. The pilot looked down from his open side-window. He had a moustache. Then the van shivered as the Lanc's engines opened up. The noise was deafening. Abruptly it subsided; the aircraft rolled away towards the runway.

'Noisy beggar. No need to rev up like that,' Phil muttered.

Charlie leant out. 'D-Dog,' he announced. 'Whose kite is that?'

'A guy named Armitage is the pilot,' said Paul, yawning.

'A new crew,' said Harry. 'This is only their second trip.

Dead keen types.'

'Armitage is the one who went with Sandy on his second dickey ride,' said Len. 'Remember that poor sod we had? Three rides with us and he finds out how the experts do it; he takes his own crew and they go for a Burton the first time.'

Phil nodded. 'Ah yes, but do you remember that poor wee bugger who went for his second dickey ride with the wingco and got a bullet in his head for his trouble? Remember? When the wingco got back, the second dickey's crew were at the dispersal waiting to hear all about the trip. But he couldn't tell them a thing. He'd bought it. One lousy bullet and it wallops him right between the eyes.'

'Rotten luck.'

'Aye, rotten luck it was.'

The van stopped again.

'All change,' said Charlie. He always said 'All change' when they reached the aircraft.

Awkward in harnesses, laden with parachutes, satchels and helmets, the crew stumbled out on to the grass.

They were experienced practitioners of a dangerous profession known as strategic bombing. They fought an impersonal war; they flew in darkness to names on maps, released their bombs on targets delineated by flickering lights, and hurried away before the flak and the night fighters got them. Staying alive was a full-time occupation; it left no time to worry about the effects of the bombs on the people below. The target was a section of a city. The idea was to destroy it utterly. The target area might contain military installations; or just homes and shops. For no longer was there any pretence about restricting targets to docks and ammunition dumps and railways. In essence there was only one target now: a people's will to continue fighting. At Bomber Command, they believed that bombing could change the course of history.

In October the crew of G-George had gone on leave. Wally and Paul planned to spend three days in London together before going their separate ways. In a taxi near Victoria they witnessed the effect of what was known as a 'nuisance' raid: a single German aircraft scudding in low and dropping bombs more or less indiscriminately. One bomb scored a direct hit on a block of flats. There was a thud, a huge ear-numbing thud. Shop-windows caved in and shattered. Glass tinkled across the road, in front of the taxi. The driver started to back up. Wally told him to stop. They would try to help.

The damage was relatively slight. One corner of the building had been hit, the rest was almost undamaged. In all, only two flats were affected. It could have been much worse. Except for one young woman. It could have been no worse for her. They pulled her from the rubble. She was smiling through a crust of grey plaster dust; her body and her face and her staring eyes were covered with the stuff. She looked like a statue but for the great dark patches where the blood was soaking through the dust. In her left hand she held a lipstick. Around her, in the mess of bricks and mortar, lay the pathetic mementoes of her life: a torn cookery book, dresses swept into a shapeless bundle by the bomb's blast, crockery, photographs, a toothbrush, a glove ...

'You want to remember this,' said a man with ARP stencilled on his steel helmet. 'Give it back to the bastards. With interest.'

They walked away, brushing the greyness from their uniforms. They didn't speak until they were in another taxi.

Wally couldn't erase the girl's smile from his mind. 'What was she smiling about?'

Paul shook his head. 'I don't know. Forget it.'

*　　　*　　　*

But the memory of the dead girl persisted. That night, he dreamt of her.

'What 'you mean?'

Wally stared at the ceiling. Where was he? Oh yes, of course. The Strand Palace.

'Pardon?'

'You were saying, "We do things like that".'

'Was I? I'm sorry.'

'You woke me up. Dreaming, was you?'

'Yes, I suppose so.'

'I saw a picture like that. David Niven, was it? Or Errol Flynn? Anyway, he was an airman and he kept on having nightmares about crashing and all that.'

'I wasn't dreaming about crashes. Go on back to sleep. I'm sorry I disturbed you.'

She propped herself on one elbow. 'You're all of a quiver, you are. Nerves jingle-jangling all over the place. Come on, I'll rub your chest for you and relax you. Would you like that? Lie back. Straight. There. That nice? I've got a nice touch, haven't I? I know I have. The Yank major told me —or perhaps it was the colonel—anyway, he told me I'd make a fortune in New York as a masseuse. Isn't that nice?'

'Very pleasant.' He couldn't remember her name. Her face was round, rather ordinary, but her dark hair was handsome and she had an impressive body. And, apparently, a kind heart.

'You're still all tense.'

'What do you expect, with your hands wandering all over the place?'

'All right, well, I'm keeping them up here, see. Not down there any more. There. Just let yourself relax, love. Let your muscles go. That's better. We'll make those nasty nightmares go away.'

Wally smiled. She sounded as if she was talking to a baby. Perhaps she did have a baby. And perhaps she did

23

talk to it the same way. He wished he could remember her name. She was a good sort.

'Your mate seems nice. The Canadian.'

'Paul.'

'Yes. You fly in the same plane together, do you? That's nice. What sort of a plane do you fly? Fighter?'

'No. Bomber.'

'Good. I hope you're giving the buggers hell, if you'll pardon my French. Give 'em what-for. I was here all through the Blitz when it was really bad, not like now; it's nothing now; bloody Jerries used to come over every night and we all had to go down and sleep in the ruddy tube station. Oo, I hated that. Nasty, snoring wretches all over the place and dirty old men tiptoeing around, having a peep in here and a peep in there. I was working in a shop then. Horrid place. I'd never go back, not whatever happened. Pay was rotten and you worked all hours and all those bitches to be nice to. I think of it when I go into shops; I think of what it was like and I'm nice to the girls because I know what they're thinking. I'd love to go up in an aeroplane,' she added dreamily. 'Must be marvellous, flying about among all the clouds ...'

'And dropping bombs on women and children.'

'What?'

'Nothing.'

'I heard you. You said you dropped bombs on women and children. Well, they dropped 'em on us first, chum. I know that 'cause I was one of the women and children they dropped 'em on. So I'm bloomin' well delighted when I hear you're giving them a taste of their own medicine.'

'I'm glad you're delighted.'

She started rubbing again. 'Don't start feeling sorry for them.'

'I'm not,' he said. 'I'm feeling sorry for myself.'

4

G-George awaited her crew, her one hundred and two feet of wing spanning the circular concrete hard-standing. She was dull black on her flanks and beneath her wings and tail, dreary camouflage green and brown on her upper surfaces, but her lines were clean and her size neatly proportioned. She dwarfed the men who had come to fly her; her main wheels were almost as tall as any of them; she seemed vast and immovable; you stood beneath her and you wondered how anything this huge could actually get off the ground.

Phil sniffed the air. Harry took off his cap, scratched his head and replaced his cap. Len thanked the WAAF driver for the ride; she drove away with a series of small leaps and bounds.

'You're wasting your time,' said Charlie.

'I know. Doug's after her. He's got his eye on her tits. And he means business, does Doug.'

Sergeant Potter appeared from behind G-George's tail. He strode up to Wally, came smartly to attention, saluted and said everything was on top line.

Wally thanked him and then walked slowly around G-George, gazing intently at wings, rudders, ailerons, elevators, tyres. It was a pre-flight ritual, a habit instilled by his first instructor. 'Always take a good, long, hard look at the aeroplane before you get in it. Make sure everything is stuck on where it's supposed to be stuck on and in the right quantity. The wings. Count them. Then count them again. Don't take anything for granted. You never know when some cretin will take a wing off and forget to put it on again. Touch the elevators. Make sure they're there. See that they move. Give them a tug. If one comes off in your hand, take it around to your fitter and have a chat with him about it.'

G-George was showing signs of wear and tear. Her leading edges were almost completely stripped of paint; bright metal showed through in a long, ragged line. The soft sheet metal of her cowlings bore a dozen dents, souvenirs of heavy-handed erks. Behind the four Merlins, oil had dyed her upper wing surfaces in great streaks to the trailing edges. Middle age was creeping up on G-George but she carried her eight and a half months with dignity. She was the oldest lady in the squadron.

Wally stood back for a final look. The control locks had been removed from the ailerons and elevators; the sock was off the pitot tube; an erk sat astride the fuselage and polished the windscreen. Everything looked first rate.

Potter said, 'If you find anything you'll put it on the 700.'

Wally promised he would. He walked briskly to the rear of the aircraft, to the entrance door with its little five-rung ladder and its sign PRIVATE BAR in neat sans serif face. Paul's work.

Inside, G-George was a long metal tube with an extraordinary number of protuberances, most of them sharp. You made your way forward with considerable care no matter how many times you had done it before. You kept your head down because the fuselage roof was low and ingeniously equipped with a selection of things to bang your head on. The angle didn't help; G-George sat tail down; you had to walk uphill. Up front, light flooded in through the cockpit canopy but along the way it was dark and you had to swallow a brief sensation of claustrophobia as you stumbled over the capricious floor panelling. Then, leg up and slide over the great transverse spar, the wings' main structural member passing through the fuselage immediately aft of the wireless operator's seat.

'Bit of gum, skip?' said Charlie. He always chewed gum in the air, never on the ground.

Wally thanked him, shaking his head. Past the bank of radio equipment separating Charlie from the navigation table: Paul sat with his back against the starboard fuselage wall, arranging his pencils and protractors. Wally squeezed past him into the cockpit: the pilot's seat on the port side; before it, the U-shaped control column, throttle console to the right, compass mounted up on the windscreen rim, over the instruments. Harry was already stationed to the right of the pilot's seat, peering at his dials; at his feet was the narrow access to her nose. G-George provided minimal space for those who rode in her; she was a slim lady with no wasted inches. But if her body was cramped it was also functional. Five of the crew were almost within touching distance; in an emergency such proximity might make all the difference.

Harry moved aside to let Wally into his seat. It was chilly; a thin damp wind blew in through the open window on his left. He slid it shut, fastening his shoulder and lap harness. Good and snug. He cranked up his seat until his head almost touched the canopy roof. Down below he saw Sergeant Potter, arms folded, daring the engines not to start at the first nudge of the buttons. They didn't dare. First the port inner then the starboard inner; port outer, starboard outer. Noise quivered through G-George.

'Pilot to crew. Testing intercom. Navigator?'

'Navigator OK.'

'Bomb-aimer?'

'Intercom OK, skipper,' Douglas responded.

Everyone's intercom was working.

The ground checks occupied ten minutes. Everything

worked. Wally called the tower: 'G-George to tower. Permission to taxi, please.'

'Tower to G-George. You are clear to taxi.'

Flip to intercom. 'Pilot to crew. Taxiing. Anything in the way?'

He looked out of the window. A mechanic stood in front of the port-inner propeller holding the chock-rope. Wally signalled; the mechanic tugged at the rope and the chock came free. Harry did the same on the starboard side. He nodded. All clear.

Wally turned, awkward in his harness, straining to see as much as possible before letting the aircraft roll. It was unlikely that an erk would leave a trolley acc plugged in —it was equally unlikely that he would be able to see it even if he had—but it was worth the effort. He wondered whether anyone had ever tried to take off with a trolley acc bouncing along behind.

Potter and his erks moved back to the grass beside the hard-standing. They had done their stuff; now it was up to the air crew ... and please God they wouldn't come back from the night-flying test with a great list of things to be done before tonight. On ops days, last-minute maintenance could be a nightmare.

Wally released the brakes and G-George rolled forward, creaking in her sulky on-the-ground manner. She disliked locomotion on *terra firma*; habitually she made complaining noises until she got into the air. Then she became a lady.

Wally, perched high in his perspex canopy, felt like a bus driver steering from the upper deck. His forward vision was partially obscured by the nose with its turret and twin Brownings; on either side there were engines and behind them the broad expanse of wing. He steered by means of the brakes; to turn right he pressed the right brake pedal which slowed the starboard wheel and swung G-George to the right.

The big lady rolled along, propelled by modest spurts

of power from the Merlins.

The peri-track ran parallel to the eastern boundary of the airfield, delimited by the main road to York. At the north-east corner, where the track swept into a ninety-degree turn, stood Brocklington Grammar School, a sombre-looking place where the sons of Yorkshire's middle classes had been educated and boarded since the 1400s. Six months before, a German pilot flying a Junkers Ju 88 intruder had mis-taken the school buildings for those of the airfield and at four o'clock in the morning had attacked, industriously and methodically peppering the place with cannon and machine-gun fire. Shells roared through empty classrooms and corridors; providentially none hit the dormitories. The Junkers caused much damage but no casualties—and he got away in spite of determined efforts by ack-ack and three Beaufighters. For both sides, it was a night of wasted ammunition, fuel and time.

Fred Sanderson's Lanc was running up beside the run-way. S-Sugar. Twenty-seven ops.

Wally glanced between the trees. A game of rugger on the main playing-field. Half the players in blue-and-white-striped jerseys, the others in plain blue. A game of some importance, by the look of it. The entire school seemed to have turned out to watch and cheer; a lot of jumping up and down and waving of caps. Perhaps the poor little blighters are just trying to keep warm, Wally thought.

One of the spectators, a short boy with a multi-coloured cap, turned at the sound of G-George's engines and waved. Wally waved in reply; he hoped the boy could see him. Then he had to push the left brake; the kite was wandering off to the side of the track.

S-Sugar began to roll as Wally stopped beside the run-way.

Harry placed his gloved hands on the throttles. He glanced at Wally. Time for the final pre-take-off check.

Brakes firmly on; control column right back in the lap. Hell of a din: checking the two stage blowers, the pitch controls, the magnetos: each Merlin blazing away to full power. Rather fun.

Harry's thumb was raised. Wally nodded.

S-Sugar climbed away, tucking her wheels in.

Wally called the tower and requested permission to take off.

He glanced to his right; there was always the possibility of some lunatic coming in to land without informing the tower and without the tower noticing him. All clear. He released the brakes. G-George creaked as she rolled on to the runway. Left brake. She turned to face the long ribbon of asphalt that disappeared over the hump in the middle of the field.

'Flaps thirty degrees.'

Harry checked. 'Flaps thirty.'

'Radiators.'

'Radiators OK.'

'Throttles locked.'

'Throttles locked.'

'Rear gunner, all clear behind?'

'All clear, skipper,' came Len's voice.

'Right. Taking off, crew. Full power, please, engineer.'

G-George shivered, not able yet to convert all the power into motion. She rolled, slowly at first, gathering speed, her propellers slicing the air, hurling it around, thrusting it back, dragging the thousands of clumsy pounds of G-George along, forcing the reluctant air to swarm over her wings and tail. At first it was of no avail; then with speed came strength; the air became a body on which G-George could prove herself. Her tail found lift and rose from the runway, tail-wheel still spinning merrily. Now G-George was in her stride. Balanced on her two main wheels she bounded along the runway, the feeling of flight in her wings.

Wally leant forward; he held the control column tightly as he watched the runway unwinding before him. At his side Harry braced himself by holding the window handles. The air-speed indicator turned steadily.

'Eighty ... eighty-five ... ninety ...'

Over the hump. Now she wanted to go. Rattling with impatience. Champing at the bit.

'One hundred.'

Fairly snapping at the air now. OK, ducky, OK, OK ...

'Hundred and ten.'

Right. Time to rise and shine. Firm pull back on the stick. Touch of rudder to correct a drift to the right. Runway dropping away ...

'Undercart up, please, engineer.'

Harry's hand was already on the lever.

'Undercarriage up.'

'Thank you.'

'And locked.'

'Flaps up.'

'Flaps up.'

The crew relaxed. Once again G-George had successfully dragged herself off the ground without a hitch. Good old George; leave it to George. Up front, Douglas turned from the transparent bomb-aiming blister and watched Elsie Trimball of the Parachute Section divest herself of her tie, her shirt, her skirt, her stockings and, finally, her underwear. Miraculously there was now room in the nose compartment for her to stand upright and exhibit her magnificent body for his delight. She couldn't resist him; again and again she turned up in G-George's nose to offer herself to him. Bit of all right, was Elsie. High in the cockpit, Harry thought glumly of Dorothy's letter; he still hadn't read it. Life was a bastard, it really was. Behind him, Paul wondered about the op. And about luck. Charlie Newton sniffed; there was a tightness in his throat; sure

31

sign of oncoming colds with the Newtons. In the mid-upper turret, Phil whistled the trumpet solo from 'In the Mood'. He was fond of the trumpet; he was thinking of buying one. Len, in the tail turret, took a deep breath, relieved to see the ground disappear. Take-offs were the nastiest part of flying, in Len's opinion.

The altimeter jogged past one thousand. Fog beaded the windscreen. Up through scattered overcast. G-George turned; the ground tilted; it was hard and grey after too many months of Yorkshire winter. Tiny crystals of ice formed on the leading edges of the wings and on the engine cowlings. The crystals multiplied, edging together to create brittle film which broke and scattered as soon as G-George reached the drier air above. Then the blue, the stunningly blue sky. The sun splashed into the cockpit, stinging the eyes with its sudden brightness. It was a tonic, looking up, absorbing the full force of it, feeling the rays seeping into every pore. Better than Guinness. Below, the world was a fuzzy carpet, dirty grey.

Wally scanned the horizon. Nothing to see but glorious colour above the mire below. He was content, still delighted by the act of climbing through cloud into the sunlight; it never failed him, the moment of bursting out of the fog; it was like Alice discovering another world: the God-like feeling of soaring above the clouds and looking down and seeing that the earth had vanished, then climbing still higher, the aircraft stretching her wings and trembling with eagerness and thrusting her nose up toward the sun; completely free.

Abruptly Wally turned G-George on to her starboard wing-tip, whirling her around in a great circle of delight, an aerial pirouette.

Len's voice rasped over the intercom: 'Rear gunner to skipper. You mind telling us what the bloody hell you're doing?'

Wally laughed. 'Sorry, chaps. Just felt like it.'

Charlie in a monotone: 'Lovely. Just what we need. The skipper's gone off his rocker.'

Everyone had something to say about that.

Wally said, 'Pilot to crew. You're an undisciplined bloody rabble and it's going to be a relief to get rid of you after this tour.'

'Navigator to pilot.'

'Yes, Paul.'

'I think I'm speaking for the rest of the crew when I say the feeling is mutual.'

'With knobs on,' said Charlie.

In mock despair, Wally said, 'How the hell did I ever manage to get saddled with such a shower?'

'Just lucky, I guess,' said Paul.

Wally settled back. A bloody good bunch, the crew. The very best. Soon they would be off on their separate ways. Shame ... it took time for seven airmen to become a crew —too many didn't get time enough. They would probably never see one another again. They would talk about reunions but there wouldn't be any. Sad. But they would have made it, they would have beaten the odds ... That trip to Essen ... the piece of flak had come smashing through the port-side window panel, missing his head by an inch ... Someone asking if the skipper was OK. Nodding, nodding ... OK, of course, OK. Piece of cake ...

And then it was all very clear. Here I am, Walter Mann, Esquire ... this is my existence on this planet. For all I know this is my *only* existence, anywhere at any time in all the eons of eternity. My life is of enormous value to me. Then why am I sitting in this thoroughly unsafe vehicle several miles in the sky, half blinded and frozen, being shot at by perfect strangers?

For democracy.

Democracy?

Also, King and Country, patriotism, all that kind of thing.

But I already explained, this is my only existence anywhere at any time ...

Certainly. And you're risking it for your country.

Which seems a bloody silly thing to do.

Everyone does it.

Which is a singularly poor reason.

It's true; no *cause* is worth the risking of my life. Not a single cause in all the world. My life is worth far more to me than any cause ...

Repeat after me. My life ...

Harry. Why was Harry staring at him? Why was he taking off his oxygen mask? Why was he leaning forward? Holding his mask out?

Reality ebbed back with every breath.

'OK now, skipper?'

Harry held up a lacerated oxygen mask. 'Lucky it didn't take your nose off, skipper. All right, are you?'

Wally nodded. OK. Stop fussing. Surly. He should have been grateful that his head was still intact. More deep breaths. It had all made so much sense. That was the depressing thing. But who gave a damn what you thought, anyway?

Turning in the sun, G-George was tested by her crew. They simulated a bomb-run; they simulated a fighter attack. They checked their weapons, the radio, the radar. They satisfied themselves that G-George was capable of doing her stuff that night.

'Pilot to crew. Letting down now.'

Throttles back a couple of notches; column gently forward. Nose inching down, G-George began her return to earth.

Harry stationed himself at Wally's side to assist during

landing. He stared out of the starboard windscreen panel; his mind seemed far away from the aircraft. Briefly Wally wondered about him. Poor chap; bad luck. Nature was so dreadfully thoughtless. Why couldn't things be a little more conveniently arranged?

The overcast approached; soon the stuff was immediately below G-George's wings. Loth to leave the sun's friendly glare, Wally pulled back slightly on the stick. For some moments G-George skimmed along, half in cloud, half out, wings slicing through the wispy tails of the stuff. But without more power she couldn't continue in level flight; she was slowing, the air-stream over her wings and tail becoming turbulent, her controls sloppy. She had to descend.

The mist swallowed her. For a moment the sun was a rosy glow above, then it vanished. The world was suddenly dark and wet and bumpy. The half-visible wings flexed and strained; the structure groaned as it transferred stresses from one component to another, absorbing and apportioning the stresses until they were tamed.

'Fifteen hundred,' said Harry.

'Thank you.'

Then the first glimpses of ground through small breaks in the greyness. Fields, etiolated green smudged here and there with white; a narrow road wending an absurdly erratic route from nowhere to nowhere. Now the glowering ceiling of cloud was above, the air was smoother.

Paul squeezed his long frame into the space behind the pilot's seat. He winked as Wally glanced back at him. The airfield was dead ahead, precisely where he said it would be. He touched Wally's shoulder, a gesture saying that he, Paul, had found the place for Wally, now it was up to Wally to land on it.

Another Lanc was in the circuit; G-George would have to wait her turn to use the runway. Wally banked, bringing a wing-tip down to point at Brocklington. A bus was pulling into the square. Stone walls divided the fields beyond the village. To the east the ground undulated, then blossomed into the Yorkshire Wolds.

Down below, the tiny Lanc landed, rolled along, slowing, passing the crossroads.

'Undercart down, please, engineer.'

'Undercart down.' Lights winked on the panel. 'And locked.'

The control tower announced that G-George was clear to land.

'Pilot to crew. Stand by for landing.'

G-George's drab-painted wing pointed at a farm. A cart moved ponderously along a path; small puddles dotted the earth. Cows grazed; inured to the roar of aircraft they ignored G-George as she boomed overhead. The ground sloped away toward the airfield. Final leg. Straighten up. A mile to go.

'Flaps twenty, please.'

'Flaps twenty,' said Harry.

'Speed one-forty.'

The village scurried by to the left. Emulating their cows, the people ignored the Lanc.

'Two hundred feet.'

The rugger game had just ended; spectators mingling with players, banging backs. Who won? Pink faces turned up. A boy waved. The same boy?

'Fifty feet. One-fifteen.'

The airfield boundary hurtled toward them.

'Full flap, please, engineer.'

The strip of tarmac wobbled; its surface was adorned by a hatching of black tyre-stains.

Sinking from flight, perfectly angled, G-George swept across the York road. A first-class approach; at runway's end she was no more than twenty-five feet in the air; she could almost have touched down in the turning-circle.

Then he saw himself, dead.

The same scene; the charcoal body with its truncated arms obscenely raised in supplication, the ghastly caricature of a face ...

G-George's starboard wheel hit the runway. The stick jarred against Wally's hand. The aircraft lurched; she was a creature instinctively seeking equilibrium. Now her port wing rushed perilously close to the blurring tarmac. Another thud. Another. Her tail-wheel touched, bounced, touched again.

Harry's startled face ... mouth slightly open, revealing tips of even Australian teeth ... ahead, the ground bucking ridiculously ... the kite rearing like a frightened horse.

The thought crystallized quite slowly, quite deliberately. I must do something, in fact I must do something immediately; if I don't we shall go off the runway and ground-loop and blow up and everyone will be killed ...

But it all seemed academic. Reason rather than emotion told him to do something. There were others to think of: Paul, Douglas, Harry, Charlie, Phil, Len ...

Harry's arms outstretched ... trying to grab the wheel before it was too late ...

Wally shook his head. 'I've got her, I've got her.'

He wrestled her from the edge of the runway; she half ran, half flew from one side to the other. Then suddenly she was docile; she trundled along sweetly, her speed slackening.

Oh Christ, he thought. Oh Jesus Christ, what the hell is happening to me?

Len broke the tension. 'Rear gunner to pilot. Are we really down now, skipper?'

Oh God. But must treat it lightly ...

'Sorry about that one, chaps.'

'That's OK,' said Paul. 'But next time tell us ahead of

time and we'll bale out.'

Paul was shaken; you could tell by his voice; he thought he had had it ...

Phil said, 'I think something cracked down here in the middle.'

Wally made himself chuckle. 'Oh, come now, it wasn't that bad.'

'I heard something go,' said Phil. 'Honestly.'

A couple of feet away Harry was smiling. With relief? He seemed about to say something; then he turned his attention to the runway.

Wally taxied carefully but not slowly. He had to act normally; he had to pass off the world's worst landing as a fleeting bit of bad luck. He had to calm the crew. Calming the crew was more important than that bloody vision. His hands tightened their grip on the control column. He looked straight ahead. He wanted a cigarette. I nearly killed everybody, he thought. What is it? A nervous breakdown? Overactive imagination? I saw the whole thing in hideous detail; I was being roasted. Not very nice. Pure imagination? I already convinced myself once of that. But it's a little harder the second time ... Could there be a connection between what I see in my imagination and what will happen? I'm not sure now ...

The intercom was silent.

The ground crew watched as G-George trundled back to her dispersal. Their eyes sped over her as she squeaked to a halt—after that landing anything could be wrong with her.

The Merlins gasped into silence.

Wally unfastened his harness. Methodically, laboriously, he checked the switches. He slid the window panel open; gratefully he breathed in the cold air. He heard the other members of the crew moving about behind him, thumping down the metal tube of the fuselage. No one was saying anything about the landing—or in fact anything about anything. Thank God for that. A crew had to have confidence in its skipper. It was vital.

Wally turned. Paul half stood in the restricted space. His dark hair fell across his forehead; his gaze was steady.

'Everything OK?'

'OK?' Wally found something to stare at, a dial to rap. 'Of course everything's OK.' He tugged the helmet off his head. 'Everyone does a rotten landing once in a while.'

'Sure they do.'

'Even me.'

'Even you.'

Wally followed the Canadian down the sloping fuselage to the exit door. The rest of the crew stood outside waiting for the van. Someone said it was cold; someone else wondered why the van hadn't arrived.

Sergeant Potter came clumping under the fuselage; he looked along the length of the fuselage, then at Wally.

Go to hell, Sergeant Potter, Wally said silently. Stop thinking what you're thinking—immediately! That's an order!

He accepted a cigarette from Paul, a light from Charlie's cupped hands. Then the van arrived.

5

The sun peeped briefly through a thinning in the overcast then vanished again. The temperature rose to thirty-nine degrees Fahrenheit. The barometer was steady.

In the scattered dispersals the ground crews readied the Lancaster for the night's work. Tractors dragged trains of bombs from the dump: dark-green cylindrical four-thousand-pounders, each close to seven feet long, bundles of stick-like incendiaries. Armourers loaded belts of .303-inch ammunition into the racks leading to the turrets, keeping their eyes open for abnormalities. A bulging cartridge could jam a gun; a jammed gun could cost lives. In the dispersals the erks laboured to correct the faults discovered by the air crews during the night-flying tests. And the chiefies and sergeants stamped around and peered at everyone's work and found things to complain about. Irascible men, they could never be satisfied. Their erks were hopeless, without mechanical aptitude of any sort. All the chiefies and sergeants had their favourite and-then-he-lit-a-match-to-see-if-there-was-any-fuel-left-in-the-tank stories. Funny but sad.

She strode across the tarmac to meet him, smiling with her mouth that was wonderfully too large.

'Hullo,' he said. 'You look desirable.'

'Do I? Thank you.' Blue-green eyes, sparkling with life.

'I feel an almost irresistible urge to unbutton your tunic and unharness those delightful breasts of yours and fondle them ...'

40

'Wally!' She pretended to be shocked. A tiny vertical crease appeared close to her left eyebrow. Wally found himself wondering how it was that the crease was off-centre; why wasn't it equidistant from her eyebrows? Typical Ann to have a slightly off-centre frown.

It isn't me talking, he wanted to tell her. I'm not being the fool; it's someone else, someone who has kindly taken over for a little while because I'm not too sure what is real and what isn't. He's doing quite well, imitating me well —except perhaps that he's exaggerating everything a bit, overdoing it, you know ...

They walked past the hangars toward the Mess. Ann asked if he was going to have lunch.

'I hunger only for your body, Sexual Officer Strickland.'

'*Section* Officer ...'

'You'll always be a Sexual Officer to me. Let's go to bed for half an hour before lunch.'

'You don't appeal to me,' she said. 'You're a nasty man. I detest you.'

'Nonsense, you're mad about me.'

'I am not. I think you have a wife and eight children tucked away somewhere.'

'How the devil did you find out about them?'

'The padre told me.'

'He should be court-martialled for spreading alarm and despondency among the troops. By the way, talking about alarm and despondency, did you see our landing?' At once he wondered why he had mentioned it; there she was, shaking her head; she hadn't seen it. He said, 'I thought the whole place was talking about it. It was the worst landing in the history of RAF Brocklington. Ropey as hell.'

'You?' She stared in disbelief.

'Me. The ground wasn't quite where I thought it was.'

'Is everyone all right?'

'Of course. I didn't prang. Just a ropey landing, that's

all. Nothing to get upset about.'

'That's good,' she said. But the little vertical off-centre line had reappeared.

'Ops still on?' Breezy, couldn't-care-less.

She said yes, as far as she knew.

'Good show!'

There! Defiance! In spite of everything, keenness to fly persists. A press-on-regardless type. But he was thinking, Oh, Jesus. She speaks and as she speaks her eyes travel over your face; she studies your mouth and your chin and your forehead; she takes a good long last look because deep down, wherever the female of the species keeps its intuition equipment, she knows this is the last day you'll be with her; you'll get into your aeroplane and you won't come back. Ever or ever ...

'Have you decided where you want to go on leave?' Keep it up.

She shook her head, smiling at the thought of it.

'How about the Riviera?' he said.

'Sounds fun. Shall we borrow a Lanc and fly there?'

'Of course. You don't think we'd travel by anything as plebeian as a train or boat! But—is it going to be Nice or Cannes?'

'What's the difference? They're both full of Germans.'

'We'll ignore them and lie on the beach and get brown all over.'

'All over?'

'All over.' Smiling, he said, 'I will take you there one day ...' It was easy; he was believing it himself. 'The war will be over soon and with any luck I won't have to do much more to help win it.'

She raised a finger to his lips. 'I know it's silly ...'

'Damn right, it's silly,' he said loudly, fiercely. 'I'm saying that I'm jolly nearly finished with operational flying. One more op to go. Saying it isn't going to make the slightest difference to my chances. But don't worry. If any kite is coming back it'll be ours. We can do it all blind-folded. We're what they call seasoned professionals. We know all the tricks of the trade: an ideal crew: we think and act as one man: we do the right things at the right times. Statistically our chances are about thirty-two times better than a brand-new crew's ...'

'What's the matter, Wally?' Her eyes searched his face again.

'Matter? Nothing's the matter.'

'All right.' Wooden voice.

A Lanc barrelled overhead, wheels vanishing into the inboard engine nacelles, flaps merging with the wing surfaces.

Ann's eyes followed it as it turned away over the school. Then she looked at the ground, and when she spoke her voice had a timid note as if she was asking a favour.

'Be extra specially careful tonight, Wally. Please.'

I am worried. For the tenth time in two days I have tried to telephone my parents' home in Cologne. And for the tenth time the operator has told me that the lines to Cologne are still under repair.

The Americans bombed Cologne two days ago. Accord-ing to the reports, it was a particularly heavy raid—a large part of the Höhenberg section of the city has been demo-lished.

My parents' home is in the centre of Höhenberg.

'Your kite's U/S,' said Owen Pinkerton. He lit a cigar-ette and banged the cartridge-case lighter on the desk with sufficient force to register the fact that he was displeased.

'U/S? It can't be.' What the hell was Owen talking about? Hadn't they just done a night-flying test? Every-thing was fine ...

'It's U/S,' said Pinkerton. 'Your landing did it. Bent the

43

starboard oleo leg. Also did something to the fuselage. Twisted it or something. They're not too sure about that; they're investigating.' He waved the smoke from before his eyes. 'You'll have to take Kenesky's kite. He and his crew are on leave.'

Take another kite? No, it was unthinkable. G-George had to be repaired; George was as much part of the crew as any man. It was a hell of a thing to ask the lads to do their last sortie in another kite. No ... But Pinkerton was busy writing; as far as he was concerned the matter had been settled. All quite simple. One kite U/S, *ergo*, procure another kite for the crew, send them off in that. Pinkerton looked up, cigarette angled aggressively.

'How the hell did you manage it?'

'*Manage* it? Good God, you don't think I did it on *purpose*?'

Pinkerton's eyes were steady. 'Undershoot or something?' Puff, puff.

'I misjudged ... The ground wasn't quite where I thought it was going to be ... Look here, Owen, surely to God you can do something about getting George repaired.'

'For tonight? Not a prayer. Out of the question.'

'But we've done the whole tour in George. It's a hell of a thing to ask the crew to take another kite for the last trip.'

'*I* didn't bend the kite,' said Pinkerton. 'Really, I know how you feel. I know you'd prefer to go in George. But you can't take George because George is U/S, so you may as well get used to the idea. Look on the bright side: M-Mother's almost brand-new. Top-notch kite. Try and be a good chap for once and go and collect your crew and take Mother for a night-flying test. We'll talk about George tomorrow.' Another puff. Glance at rectangular wrist-watch. Crisp stainless steel on bed of crisp black hair.

Wally said, 'They can replace an oleo leg in an hour or two.'

'They aren't going to.' Mouth becoming taut. 'The fuselage is damaged also. I explained that. You're flying Mother tonight. Kindly go and collect your crew.'

Tell Owen? Tell him everything? Explain precisely why George came within a hairsbreadth of being ripped into very small pieces? No. Poor Owen. Poor bloody Owen. It really would be the last straw, wouldn't it?

'As long as M-Mother's a good kite I don't see that it matters,' said Charlie with a sniff.

Phil shook his head. 'Bit of a shock, in a way, having to take another kite ... you know, after all this time with the same one.'

Wally said he was damned sorry about it and it was all his fault, but at least Mother was a new kite; perhaps it would be a pleasant change.

Paul smiled in his wry, crooked way. What the hell, one kite was just like another.

Charlie looked at Wally, his eyes asking: Are you worried about it, skipper? If you're not I'm not.

'Hell of a way for George to go,' said Harry. Then he glanced at Wally. 'Sorry, skipper, I didn't mean ...'

'No need to apologize. I agree with you. It was a hell of a way for her to go.'

'It'll be nice to have a new kite for a change,' said Len.

'She's probably got a half-decent heating system which is more than you could ever say for George.'

'All Lancs are the same. Hot as hell for the wireless op and freezing for everyone else.'

'Whose kite is Mother?'

'Sergeant Kenesky's. He and his crew are on leave.'

'Lucky bastards.'

'We'll be going on leave soon.'

'Damn right we will.'

They looked at him, as if seeking reassurance.

M-Mother performed admirably. The crew liked her because she was tight and new and handled well; indeed she seemed a trifle lighter on the controls than George, a mite more perky.

At 1457 hours M-Mother swept across the York road, wheels down, flaps at twenty degrees.

'One hundred and fifteen.'

Harry's eyes bounced from the airspeed indicator to the runway and back again.

Wally acknowledged. Mouth unusually dry; crew unusually quiet. Who could blame them, mouth or crew? Neither had any choice; they simply had to go along for the ride and hope for the best.

'Full flap, please.'

Harry's hand sped toward the lever.

'Full flap, skipper.'

Barely a thump. Three wheels kissed the tarmac simultaneously. Rumble, rumble; ladylike, M-Mother rode down the runway, tail-wheel slicing the centre line.

After the world's worst landing, the world's best.

6

He took off his shoes, unknotted his tie, slipped his collar from the front and back studs and placed it, tie still in place, upside down on the dresser. His right trouser pocket contained a half-crown, two sixpences and four pennies; he made a neat pile of the coins within the semi-circle created by the collar.

Three and tenpence and a crumpled packet of Player's.

He lay on the bed and closed his eyes. Immediately the runway came swaying toward him again. He opened his eyes, turning on to one shoulder. What the hell did I come here to my room for, he wondered. To sleep; an hour's sleep, you said. Remember? You had to play the ever-so-cool skipper for the benefit of the crew. By the merest fluke you managed to pull off a passable landing. But you weren't satisfied with that; you had to impress the lads more, so you casually announced that you were going to have an hour's snooze to ensure your wide-awakeness for the night's jollities. You should have stayed with the lads, you clot.

Yes, he should have. It was absurd to think of sleep. Rarely had he been more awake. Still, it did some good just to lie for an hour and try to relax.

He rolled on to his back again. It was weird trying to separate reality and unreality. Something had happened to time. Was it really only this morning that he had stood and watched the Oxford land? And was it only three hours or so since he had written off George? It was as if he had dreamt it. And yet it was no dream. One had only to trot over and have a look at George to see that it was no dream. He sighed. Hopeless, trying to reason it out—because there was no reason in it. He asked himself: Am I frightened? He thought about it. No, puzzled, but not frightened. Was that a good sign or a bad sign? Once, twice—would the third time be the real thing?

I suppose, he thought, if one was religious one would be able to accept this sort of thing with tranquillity. One would start setting one's affairs in order, returning library books and so on.

He kneaded his forehead with his fingertips. It was maddening not even knowing whether to take the thing seriously or not. It was quite likely that in a few hours he would be chuckling over the memory of these moments, mentally nudging himself in the ribs for being so easily rattled. Then again, perhaps life *was* predestined ... What would the nice old Station Chaplain have to say about it?

'A premonition? Dear me. How very nasty. Nearly pranged, did you? Well, well, we'd better think about it, hadn't we? What did you have for breakfast? The usual? Porridge, toast and tea. Well, well, nothing too dubious there. What about dinner last night? Normal repast, eh? And, tell, pray, did you perchance linger too long at the bar? No. Well, well, that eliminates the usual gastric causes. Let us consider another possibility. Let us consider your sadly battered conscience. You are distressed to think of what you are doing to people in the cities you bomb. I want to understand this clearly. You are in agreement with destroying the enemy's cities and factories and railways and power stations and things of that type. Very good of you, I'm sure. But as I understand it you are concerned because you are doing ghastly things to untold numbers of people in the process, particularly civilians, women, children, old folk, etcetera. Am I correct? This is the problem? Good. Well, tell me, if you will, does it concern you that other crews are doing the same thing? Yes, but not so much. Ah! I see. It's only your own participation that concerns you; all you want to do is finish your tour and get out of Bomber Command, instruct or something until the war is over and then try to forget the whole rotten business. Interesting. Well, well, could it be that you are only saying this to conceal your real concern: your precious hide? This love of mankind, isn't it rather too sudden, too convenient? You care so little about other crews blowing people to pieces. Doesn't this, my boy, suggest a fundamental hypocrisy? In other words, it's not the *act* that concerns you but rather the fact that you are required to participate. You're like the man who enjoys a good steak but who feels ill if required to help kill the cow.'

Wally shook his head. The conversation had gone wrong somewhere. He crossed to the dresser and lit a cigarette. It was easy to make fun of the chaplain; no one was more vulnerable. So what? So bloody what? He rummaged in a drawer for his note-pad.

I still can't get through to Cologne. Worry nags at me like a toothache. I try to read a magazine but I can't concentrate.

Veit is asleep in an impossibly uncomfortable-looking wicker chair. A veteran, Veit; he has been flying for nearly three years; he started out on Me 109s; he transferred to night fighters a year ago. A kindly fellow, he took pity on the fledgling; he has taught me a lot—and still he keeps forgetting my name. No doubt he'll remember it when I become a fully fledged member of the Staffel, when I do something to earn his respect.

I wonder what the Amis will send over during the next twenty-four hours. What a choice they have! Fortresses and Liberators during the day and Lancasters and Halifaxes at night—plus assorted fighters and fighter-bombers and strafers and photo-reconnaissance machines—anything they deign to pick from their limitless stores!

Although we are a night-fighting Staffel, the controller may send us up during the day to fight the Americans. So Veit tells me. He also tells me the Me 110 is no match for a Fortress or a Lightning in broad daylight. Too slow, too ponderous. You need speed and agility to stay alive during the day. And luck.

Incredible, the way Veit can sleep. He can relax in an instant, although he knows he may be sent out at any time. A week ago Veit attacked a Fortress head on. He hit it too, he said. He saw one engine burst into flames and he saw pieces flying off the body near the cockpit. The trouble is, everything happens so fantastically quickly in head-on attacks. He went down beneath the Fort and started to turn. Immediately two Thunderbolts were on him like angry bloodhounds. He was lucky to get back to base. I saw him land. His machine literally fell apart as soon as it hit the ground. But Veit stepped out of the mess. They gave him a brand-new aircraft.

How long will I last?

Werner was killed last Thursday. Happich on Saturday. Müller Sunday. Martin crashed on landing two days ago; they still don't say whether he will pull through.

I have flown twice on missions. Both at night. Both accomplishing absolutely nothing.

Patience, Veit tells me. It takes time. At first everything is confusing, he says; you make the mistake of thinking before acting; you have to react like an animal, instantly, correctly. Soon it will begin to make sense, he assures me. The first thing I must do is forget all the crap they taught me at training-school ...

Veit can afford to be tolerant; he has twenty-nine victories.

What a dream world at training-school! I swallowed it

all: all the stuff about the Amis being cowardly Jews who run at the first sight of us, about our aircraft being infinitely superior to anything they have to fly, about our five- and six- and seven-to-one ratio of victories. I have been here only a few days and yet I have learnt that we are not winning the war in the air; we are fighting bravely but we are not winning. We shoot down dozens of bombers but there are untold numbers of bombers to take their places. The Amis possess incalculable strength and with each day they get stronger and we get weaker. It is that simple—and that depressing. Already the odds are savage. Soon, say some of the pilots, it will be suicide to attempt to take off during daylight.

Soon their armies will invade. Everyone says so. Can we stop them? I wonder. I think of the pilots still under train-ing. I presume they are being told, as we were, of imminent victory, of incredible new aircraft coming off the assembly lines in their thousands, ready for us to fly as soon as we reach our squadrons. And what do we find? Messerschmitt 110s. Ancient crates. The designers keep modifying them, adding new equipment, radar and cannons, but the basic aircraft is simply too old. The 210s and 410s are better, they say, but not much. We have none of them here. I wish they'd selected me for single-seaters. 109s or 190s.

Veit stirs in his sleep. He smiles. What is he dreaming about? Victories over Lancasters or women?

I glance at my watch. A present from Mutti and Papa for the brave warrior going off to the front. Jewelled movement. Swiss. The very finest the grey market can provide. Four o'clock. Soon I must try the line to Cologne again.

Slowly, reluctantly, the sky cleared. Eyes turned upward wide with astonishment. The sun! There really was one! Everyone but the air-crew types had forgotten its existence. When was the last time it had shone? No one could recall. Two weeks at least, probably three. Blimey, perhaps winter

51

really would come to an end one day. Come to think of it, the first day of spring wasn't so far off; just a few days. In the cockpits fitters grinned and told each other it was getting *hot* with the sun shining in through the perspex. Nice, for a change.

The last bombs were cranked up from the trolleys, grasped by steel fingers within the bomb-bays. Thirty-three-foot-long bomb-bay doors wheezed shut. Hundred-octane fuel gurgled into the tanks (six to an aircraft; total capacity: 2,154 gallons); final adjustments to controls and levers and lights and sights and seats and mirrors and compasses and triggers. Then the job was done. The aircraft were ready. Laden, they rested on their slender undercarriage legs and waited for their crews.

The wind freshened. A Churchman's wrapper, crumpled and empty, blew across the concrete hard-standing to play against the left main wheel of G-George. The wind pressed against fins and rudders; the aircraft stirred; its door banged against a bulkhead; the noise bounced along the stringers and formers of the empty fuselage. Tomorrow they would decide G-George's fate.

Atop the hangar, the windsock ballooned.

A Boeing Fortress appeared from the east and flew across the airfield at five thousand feet. It turned, displaying its huge tail assembly. Silver and shining in the sun. And lost. A nasal voice asked Brocklington tower where in hell was Honington, Suffolk. Brocklington tower gave directions. The Fort said thanks and headed south.

Wally wrote a letter to his parents. It was a cheerful letter, the sort of letter to make parents nod and smile through their tears. He told them he was at peace with himself (whatever the hell that meant) and that they shouldn't remember him as totally good or totally bad; he had disappointed them in so many ways (of course)

52

but he could honestly say he had never set out to hurt them. Or anyone, for that matter. He loved them very dearly although he supposed that he had never really taken the trouble to tell them so. End of letter.

He folded the letter, slipped it into an envelope, sealed the envelope and wrote the address and put a stamp on. Then he took another sheet of paper and wrote: TO BE POSTED ONLY IN THE EVENT OF MY DEATH. He clipped this to the envelope and placed it in the centre of the chest of drawers.

There. He had done it. Something he had sworn never to do.

Damn. He looked at himself in the mirror. Tousled; no collar. Angrily, he lit a cigarette. He inhaled and blew smoke at his reflection. Perhaps he would never see his face again in all eternity ...

He picked up his collar. Rather a limp-looking effort. He dropped it, opened the drawer and took out a freshly starched collar. He fastened it to the stud at the back of his neck, then slipped in the tie before passing the front stud through the slots. A couple of tugs: tie positioned neatly. Neatly enough for ops.

Anyway, what about all the times people said things they had never said before and then got into the aircraft and flew off—and came back? Eh? What about all those times? No one remembered those times, did they?

He blew smoke at his reflection again. Putting his cigarette on the edge of the dresser he slipped into his battle-dress blouse. Two buttons to fasten at the rear to prevent the blouse slipping up—he would undo them before putting on his flying gear. A row of buttons up the front, a quarter-belt to trim the middle. His epaulettes bore the single stripe denoting Flying Officer rank—for which His Majesty's government paid the princely sum of eighteen shillings and twopence per day. The pilot's wings over his

53

left pocket were well dulled, thoroughly operational. He brushed his hair. You look bloody gorgeous, he told his reflection.

He swallowed. His mouth was suddenly dry. He gripped the edge of the dresser and squeezed his eyes shut and fought the panic that exploded within him.

Oh, God, he breathed, when it was over. I'm so bloody scared.

7

Men emerged from huts and barracks and messes and offices and, singly and in groups, some two hundred of them made their various ways along the main thoroughfare of the station, turning left at the hangars, past the control tower and the flight offices. All the men wore air-crew badges, the double-wing badge of a pilot or the half-wing signifying one of the other air-crew trades. About one-third of them were officers, the rest sergeants, flight-sergeants or warrant officers. A few men, mostly pilots, wore ribbons, the diagonally striped blue-and-white ribbons of the Distinguished Flying Medal and Distinguished Flying Cross most numerous. The airmen wore a combination of standard uniform and flying-gear; fleece-lined jackets were popular, so were flying-boots. Dozens of men, particularly the gunners, sported huge white naval turtle-necked sweaters in lieu of shirts and collars and ties. Unlovely garments but most practical for long winter flights in indifferently heated aeroplanes, the sweaters hung below the wearers' battle-dress blouses like great hairy skirts.

The men made their way to the briefing-room.

They talked among themselves. It was important to everyone—including yourself—to discuss the forthcoming op in the most casual of terms. Or preferably not at all. The dangers were best kept to yourself. No one wanted to hear about them; everyone knew.

Wally and Paul walked in company with Flying Officer Bert Dunn, pilot of P-Popsy and veteran of twenty-two ops. Flying Officer Bert Dunn had a hobby: model aeroplanes.

He had just started work on a 1/36th scale Bristol F2b. He said it was a devil of a problem to get the right effect on the wings. The wings of the original were of wood construction, fabric covered. When the fabric was doped it created a charming scalloped effect between the solid ribs. Flying Officer Dunn's problem was how to achieve that same effect in a small model. One solution, he said, was to make the wing as they had made it in 1917: build it up rib by rib then cover it but, by George, it seemed one hell of a lot of work.

Paul suggested glueing bits of thread across the wing to simulate ribs. Flying Officer Dunn said he had tried that on a Spad; when the thread was painted it shrank and pulled the wing out of shape. It was a jolly tough problem.

Wally said yes, a jolly tough problem indeed.

Long, narrow and Spartan was the briefing-room. Its bare wooden floor bore an untidy collection of trestle tables, benches and fold-up chairs. Maps and aircraft recognition bulletins adorned the walls; the latest Keep-your-mouth-shut posters were prominent. Jet-black aircraft models hung on wires from the ceiling: a Stirling, a Focke-Wulf 190, a Blenheim, a Hurricane, a Heinkel 111 and, for some reason, a Gladiator. Against one wall stood a glass case containing two Luftwaffe uniforms; no one was sure why they were there. At one end of the briefing-room, behind a low stage, hung a large coloured map of Northern Europe. Beside the map was a blackboard; a second blackboard rested on an easel to the left. At one side of the stage, incongruously, there was a pulpit. On Sundays the briefing-room became a chapel.

Today, as each airman entered the briefing-room he glanced at the large map. The map had the gen: a bright red ribbon extended from the familiar dot in England that represented Brocklington, out across the North Sea, then angled south into Germany.

Berlin again.

Christ almighty.

'They've got one-track bloody minds,' said someone.

Berlin was a long way away. And a long way home.

The airmen found seats. They lit cigarettes and glanced again at the red ribbon and talked of other things and thought of nothing else. Then the side-door opened; there was an explosion of scraping chair-legs. A short, sturdy figure strode rapidly into the briefing-room: the Station Commander, Air Commodore Bailey, a man in his early forties who had flown Foxes and Harts and Heyfords in the 'twenties and 'thirties and, during the first year of the war, an underpowered contraption called the Battle—against stupefying odds he had somehow survived. Behind the Station Commander came the Squadron Commanders, the Intelligence Officer, the Met Officer, the Navigation Officer.

The group made its way to the stage.

The Station Commander told everyone to be seated. He wished them all good afternoon, his voice booming as a commander's voice should boom; you felt that in earlier days he might have addressed troops on a hillside before leading them into battle—and they would all have heard what he had to say. He remarked that it was good to see everyone assembled once again; he apologized wryly for the cancellation of last night's show; he felt reasonably sure, however, that everything would go according to plan tonight. He took a pointer from the easel ledge and thrust it at the dot marked Berlin. He said he was sure it was going to be a very good show.

He grinned fiercely and tapped Berlin with his pointer.

Endicott, the plump, balding Intelligence Officer, told the airmen that they would be part of a sizable force.

He walked to the map. He glanced at the map and then

57

at the easel. He wanted the pointer but he observed that
the Station Commander was tapping his left toe with it.
Endicott made do with his finger. He indicated the route
selected by Bomber Command at High Wycombe with
modifications by Group. His finger followed the ribbon east-
ward across the North Sea to a point close to the German-
Danish border, straight across the narrow strip of land,
over water again, then sharply south, angling in to the
target. The crews thought of the interminable miles in
winter darkness, over sea and then unfriendly land. Endicott told them of the other squadrons which would be par-
ticipating, how they would swarm out from their airfields
along the eastern flank of England, their paths converging
at a nameless spot near the German coast, to form an
immense stream. The Brocklington contingent would be
among the leaders. Endicott's finger stabbed at the coast
and he described how the aircraft would slip into enemy
territory between the various flak locations. He made it
sound as though some four hundred bombers would be able
to sneak across the border without anyone knowing about
it. The cleverly arranged course would throw off the
defences; they wouldn't know what the target was until the
very last moment.

'Like bloody hell,' murmured a veteran's voice.

'We'll be among the first on the scene,' said Endicott
although he personally wouldn't go near an aeroplane that
night. 'The aircraft not yet equipped with H2S will be
bombing on the Pathfinder markers. Zero hour is 2130
hours. At zero minus three minutes the Pathfinders will
sky-mark the lane to the target with red flares that will
change to green after one hundred and twenty seconds. At
zero minus one the target markers will go down. The Pathfinders will also drop red and yellow flares twenty miles
beyond the target and you will turn on these flares on your
way home.'

It sounded clear enough. The trouble was, there would be God knows how many more lights of God knows how many different shades below. The Jerries were diligent in the burning of false markers. It could be thoroughly confusing; and the flak and the fighters didn't help.

Endicott consulted his notes. He said he had some brand-new gen on flak and night-fighter forces—and a Lancashire voice said about time too. Endicott smiled vaguely; the Station Commander glanced along the men in the front row, touching his left eyebrow and tapping his foot with the pointer again.

The airmen learnt that all friendly aircraft in the vicinity of the target would be four-engined: so shoot at anything else without hesitation! Loads would consist of 4,000-pound bombs plus incendiaries. The attack was planned to last precisely thirty minutes.

Endicott sat down and the Met Officer took over. A bristly Scot with curly red hair and a double chin, he told the airmen that the weather was clearing very nicely indeed, in fact, even more rapidly than had first been calculated. It should be almost totally clear over the target. A trough of low was moving in from the west and by the time the Lancasters reached the English coast on their return journeys the weather would be overcast once more. All in all, the weather was a welcome change after that of the past few weeks, he observed.

The newer crews made copious notes and diagrams of searchlights and flak batteries—most of which information would be of little value during the mission. The more experienced the crew, the fewer notes and diagrams. After half a dozen ops you got to know what was of real importance among the data the briefing officers dished out.

Finally the Station Commander stood up and wished them a very good trip indeed and the very best of luck to them, one and all.

He half saluted, half waved as he strode off the stage. He observed the airmen shuffling to their feet. He knew what was going through their minds; he had experienced the same fears and uncertainties, the same impatience, the same resentment against a comfortable authority that picks targets and routes and loads and heights for other people to fly.

The airmen looked younger and pinker every day to the Station Commander. Half of them were little more than schoolboys; some of them attempted to look older by sprouting outrageous moustaches—and succeeded only in looking like actors in school dramas. The Station Commander hoped they would all get back safely; but he knew it was unlikely. Berlin trips had always cost crews; the combination of distances and ferocious defences stacked the odds too high. The statistics declared that 1.72 aircraft would be lost. Well, a year ago it had been worse: 2.13 was the average cost of sending a force against the German capital. And in those days the results were far less impressive; the squadrons still flew Wimpeys, twin-engined relics of an earlier age of aviation. Lancaster crews lasted longer.

Tonight, inevitably, one or more squadron of Lancs would be lost, would plummet out of the sky and be blown to fragments or splash into the icy waters of the North Sea to go sliding down, turning over and over, disintegrating on the journey to the sea floor. The crew? The chances were against them. Almost invariably someone died when a kite was lost. Six of the seven men might bale out safely but the cursed statistics proved how unlikely it was for everyone to make it. And the unfortunate one was so often the skipper. The reason was cruelly simple. A mortally wounded aircraft flies badly; the pilot must work hard at the controls to keep the machine on an even keel while his crew jumps. But when the last crew member has jumped who is there to hold the aircraft steady while the pilot makes his escape?

Pinkerton cornered Wally on the way out of the briefing-room.

'How's the kite? Any complaints?'

Wally shook his head. 'No, it's first-rate.'

'Good. That's good,' said Pinkerton. He seemed anxious to be understanding. 'I know it must be a bit of a bind having to take a new kite on your last trip after using the same one all that time. I'm glad you found Mother satisfactory. Don't bend her, will you—Sergeant Kenesky will be awfully annoyed if you do. He's very proud of her.' He grinned. He had a pleasant grin; it was a pity one so rarely saw it.

Wally promised not to bend M-Mother.

'Good man.' Pinkerton glanced up. 'Everything else OK?'

'Yes, thank you.'

'Glad to hear it.'

Wally wondered whether Pinkerton was really asking: 'Tell me, Wally, are you going potty? Losing your loaf, are you, old man?'

I must be what is known as a border-line case, Wally thought. Not quite gone enough to call for the men in the white coats, but a great big question mark as far as flying is concerned.

On the stage a corporal carefully removed the red ribbon, placing the marking pins in a cardboard box. Without the ribbon the map looked curiously forlorn.

Well-meaning, Pinkerton said, 'It should be a good show tonight.'

Wally nodded. 'I can hardly wait,' he said.

The boys stood around outside, casual as ever. For a

moment, Wally looked at them. He thought: Do you realize you're playing around with the lives of these fellows as well as mine? If I get the chop they'll probably get it too. Hardly fair, is it? He wondered who he was talking to. God, he felt so tiny and vulnerable; he wanted to run and find Ann and cling to her and hide his face in her hair. But the rules and regulations were quite clear: under no circumstances could there be any running and clinging and hiding of face in hair. That's where she was: over there, in the control tower, the square, grey place. Perhaps she was watching him at that very moment, noting how jaunty he looked, chatting with his crew, grinning at the old chestnuts about Paul getting lost and finding the way home by reading the names on railway stations, about Charlie listening to the BBC Forces Programme throughout the trip, about Douglas scoring the first direct hit of his career—on Blackpool Tower. Ha bloody ha. Jesus Christ, Ann, he thought, am I really going to die? Have I been told *officially*?

He didn't know; he didn't know anything ... except that it was just over there ... fifty yards away, that he had first spoken to her. One morning just before Christmas. She walked by; he had watched her and had imagined how her body looked beneath her clothes, the flesh of her flanks and thighs moving and catching the light. He had pondered the matter of her breasts. Were they truly as developed as they seemed to be? Were her nipples of generous diameter? Then he felt ashamed because he was taking stock of her as a farmer might take stock of a cow. But quickly, glibly, he had invented an excuse for himself: the individual's capacity for civilized feeling is indirectly proportional to the tonnage of high explosive he has dropped on perspiring, praying humanity. At least he had been honest enough to shout Bullshit! at himself ...

'I say, I saw you at the White Hart the other night. I

was the one who whistled at you. I'm sorry. I had a couple of drinks too many. Normally I'm quite well behaved in pubs.'

Her look had seemed so impossibly wintry; positively Princess Elizabeth. It said that her father must be an air marshal and she must have scores of boy friends, all wing commanders and up, all catalogued by income, connections, pedigree and size of organ ...

'I didn't notice you,' she said. Wizard voice.

'I think you did. You were with Norman Livesey. I was wishing you were with me.'

'Was that why you were rude?' Still very Frigidaire, but perhaps there was a glimmering of hope.

'Let's go to York next Saturday,' he said in a rush. 'We can have tea in a little place I know near the market, then we can go to the pictures and have some dinner somewhere and have a walk along Fossgate and Petergate and the Shambles and look in the shops and have a drink in Betty's Bar and I'll be most polite and all that because it'll be our first evening together; however, all the time we're together I'll be conscious of what an attractive person you are and how very much I'd enjoy sleeping with you.'

She nodded slowly, thoughtfully. 'You're quite attractive yourself,' she said. 'The girls in the Waafery said you're a bit of a charmer and I see they're right. You say your piece awfully well, by the way. It has just the right set of ingredients: an invitation to do pleasant things in nice places in the company of a man who's fairly good-looking and quite attentive and courteous and yet has just the right sort of elemental instincts, kept under control with difficulty. It's a good piece—but I've heard it done better by a captain from Omaha, Nebraska, a squadron leader from Brighton and a lieutenant from Owen Sound, Ontario. Oh yes, and a corporal from Calcutta. Now you really must excuse me. Good day!'

She strode off leaving Wally to stare at a sparrow fluffing its feathers on the flight-office roof.

Suddenly he found himself bellowing:

'I say! You're a smasher!'

Six airmen turned to look. Ann stopped in her tracks but she didn't turn. After a moment, she started off again.

'Wait a minute! Hey! Wait!'

She stopped again but still didn't turn. He ran after her, watched by the six interested airmen and a pilot officer and a WAAF who had poked their heads out of the flight office to see what all the commotion was about.

'I like you,' he said with enthusiasm. 'I like you very much and I don't say that to many girls.'

'Don't you dare shout at me again,' she said, her lips tight. 'Don't do it again or I'll do something violent to you.'

'I sincerely hope so,' he said. 'York next Saturday?'

She shook her head. Someone Else. Somewhere Else.

'Sunday?'

'There's nothing to do in York on a Sunday.'

'We'll find something.'

'No, thank you.' Pause. Then the hint of a smile. 'But I think I may go for a walk on Sunday. I really haven't seen Brocklington yet.'

'I'll guide you,' he told her. 'I know the village as Sandy McPherson knows his organ, if you'll pardon the expression. I'll take you to the Forbidden Quarter, to the Slave Market, to the Temple of a Million Delights, otherwise known as the Oddfellows' Hall ...'

But on Sunday there had been no need to think up absurdities to keep her amused. On Sunday they walked to Brocklington and into the country beyond and discovered happiness in each other's company. They told each other of their lives; they walked eight miles that Sunday and hardly realized it. The following Tuesday they went to

64

the station cinema and joined the hooting at *A Yank in the RAF*. Afterwards they walked along the York Road; in the darkness they kissed. It began to rain but for some minutes they were unaware of it. They tried to shelter under a tree but it was leafless, useless. The White Hart was a mile and a half in one direction, the village two miles in the opposite direction. In between, there was nothing, save the airfield. They walked back to the main gate.

'Tyrone Power would have done better than this,' Ann told him. 'He would have found a cosy little hut complete with fire and sofa and dry clothes.'

Wally said, in a voice suddenly husky, 'I'll do better next Saturday. I'll book a room at the Carlton.'

And she had said, 'All right, Wally,' as if it was the most natural thing in the world. Which it was.

8

It was the in-between time. Time to kill. Too much time. A meal to be eaten, flying-clothes to put on. And that was all, except waiting.

You might spend the time reading. Or you might send a letter home. You might chat but suddenly there seemed very little to talk about. You might sleep the time away. You might pace it away. Hardly a man admitted to worrying about the op. Hardly a man didn't worry. If a man was a veteran of half a dozen or more ops he worried about the things he had seen: the flak, the fighters, the searchlights. If a man was new to the business he worried about the unknown, about the things he had seen only in photographs and the things he had read and the things he had heard in the Mess. Some men worried about their inadequacies, real or imagined. For most the fear of letting the side down loomed larger than the fear of being killed or wounded.

Some men worried about their pilots; some pilots worried about their navigators. Some men worried about their wives and children. Many men had individual fears: the fear of mid-air collisions. To such men, take-offs and landings at night were the worst times of every op; other men feared fire above all; some trembled at the thought of ditching in the sea. Even the parachute, saver of countless lives, was regarded with terror by some; men would die because they could not force themselves to jump from stricken aircraft.

But airmen didn't speak to one another of such things; it wasn't done. What was done was to make believe that the op was a 'show'. Everyone was going to have a fine time;

it was going to be a 'good show'—except of course for the crews that got themselves shot down and for the people on whom the bombs would fall. (It wasn't done to talk about them either.) After the raid the crews would receive Target Tokens: cards upon which were pasted copies of the photographs taken by their aircrafts' automatic cameras as the bombs hit the ground.

Souvenirs of a good show.

The crews ate their ops tea together, officers and NCOs side by side on long deal benches. The op was already in motion, thus rank became progressively less important. The only boss was the pilot, the skipper, and everyone obeyed him, even though he might be a sergeant and the navigator a flight lieutenant. Or even, in theory, an air commodore.

The crews received bacon and fresh eggs before the op: three rashers of bacon and two eggs per man. In the centres of the tables were great piles of sliced bread flanked by pound chunks of Ministry of Food margarine with its curiously cardboard taste. The room was a warm, continuous bellow. Everyone talked now, particularly the ones who could find nothing to say ten minutes ago. Eating seemed to help. Topics were trivial in the main: leaves and popsies and West-End plays and what Tommy Handley said the other night. But some men had no appetites. A problem with the gullet: food simply refused to be swallowed. They drank gallons of tea, warm and sweet, and they cut their eggs and bacon into the tiniest of portions and still it wouldn't go down. Finally they pushed the food to one corner of their plates to make it look as if they had eaten more than they had. They drank more tea and waited impatiently for the time to get up and get going.

Of the two hundred-plus men only a handful were thirty or more. The average age was twenty-two. Good looks were the rule rather than the exception because the men were healthy and of above-average intelligence. Even in the fifth year of the war, air-crew qualifications were strict; only the best would do. The majority of the airmen were conscious of the fact that this might be their last meal on earth. The target was Berlin: therefore somebody would almost certainly get the chop. It would almost certainly be somebody else, of course. Of course. And the very best of hard cheese for whoever it would almost certainly be. Thus, a score of rabbits' feet nestled in trouser pockets; four-leaf clovers lay squashed flat in wallets and notebooks; 'lucky' scarves abounded, most of them red. One airman carried his daughter's first tooth; he never flew without it. Another carried a garter purchased from a London prostitute for a pound. One pilot wedged a photograph of his wife and son on the instrument panel before take-off. A mid-upper gunner had never been off the ground without his favourite pornographic postcard ('The Party at the Nunnery') in his pocket. Another gunner hung a small gold cross on the breech of his Brownings.

As he munched his eggs, Charlie Newton told Douglas darkly that one day there would be peace. And it would be bloody awful. Back to civvy street; back to hard times. 'Don't you believe all that cock the politicians talk about the marvellous world they're going to build for all us heroes. Don't you believe it, mate. It'll be a marvellous world for heroes with money; it always has been, it always will be. The same last time. The Great War. Great for whom? They all said, C'mon lads, join up and fight for England, home and beauty and the Conservative Party and Ascot and the Bank of England and Threadneedle Bloody Street and your chum and mine, King George. Come on and risk getting your silly head blown off to defend the British way of life. But they really meant, ways. See, there are two ways: one way for you and me, mate, and the other way for the geysers with the money and the families and the nice accents. And it's only *that* way of life that's worth fighting for and we don't even get in on it! Bloody marvellous, isn't it? The rich get all the poor sods fighting to help keep the rich rich. I don't know, I really don't. And when it was all over, what happened? Why, the gallant bleeding lads in khaki suddenly became something called the militant unemployed. A menace to society. I remember the General Strike in '26. All those poor sods marching again, only this time they had working clothes on instead of uniforms. And the same bleeding politicians who had taken off their top hats to them in 1916 now wondered about using machine guns on 'em. And the slump. I saw nippers growing up on dry bread, their teeth going black in their heads. No money for dentists; no money for nothing. It went on and on. And what did anyone do about it? Well, by Jove, there simply wasn't anything anyone could possibly do about it, don't you know. Most regrettable and all that but the situation was caused by international stock-market problems and trade indices and balances of international finances. Nothing to do but tighten the jolly old belt and see it through; the good old capitalistic system would survive, have no fear. And then, all of a sudden, there was all the money in the world to buy tanks and planes and guns. Why? Because of Hitler. Hey-bloody-presto, no more stock-market problems, everyone working, making lots of things to be blown to smithereens. Three cheers for the flaming capitalistic system. And now this lot and what happens? Same thing. We can't bloody wait to join up to fight for *them*. I dunno; I really don't; it makes you sick. We should have told the politicians: Up yours, cock. But we didn't. We listened to the BBC and they told us the same bloody tripe as before. And we swallowed it. And here we are. And we bloody well deserve to be.'

Len said, 'You didn't do too bad mate. You're a W/O. You're sitting pretty.'

'Right,' said Charlie. 'I'm doing all right because they need me. And you. But wait till they don't need you any more. Just wait till then.'

Phil said, 'You're a miserable old bugger, Charlie. It'll be better this time. People aren't going to put up with things the way they did.'

'Oh, and just what are they going to do about things if they don't like them? What you don't understand, mate, is that you don't run things. You don't run anything. You don't even run yourself. *They* run everything. They decide how much you're going to make, how much you're going to pay for your food, for your clothes, and for every other bloody thing. You're powerless, mate. You just do whatever they tell you. And the funny bloody thing is, half the time you don't even *know* they're telling you. You think you made your own mind up about something. But you didn't. You're just thinking what *their* newspaper told you to think.'

'I don't know,' said Phil thoughtfully.

'Too right you don't,' said Harry.

Len said he had heard enough about politics; he was more interested in the end-of-the-tour party; had any decisions been made? Was it to be the White Hart? Or somewhere in York? Or Hull?

Everyone turned to the skipper. He smiled, half shrugging. Dreadfully sorry, hadn't really made any definite plans yet. What was the consensus? York? Who was in favour of York?

Phil beamed. 'It doesn't matter where we go as long as we can get young Douglas fixed up.'

'Fixed up?' said someone. 'What, with a woman, you mean?'

'I wasn't thinking of a Dalmatian, chum.'

Suddenly everyone was looking at Douglas, whose mouth had opened slightly and whose eyes were pale and shrinking, like a frightened doe's. His left hand held a fork poised midway between plate and mouth. A piece of egg fell off the fork and landed damply back on the plate. He seemed utterly stunned by Phil's suggestion.

Len said he thought it was a very noble idea; Harry nodded; Charlie shook his head, clearly pained at the turn the conversation had taken. Paul laughed quietly.

Phil said, 'What sort of bints do you like, Doug? Big ones? Little ones? Fat? Thin?'

Douglas's mouth flickered nervously from an I-know-you're-just-joking smile to an oh-God-they-mean-it quiver and back again; again and again; and all the time his eyes darted over the faces of his crew-mates, seeking reassurance. He had turned bright pink; he was apparently incapable of speech. His crew-mates told him of the wondrous variations on the female theme and how all he had to do was state his preference and it would be taken care of. Harry said Douglas was lucky to have such friends; Len suggested that possibly Doug's preference was for something on the exotic side, Oriental or chocolate brown; a fellow should have his choice his first time up.

Wally said, 'But perhaps this isn't Doug's first time up.' Stares.

Paul took the cue. 'Right! Seems to me you guys are assuming a hell of a lot. Doug's been around.'

More stares. Disbelieving stares. Len turned to Douglas. 'Well,' he snapped, like a Gestapo interrogator, 'is it?'

Douglas gulped. He found voice. 'Is it what?' he countered, the 'what' emanating as a tinny shriek.

'You know what. Come on, mate.'

'Yes, come on, Doug. Tell us.'

A new game: Is Douglas Indeed a Virgin Or Has He a Past No One Ever Suspected? It was more fun than the last game. Certainly it seemed to make Doug even pinker; you could see how ruffled the poor little squirt was: a strand of hair toppled away from his normally impeccable head to dance in front of his eyes. He stuttered: None of his crew-mates' business; they had no right to pry; he didn't pry into their private lives; they shouldn't pry into his ...

Then all conversation ceased at nearby tables and faces turned as Douglas jumped to his feet and pushed his way through to the door. Harry stood up then sat down again. Paul scratched the tip of his nose. Len seemed deflated. Phil observed that the lad was a wee bit touchy.

'Always was rather a sensitive bloke,' Charlie observed.

Len stood up. 'I'd better go and ...'

'No, leave him be,' said Wally.

He sipped tea pensively. Everything seemed to be going wrong with this op.

There wasn't much time left in which to be yourself. Soon you would have to struggle into bulky flying-clothes and collect your gear and go out to the aircraft. You wouldn't be quite yourself any more; you would be a component required to perform certain important functions. The other components would depend on you.

Wally walked across the sodden turf beyond the hangars, a long way from the Mess and the faces and the uniforms.

He paused and looked back. Hundreds of people milling about over there but here he was quite alone. Curious places, airfields, curious and frightening and fascinating. The buildings were becoming evanescent in the deepening evening, merging with the trees and the hills behind.

He turned up his collar and thrust his hands deep into his pockets. I was scared, he thought, now I'm not. I'm not at all scared.

'When I see daylight again I'll have done my last op,' he said aloud. 'I hope,' he added.

A cold wind scurried up his trouser leg. It was strange, the fear had gone like a minor headache. He wondered where it had gone, where it was lurking. He remembered the girl in the wrecked flat, the girl who was dead. Please don't let my bombs do anything like that. He huddled down in his shoulders. He told himself that if he had any sense he would be snuggling up to a nice warm Ann instead of standing out here doing ... what? He was going to feel bloody silly tomorrow morning when he remembered all this. What *was* he up to? Introducing himself to his maker in case he happened to bump into Him during the night?

He sniffed. The cold was making his nose run.

If I do get the chop, he thought, it will be quite interesting to find out what really does happen after death. He recalled conversations with Jack Hellier on the very same subject. Since those conversations Jack had found out: he had spun into the Wadden Zee one night in January. Perhaps he had discovered that there really are pearly gates and cumulus floors and a great big desk and a book with your life described to the last sordid detail.

Wally told God: To be perfectly frank I don't think You give a damn for the human race.

He looked around the darkening airfield and described to God what was happening and why. Nasty business, eh? Unholy, you might say. Well, if You really do care why do You permit it?

Behind the Armoury he encountered Douglas, hands in pockets, battledress collar turned up. Huddled against the building, hiding from the wind, he looked frozen and forlorn.

Wally greeted him. 'Nippy, isn't it? I've just been for a walk. Have you, too? We must be out of our minds. Coming?'

Douglas nodded, half smiling in the automatic way of people who haven't yet learnt to be sure of themselves.

'I'm sorry ... I made rather a scene in the Mess.'

'Did you? Yes, I suppose you did. Never mind; it really doesn't matter very much.'

'I think it matters,' Douglas said. 'I made a fool of myself.' Evidently he felt strongly about it; he added: 'A bloody silly fool of myself.'

Wally shrugged and said that everyone makes a bit of a fool of himself at one time or another; it seems serious as hell at the time but it really isn't. They're a good bunch of lads. A bit basic, perhaps, but they don't mean any harm. In a way, it's an indication of how fond they are of you.'

Douglas stared at him. 'I don't think it's a very nice way of showing it,' he said seriously.

Wally chuckled. 'I wouldn't worry about it if I were you.'

'I wouldn't either, if I were you.'

There was something in the way he said it; something disarmingly sincere and honest. Wally had an uncomfortable feeling that it was admiration; and he had an equally uncomfortable feeling that he'd been talking in a cruelly flippant way. It was all frightfully amusing: to everyone except Douglas. To Douglas it was horrifying. But why? Wally wondered.

'I like women,' said Douglas as if reading his skipper's thoughts. 'I like them very much. I think about them all the time. In fact, to be perfectly honest, I hardly think about anything else. Sometimes I think I'm a bit odd, because I think about them so much. But when I'm really with a woman it's all different; it's awful. I can't think of anything to say; I do the wrong things. I'm an absolute idiot.'

'No, you're not,' said Wally. 'Lots of chaps feel like that. But they get over it. You will too.'

'I don't think so, skipper. I think I'm just one of those people who are doomed to spend lives of lonely pointlessness.'

Wally smiled to himself; some Hollywood hack must have banged out that phrase for some Hollywood actor to mouth—and six thousand miles away a foreign airman finds that it fits his own problem to a T. Ah, the miracles of modern communications.

Douglas said, 'It was nice of you to say ... well, you know, what you did say ...' He looked at Wally. 'Thanks ... thanks very much.'

Touched, Wally told him it was nothing, nothing at all.

Veit yawns and stretches and shakes his head like a dog coming out of water. Now he is wide awake. He looks at me, blinks. He unwinds himself from his chair and walks across to the window, scratching the small of his back with both hands. He studies the sky; his eyes rove from east to west; he peers into the twilight as if reading a distant sign. I watch and wait for his verdict. Veit knows sky.

'I think our friends will be paying us a visit tonight,' he announces and goes back to his chair.

'Dear me,' said Greening as he breathed noisily on his spectacles and began rubbing them with a handkerchief.

Wally looked at the VD poster informing that delay in treatment could have a number of dire consequences, including death. 'It's a bit tricky,' he said, 'because the chap in question is married already. And he asked me to ask you whether there's some way of, well, bringing the young lady back on stream, so to speak.'

Greening put his glasses on and sighed at Wally. 'You're asking me to suggest something?'

Wally nodded and thought, That's what I just said, you sanctimonious twerp.

'How late is her period?'

'I don't know precisely. A week or so, I think.'

'That's not long, is it?' He sounded like a schoolmaster

who has been given an incorrect answer in class.

'Isn't it?'

'When I was at med. school we had a party for a girl who was celebrating the return of her period. She hadn't menstruated for three months. She was in the midst of examinations. The strain, the general anxiety simply upset the metabolism of her body and she failed to menstruate.'

'I don't think this girl is taking any examinations.'

'Perhaps not. But what I'm trying to explain is that all sorts of things can prevent a girl having a period, not only pregnancy.' He gazed at Wally and clicked his tongue. 'She might try taking very hot baths with mustard.'

'Hot baths with mustard?'

'Very hot. They sometimes seem to help. She might also try taking castor oil. The resultant, um, upheaval might well bring her on.'

'Parboiling and purgation, eh?'

Greening nodded primly. 'Other than that, I'm afraid there's nothing I can do for you, Wally. Nothing at all. I'm sorry for you; I'm sure it's very inconvenient and all that, but there's nothing I can do. I'm sure you understand why.'

Wally said, 'Look, I explained, it isn't *me*, it's my engineer, Harry Whittaker ...'

'Quite, quite,' said Greening.

Wally stood; he started to repeat that all this was for someone else; then he laughed. What the hell difference did it make?

The room was full of steel lockers in which the airmen kept their working-clothes: their flying-suits, fur-lined boots, gloves, helmets, oxygen masks, Mae Wests. The room smelt of leather and rubber and kapok and fur and sweat and nervousness. The airmen tugged and zipped and buckled and tied themselves into their flying-clothes, emptying their

76

pockets as they did so. They had been told umpteen times by umpteen officers not to take personal possessions on ops. ('You'd be astounded, gentlemen, if you knew how much a capable intelligence officer can deduce from something as innocent as, say, a tram ticket.') They looped the harness straps over their shoulders and around their bodies and between their legs. ('If you should happen to have occasion to jump out of your aeroplane and your harness should happen to be slack, well, you will probably break every bone in your body when the parachute opens; moreover, you can count on coming down with a very high voice, a very high voice indeed!') The airmen carried their chest-pack parachutes suitcase-style, using the edge handles provided, taking care not to lift the pack by the metal ring in the centre. Everyone knew of clots who had opened parachutes in crew rooms and in taxiing aircraft and in vans and even in lavatories.

Bulky in their padded suits, the airmen made their separate ways outside to gather in groups around the door while ground personnel eyed them from respectful distances; then more airmen came through the door and the gatherings burgeoned and spilled off the narrow path on to the grass and the ground personnel moved back to make more room for the men who stood a fairly good chance of having their heads blown off during the night. Crews assembled casually and for the most part efficiently but here and there a skipper balanced on tiptoes and asked loudly where the hell his navigator or rear gunner had got to. The airmen talked and laughed; everyone played the game of excessive pre-op cheer. It was expected.

The wind had strength now. On the hard-standings the Lancasters stirred heavily as the day dissolved into night.

9

The van squealed to a halt.

'All change,' said Charlie.

'I'm going to miss you saying that,' said Len. 'But not very bloody much.'

For the third time that day the seven members of the crew stumbled out of the van. They passed their gear and bags from man to man and dumped them on the grass under M-Mother's perspex nose. They weren't yet inside the aircraft but they could smell the metal and fuel and oil and plastic odours that combined to create that unique Essence de Lanc. Lancaster crews said the aircraft smelt like none other; they could pick one out blindfolded.

Charlie belched. 'Greasy bloody eggs,' he complained.

'Better now?' asked Len.

The skipper went off to walk around the kite and make sure all the parts were tied on. He returned in a couple of minutes and then they all made their way up the short metal ladder and disappeared into M-Mother's fuselage.

The ground crew watched the strangers take over their kite. The sergeant planted himself a few feet to the left of the nose. He glared at the engines and then at the pilot's window. Treat the engines proper and they'll start, his glare said.

Inside the cockpit Wally settled himself into his seat. Harry moved in behind him, plugging his intercom into its socket.

'Switches off.'

'Switches off.'

The litany of preparing for flight ... take nothing for granted inside or outside the aircraft ... check and recheck.

M-Mother quivered as the port inner clattered into motion,

then the starboard inner; the port outer; finally Wally punched the button for the starboard outer engine's booster coil: the propeller wheezed and spun and became a blur.

The ground-crew sergeant nodded, still glaring.

'Pilot to navigator. Checking intercom.'

'Navigator to pilot. OK.'

'Bomb aimer?'

'Intercom OK, skipper.'

Engineer, wireless op, mid-upper gunner, rear gunner: everyone was in communication.

M-Mother trembled as Wally opened the throttles running them up to zero boost, testing the magnetos. Harry's eyes raced over the instruments: pressures, temperatures, revs—everything on top line. Thumbs up.

'Pilot to crew. Any complaints?'

'No complaints.'

'Wireless op? How's your stomach?'

'Better, thanks, skip.'

'Good show. OK. Time for a smoke.'

The Merlins rumbled into silence; the propellers became great three-bladed metal contraptions again. Surprisingly, you could hear an erk walking across the concrete hardstanding; his voice seemed loud in the sudden stillness.

Now, the last lap of waiting. The crew squeezed themselves out of their seats and thumped down the fuselage and out on the grass again. The ground crew stood in melancholy assembly near the tail; they drifted away when told everything was working. No last-minute flaps; thank God.

A small car appeared; it turned into M-Mother's dispersal. Automatically suspicious, the air crew watched it stop beneath the aircraft's nose. Then they smiled and turned away because it was only Brigden, the Armaments Officer: no one of importance.

Three minutes later Reynolds the wireless man came buzzing along to ask after M-Mother's radio and radar.

No problems, Charlie told him.

'Good show,' said Reynolds warmly. He had a pale round face and he wore glasses. 'This is your last op, isn't it? Jolly good show. Have a good one. Drop one for me.'

'On you?' Paul asked him.

But Reynolds was already scurrying away to the next dispersal.

Wally lit his last cigarette and tossed the empty packet at Paul; it missed him and hit M-Mother's tailplane. Was Ann at her desk or out on the tarmac to watch the take-off? Many of the WAAFs braved the cold night air to give the boys a wave—and the boys appreciated it. It was hard not to feel a tingle of pride as the motors gunned and the kite started to roll; surely the knights of old must have felt the same things as they rode off to battle amid a flutter of ladies' handkerchiefs.

But knights of old didn't drop bombs on civilians.

'I can't say I really feel like going flying,' Paul said. 'What do you say we call the whole thing off and go into town and get laid instead?'

Wally smiled. 'You're reading my mind again.'

'If they scrub this one that's exactly what I'm going to do,' Paul declared. 'A guy can stand so much. I'll get blotto.'

'I've never seen you blotto.'

'I have been,' said Paul. 'The last time was a party they threw for me when I came overseas. It was in a house on Bathurst Street; I remember that quite well; and I remember the girl. They tell me I fell asleep on her. *On* her. Can you imagine? But I don't recall a thing about it. I woke up at home, under my bed. And with the worst hangover in the history of the Taylor family. I had to catch a train at Union Station at ten after nine. Wow.'

Wally glanced at his watch.

'I think it's about time, chaps.'

They clustered at the leading edge of the starboard tail-plane, struggling to get through layers of thick winter flying-gear.

'Ready?' Wally asked.

It was a ceremony of long standing.

'Just a mo',' said Phil.

'Hurry up. Mine's getting cold,' said Harry.

'All right,' said Phil. 'Ready.'

'Right,' said Wally. 'Fire.'

They emptied their bladders on M-Mother's tail-wheel.

Afterwards they buttoned and zipped themselves up again, satisfied that they had done everything to ensure a successful op.

'There's the flare.'

They turned toward the control tower. The light soared into the night sky and scattered into fragments as it fell.

The crew took the final drags of their cigarettes then squashed them into the grass.

'Well ...,' said Wally. For a moment it seemed as if he was going to make a speech, a few words from the captain on this auspicious occasion, etcetera, etcetera, but then he just smiled and turned and went up the narrow ladder once more and the others followed him. The door closed behind them; it was opened and closed again sharply and finally from within.

The ground crew was practised. Two men handled the chocks, two more took care of the trolley acc. Another man carried shielded lights with which to guide M-Mother from her dispersal.

And from dispersals in every corner of the airfield the bombers came, slowly, timorous monsters sticking their noses out of their lairs, leaving the protection of the trees. They turned, tyres squealing, on to the perimeter track. Then they picked up speed, hurrying toward the runway, red and green lights dipping and rising, engines spurting bursts of noise.

There were times when the squadrons' departures were occasions of some ceremony. When notable somebodies visited the station or when the Ministry of Information sent cameramen to obtain citizen-stirring footage of our bomber boys going out to clobber the foe, the squadrons' aircraft would be marshalled on either side of the runway, angled smartly—'like the feathers at the end of an arrow', one newspaper described it. The Lancs would lumber out, the first from one side of the runway, the second from the other side and so on. Before the first Lanc was off the ground the second would have started to roll. All very neat and crisp and businesslike. The visiting notables would be impressed and the cameras would whirr and presumably the citizenry was stirred.

But this was late winter. And it was dark. No ceremony tonight. All that mattered was getting the kites sorted out and into the air as rapidly as possible.

As each aircraft arrived at the end of the runway the wireless operator signalled the control caravan, announcing the code letter by Aldis lamp. (R/T was forbidden because the enemy would simply monitor the transmission and know that aircraft were taking off on a raid. Using R/T was tantamount to sending a cablegram to the Reichstag informing them that the aircraft would be over German territory at such and such a time. Radar would tell the Germans of the approaching bombers soon enough—no point in making it easier for them.)

The control van winked a green eye at the Lancasters one by one; and one by one the Lancasters waddled out from the queue at the entrance to the runway, flaps drooping, engines howling, and crept then ran then sped away into the night.

M-Mother was eighth in line.

The runway was two lines of lights converging somewhere out of sight beyond the hump.

'Flaps thirty.'

'Flaps thirty.'

'Radiators OK?'

'Radiators OK.'

In the tail, Len swung the turret to port as far as it would go; now he and his Brownings were pointing along the tailplane. He could feel the sliding exit-doors at his back. Comforting. If anything went wrong during take-off, he would need only an instant to unbuckle himself, another instant to open the door, a third to tumble backwards and out.

'Throttles.'

'Throttles locked.'

Amidships, Charlie popped a piece of gum into his mouth and watched for the green light from the control caravan. His head touched the smooth perspex of the astrodome; he stared fixedly at the caravan; as the communications man of the crew it was his official job to inform the skipper when they were given the OK to take off.

Green light!

'We're away, skipper,' Charlie barked.

'Thank you, Charlie,' Wally acknowledged, although both he and Harry had seen the signal. 'Pilot to crew. Taking off now.' He shut the window panel at his left. A hiss as the brakes released their grip. 'Full power, please, engineer.' The Merlins dinned; Mother trundled forward, heavily, sulkily, then picking up speed, creaking as the runway's bumps and hollows jarred her structure.

Behind the row of lights, vague figures ... hands waving.

Wally gazed at the black ribbon between the lights that now rushed at him and swept away on either side. Over the intercom came the monotonous recitation of air-speeds—forty—forty-five, fifty, fifty-five, sixty. Now Mother was shaping the air over her wings; she began to ride. Tail up, she dashed along the strip of tarmac, belly crammed, tanks brimming. A lurch; over the hump. Now the flare-path had an end ...

'Seventy-five ... eighty ...'

Of course she would unstick. Of course she would. A good kite, George. But this wasn't George, was it? No, well, Mother was just as good. Think of all the things that could go wrong. Didn't someone claim there were seven thousand eight hundred and twenty-something things that could go wrong with a Lanc on take-off? Seven thousand eight hundred and twenty-something *different* things. All of which could prove fatal, so the someone said.

Warning lights ahead. Runway's end. Climb now or forever hold your peace.

Mother was already aloft. Speeding lights slowed as they dropped away. They vanished, left behind. Darkness. Noisy darkness.

'Undercarriage up.'

'Undercarriage up. And locked.'

'Thank you.'

Two green lights announced that the wheels had nestled in position behind the inboard engines, doors folding in behind them. A bump: flaps up. M-Mother's wings were clean. She climbed steadily, turning.

Hauptmann Langer is sympathetic. A direct hit, he explains. They could have felt no pain. Killed instantly. Is there anything he can do? Any relatives to be informed? What about funeral arrangements? Leave will, of course, be arranged.

I don't know what to think. Now that my worst fears have been realized I am strangely numb.

'What do you suggest?' I ask. 'What am I supposed to do?'

'For the present, nothing,' says Hauptmann Langer.

'Communications are very difficult at the moment. I think perhaps I must make some further inquiries of the civil authorities.'

I tell him I have been trying to telephone for two days. 'They kept telling me the lines were being repaired. I wonder why they didn't tell me the number I was ringing had been blown to bits.'

'These are difficult times,' says Hauptmann Langer.

'Perhaps my parents were lying there for two days before anyone came and found them.'

'No, I feel sure that wasn't the case.'

'The report says it was a direct hit?'

'Yes. The report came from the office of the Polizei-präsident. A direct hit. Your parents and some other occupants of the building were killed.'

Other occupants. The Schommers. Tenants of the top floor. For some reason I find myself telling Hauptmann Langer—who is a very busy man—that my father was less than fifty years old, my mother only in her middle forties. My father would have been in the Army but for his right eye. He lost the eye in a car accident a year or two before the war. It was a bad accident, I tell Hauptmann Langer; it could easily have been fatal: a head-on collision between our small Opel and a truck. My father was extremely lucky. But perhaps, I explain laboriously, if my father had gone into the Army he would now be alive. So the car accident was fatal after all, wasn't it? Through it all Hauptmann Langer listens patiently. Nodding. Agreeing. If it was Veit before him I could understand his patience. Veit is, after all, a valuable pilot who has more than justified the expense of his training and his equipment. I have accomplished precisely nothing.

I thank Hauptmann Langer. He says he is extremely sorry.

I go outside. It is dark. The sky has cleared.

I take deep breaths. I hope the Tommies come tonight.

10

One's nerves invariably settled down as soon as one was airborne and actually on the way. Relaxing, Wally lowered his seat to cruising position. The control column throbbed healthily beneath his hands; the engines sounded clean and noisy. Piece of cake.

He turned M-Mother until the compass needle joined the plotted course in a neat twelve o'clock. With his right hand on the U-shaped control wheel he could steer Mother almost like a car; the difference lay in the necessity of controlling the dimension of height.

'Pilot to navigator. On course oh-eight-eight. OK?'

'Navigator to pilot. Spot on, skipper.'

Paul had his own compass at the navigation station; it was sensible to check periodically that both compasses were telling the same story. Particularly when the trip involved a long trek over the North Sea.

'Pilot to gunners. Watch out for other aircraft, please.'

Immediately Len's voice came back: 'Rear gunner to pilot. There's a kite right behind us. He's gone now. He was close.'

'Roger. Keep watching, chaps. Lots of aircraft around.'

He switched off his microphone and unclipped the oxygen mask so that it dangled from one side of his helmet. At twenty thousand feet one had to breathe the stuff continuously; for the time being, however, it was pleasant to do without the mask.

His eyes travelled from the invisible horizon to the airspeed indicator to the compass to the altimeter; then his
86

eyes made the same journey again. And again. They would keep making the same journey as long as the aircraft was aloft. When Wally first learnt to fly he had to instruct his eyes: look at the horizon, make sure it's in the right spot: it should be just above the nose, according to the instructor. He said if it's higher the kite is in a dive; if it's lower the kite is climbing. Stick forward or back, automatically. Now study the air-speed indicator. It's supposed to say ninety knots. If it says more it's undoubtedly because the afore-mentioned horizon is too high, meaning the nose of the kite has gone down, therefore pull back on the stick because you are descending and if you continue to descend you will break yourself into rather small pieces. But not too much on the stick, otherwise the kite will start climbing and the speed will drop off and if you don't do anything about it the kite will stall which means that it will simply cease flying. And the instructor will be more than a little cheesed off. At the same time as all this, make sure the kite is still heading in the right direction. You know what course to fly: one-seven-two. You turned the barometer-like thing until it read one-seven-two and you turned the kite until it was pointing in that direction. Is it still reading one-seven-two? Don't spend too long looking! The horizon's drop-ping! Stick forward. Look at the air-speed indicator. Quickly. Now you're wandering off course!

It had seemed so impossibly complex in those days. One simply didn't have enough eyes and hands to keep every-thing happening correctly at the same time. But slowly one discovered that one did. It was like trying to learn to ride a bicycle—anyone could see that the thing was absolutely impossible; how could anyone be expected to steer and pedal and correct one's balance all at the same time? But one managed somehow. And eventually one started doing all those impossible things without even thinking of them. They became part of one's instinct. Balancing as one steered

87

and pedalled; correcting for altitude and direction and speed. Piece of cake.

By now all the kites would be away from the airfield; calm would reign once more. The controllers and the spectators and the ground crew would disperse like the audience from a football match. Except that these players would be returning in a few hours—at least the players bloody well hoped they would be returning in a few hours.

'Bomb-aimer to navigator. Coast ahead.'

'OK, bomb-aimer, thanks.'

Twice I have seen myself die, he thought. Twice today. Dead. Overcooked. He tried to recreate the pictures in his mind. He wanted to study them, analyse them. But it was like thinking back over a dream: the remoteness of it: mere wisps of imagination floating aimlessly about in his brain; it was stupid to attempt to attribute form and logic to it. Surely the brain was constantly crammed with random thoughts; well, wasn't it possible that some of these random thoughts might connect and, purely by chance, make sense of a sort? Might not an infant playing with alphabet blocks accidentally spell *glockenspiel*?

Infants. Ahead there was a city. Infants kneeling at bedsides asking God if He would please take care of Mutti and Papa and Oma and Opa and Onkel Heinrich and Tante Erna and the Führer and Reichmarschall Göring.

In the bomb-bay a four-thousand-pounder nestled among sixteen cans of incendiaries.

'Bomb-aimer to navigator. Crossing coastline now. Coming aft.'

'Roger.'

The whole thought-process was depressing. The curious thing was that it didn't depress him. He could examine his feelings quite objectively. He knew that he cared more about the consequences of his not flying on ops than about the results of those ops. Living among the very-much-alive it was too easy to forget the very-much-dead. He could tell himself that he had volunteered to fly and that he was obligated to complete his tour of operations. It was part of the bargain. The authorities gave him hero status; in return he had to do their bidding. All of which added up to one thing: moral courage—a complete lack of same.

Doug's head emerged from the nose compartment. He smiled up at Wally as he squeezed himself through the narrow hole. Then he scrambled to his feet and disappeared aft. He would assist Paul, verifying their position over the North Sea by means of Gee-readings.

Wally glanced up through the transparent roof of the cockpit canopy. The clouds were clearly visible: scattering and stretching as though someone was pulling at both ends until they broke and dispersed.

Actually, Wally thought, it's getting a bit *too* bloody clear.

The wind was stronger now, tending to blow M-Mother north of course. It was necessary to steer south a few degrees, continually correcting and recorrecting so that the end result was arrival at the nameless point in the North Sea designated 'A' on the navigational route-sheet. The position of Point 'A' was 5440 0500. It marked the end of the first leg of the trip. Point 'B' was over German soil.

Beneath Paul's hands the navigation table shivered, as if labouring to assist M-Mother up to cruising altitude.

'Navigator to pilot. Steer one hundred.'

'Roger. One hundred. Thank you, navigator.'

The form before Paul bore the impressive Air Ministry code number Wt. 51687-04190 500m 3.44 R.M. 51-9090. Paul presumed this meant something to someone somewhere. He drew the line of the new course and immediately began a fresh set of calculations. He would be hard at work until he wrote in the time of landing—with a large sigh of relief.

Suddenly M-Mother's wing dropped. The aircraft slumped

to the left as though it had lost its footing in the air.

Len said indignantly, 'The silly bastard nearly hit us!'

'I know that, rear gunner.' The skipper sounded vexed.

'I didn't see him coming, skip.'

'He must have gone under us,' said Phil.

'All right, that's enough chatter,' came the skipper's voice. 'Let's just keep our eyes open, shall we?'

Paul was thinking of Sawley. He had first come across his work in the Art Gallery of Ontario a couple of years before the war, a simple study of a man staggering slightly under the weight of a large barrel on his shoulder. 'Sawley '09', it was signed. Paul had never heard of him. Then he learnt that Sawley was an Englishman who had enjoyed a brief fame shortly before the First World War, but had soon disappeared from the front ranks of British painters. He lived somewhere in the north of England. Shortly before being posted, Paul discovered that the 'somewhere' was a village called Brocklington, and that was precisely where he was eventually sent. It had been fantastic luck and the only possible explanation was that the authorities had had no idea that he *wanted* to be posted there.

Paul had found Sawley's place without difficulty—Brocklingtonians knew one another and one another's business. It was a sagging cottage of grey stone with a brown tiled roof. The tall hedge around the garden was unkempt; only flakes of paint remained on the front gate; he had to lift it on its rusty hinges to make it open. He walked the dozen paces along the flat path and he was terrified. What right had he—immature, overdressed, overpaid—to waste the priceless time of this genius? He paused. He came close to turning and fleeing; but then the front door opened. A tiny elfin face stared up at him. It was fastened to an elderly lady. Her eyes darted up and down the length of him. Who was he? What did he want?

'My name is ... Paul Taylor.'

'You're an airman. What'you doing here then? The airdrome is over there. You a Yank? You sound like a Yank.'

'No. I'm Canadian.'

'Oh.' Sniff. 'Well?'

Well, he would like to see Mr Sawley if it was possible; perhaps he might speak with him if it wasn't too much trouble.

'What if it is too much trouble?'

She was an unpleasant little creature—but she had a point. Frederick Sawley probably had hundreds of thousands of admirers; what if they all came calling simultaneously?

'He's taking a nap.'

'I see.' Feeling something akin to relief, Paul turned. He was anxious to get away from this acetous female. 'I'll try some other time,' he told her.

She shrugged with her eyebrows and closed the door.

He had gone back two days later. It had taken some drumming up of courage but the thought of being in Brocklington and not seeing Sawley nagged at him. He had to express his admiration. He had to ask a question or two. He had to see what manner of man could produce work with such a marvellous crude vigour.

He returned to the sagging cottage and the peeling gate and the old woman. (Was it Mrs Sawley? Or a maiden sister? An aunt? A housekeeper?)

'You're the one who wants to see him because you admire him so much, don't you?' The notion seemed to amuse her; she smiled; then she touched her mouth and the smile vanished.

'What the hell's all this about?' A man's voice from within the house: a gruff, old man's voice. 'Bloody draught going right through the place.' He came into view: stocky but bent with age: at least seventy-five: hard blue eyes, an obstinate jaw: white hair hanging limply across his forehead.

Excited, Paul interjected, 'I came to see Frederick Sawley, sir. I admire his work. Very much.'

The old man took a pipe from his pocket. 'Well, you must be the only one left who does.' He blew noisily through the pipe. 'Aye, well, you've seen Fred Sawley, young man. Satisfied?'

Paul swallowed. 'I saw one of your works in the Art Gallery of Ontario, sir, in Toronto. A man carrying a barrel. It was dated '09.'

'A long time ago. I don't remember it.'

'I do,' said the woman. 'You did it in Ripon.' The old man shook his head, apparently disinterested. 'Yes, you did.'

Paul said, 'I was very impressed by its ... its power ... its vigour. I found out you lived here in Brocklington.'

The moments fled. So many questions—but Paul couldn't think of one. Here was Frederick Sawley, in person, just a few inches away ... but what should he say to express his feelings?

'Might I come back, sir, some other time?'

'He's too busy,' said the woman.

Sawley ignored her. 'Aye, I suppose you can if you want to,' he grunted, then he turned and walked slowly upstairs.

It had taken time to get to know Sawley even slightly for he was by nature a taciturn individual and he had been forgotten and hurt by the outside world; he disliked most people, he distrusted all. Although Paul came to know the old man quite well he knew he couldn't claim to be a friend. The gap was simply too vast. Sawley tolerated Paul —and Paul was perfectly content to have it that way. Sawley gave up a little time once a week or so to listen to fervent compliments in a strange accent. It seemed to amuse him slightly. For Paul, however, Sawley's studio was a place in which he never failed to be outrageously happy (in spite of the necessity of encountering the ophidian woman, who turned out to be Sawley's wife). His respect for Sawley's work—and for Sawley himself—deepened as the weeks became months. The old painter was a man to admire, a true artist who lived as he painted, never compromising, never pretending, an honest man, a real man.

A man to emulate? Yes, but who had the courage and the will?

The honest man, the real man, had some of Paul's own work in his studio. Paul had told him of his efforts. Characteristically, Sawley hadn't responded or even commented at the time. Then, two weeks later, as Paul was leaving the studio, he had said, 'Bring some of your work if you like. We'll have a look at it and see what you've been up to.' But when Paul brought the paintings (a simple landscape, a charcoal sketch of a shot-up Lancaster and a portrait of a girl from Oakville, each selected after hours of agonized wondering), Sawley had put them in a corner. He'd look at them one day soon, he said, when he felt like it.

M-Mother rode on through the night, gently climbing, pulling her load of humans and high explosives higher and higher above the lonely sea. In ten minutes she would reach Point 'A'. Then a change of course would bring her over enemy territory. Scores of aircraft rode with M-Mother; occasionally they could be seen, their exhaust stubs like tiny embers in the sky.

Radar still connected the aircraft silently and invisibly with home and told them where in the featureless air they were. Soon, however, the Gee-signals would elongate and finally fade. The last link broken.

Pilot Officer Duquette's port inner had seized up without warning; at once his port outer started heating. Duquette swore volubly in Quebec City French and jettisoned his bombs—which led to reports that an aircraft had crashed

93

into the sea. Duquette limped back to Brocklington and reported his problem and requested permission to land. Whereupon Duquette was told by his engineer that the undercart wouldn't lock down. He told his crew to bale out. When the last man had jumped, Duquette attempted a wheels-up landing. He came in low, sweeping over the village and the school, cutting the throttles moments before touching the ground. There was a rending, screaming din as the fuselage tore itself open on the ground; then one wing dug into soft earth on the right. The Lancaster, twenty tons of metal travelling at some eighty miles an hour, swung viciously to that side. Its structure buckled and fractured under the awful stress. The fuselage broke in half just behind the trailing edge of the wings; the port outer engine went careering on, bouncing across the earth, spewing great swathes of burning fuel. The front section of the fuselage tore itself free of the starboard wing and crumpled into shapelessness as it spent its impetus skidding across the grass, dragging the remnants of the port wing which exploded into an inferno as the fuel tanks were ruptured.

Emergency crews sped to the scene. Asbestos-suited fire-fighters sprayed foam on the wreckage, trying to smother the flames; others tried to chop their way into the fuselage with hatchets. But the heat was murderous; it was impossible to do anything in spite of the Station Commander's exhortations to get the crew out. Someone told him that the crew had baled out; only the pilot had remained aboard.

'Get him out!' the Station Commander bellowed.

Then a voice at the Station Commander's shoulder said there was really no point in trying to get the pilot out. Angered, the Station Commander turned, about to state in the most definite way that there was always hope, etcetera.

But it was Duquette standing there, his face scratched, his flying jacket badly ripped.

'I'm the pilot, sir.'

'What, of that aircraft?'

'Yes sir.'

'Good God! How on earth did you get out?'

'I'm not at all sure,' said Duquette. 'I think my seat must have broken away or something. I found myself lying about ten yards ahead of the kite just as it went up.'

'You're an uncommonly lucky young man,' said the Station Commander inadequately.

'I think so too,' said Duquette. He stared at the blazing wreckage. 'She really is written off, isn't she?'

In a kind voice the Station Commander said, 'Don't feel too badly about it, my boy.'

'I don't sir,' said Duquette. He smiled weakly. 'I'm glad she's written off to tell you the truth. I told Wally Mann about her this morning. She was a cow, that one, a real cow.'

Charlie's job was to listen. If a signal happened to be transmitted from England saying that the op had been scrubbed and everyone was to turn around and come home, it was Charlie who would receive the signal on behalf of M-Mother and pass it on to the skipper. Every wireless op shuddered at the thought of failing to receive such a signal —and it could happen for God knows how many reasons. The result would be that a solitary aircraft would mount a single-handed attack on Berlin or Bremen or somewhere equally unfriendly.

Charlie listened. He often heard voices. Sometimes they were the voices of Pathfinders already over the target instructing the oncoming kites where to drop their bombs; sometimes they were enemy voices, jabbering away incomprehensibly; sometimes they were the voices of men who were lost and low on fuel; sometimes they were the voices of men who were dying and knew it. Once Charlie heard a wireless op with a Welsh accent telling anyone who could hear that his aircraft was ditching and its position was such and such; it was gliding in, he said, badly damaged and losing all its fuel. Then suddenly he said, in a mildly annoyed tone, not to bother, a wing had just broken away; there wouldn't be anything left to fish out of the sea. It seemed incredible that a man could speak so matter-of-factly at such a time. Charlie told himself he would have yelled his head off ... but perhaps not, he conjectured, perhaps a man suddenly faced by the certainty of death could be calmer than if he was going to the dentist. Nature could be kind as well as cruel.

After this op the crew would break up. Charlie would never see any of them again—or perhaps he would, after the war, when everything had settled down again. He'd be strolling along Oxford Street one bright spring day and who would he bump into but the skipper! Charlie ... Wally ... Delighted ... Looking Well ... In the Pink ... Not a Day Older. And all that. Pop into a smart little bar. Hoist one. Here's to old times. Ah, they were good times. Talk about the crew, where they were: Paul and Harry, making fortunes in Canada and Australia, of course. Phil running his pub. Len doing something illegal and profitable. Doug? Doing well, anyway. At something. And the skipper? Stock Exchange or something like that. Next: Charlie Newton. Yes. What about Charlie Newton? Thirty-plus, knowing nothing, being nothing, a big question mark with a big family to support. Of all the lads in the crew, Charlie told himself, you've got the biggest responsibility and the least bleeding ability to handle it. See the Education Officer? What, at his age? Go back to school? Why not? Yeah, why not? I wasn't too old to learn my trade in the RAF, Charlie thought. I'm a warrant officer, aren't I? That must mean something. It might mean that they got my name mixed up with someone else's, but I'm the one with the badge.

Then he thought of it. The article he was reading in *John Bull*: airlines: after the war everyone travelling by air, all over the world. Charlie would be a wireless op on an airliner! He would travel all over the world, being adored by the female passengers, envied by the male passengers, respected by one and all. Charlie Newton, Success.

Charlie was delighted with his idea. A real corker! Airlines would be needing wireless ops—and he was a wireless op. A good one. So when he happened to run into the skipper on Oxford Street he would casually declare that he'd just flown in from Calcutta and he was off to Rome that evening so he really shouldn't have another ... well, perhaps just a little one ... Charlie thought: Life's funny, really funny, this rotten war could turn out to be the best thing that ever happened to me ...

Ten tons of light aluminium alloy formed M-Mother's body and flying surfaces. She consisted of some seventy thousand separate parts; half a million factory operations and thirty thousand jigs and tools were required to manufacture her. She was a Lancaster, the best bomber in the RAF, some said the best bomber in the world. Certainly she could tote a far greater load than the American Fortresses and Liberators, even the B-29; but, then, she didn't have to carry platoons of gunners to defend herself in daylight raids. She was a lady of the night.

11

'Pilot to crew. Oxygen on, everybody.'

Hands, already chilled, fastened the masks with press-studs on the right-hand side of the head. Seven faces now became snouted and ugly and indistinguishable. M-Mother fed them oxygen through seven umbilical cords so that they might survive in the rarer atmosphere into which she was conducting them.

Douglas stared at the cathode-ray tube with its green blips of light. A blonde stared back. She was the second nude in the latest *Men Only*; the first nude was dark-haired and her photograph was so artistically out of focus that it was more than a little difficult to become enthused. The blonde, however, was a vastly different kettle of fish. A superbly sharp shot. Taken out on the beach. (Which beach, for God's sake?) She was leaning back against a big rock and close examination of her shoulder and left breast revealed a scattering of sand.

M-Mother jogged, sank a dozen feet, then righted herself.

Douglas didn't notice. He was wondering whether the boys really intended to fix him up with a woman. Awful. Yet marvellous. How wizard to be like the skipper, or Paul, or Len, or Harry. They knew how to handle women. But even for each of them, there must have been a first time.

Everything was terrifying the first time. Hadn't he been terrified the first time up in an aircraft? Hadn't he gone through the most fiendish torture, working up courage to go onstage in the school production of *HMS Pinafore*?

Oh, to have a natural way with women—like the sailor in the train to London. He certainly had a natural way with them. 'No use wastin' 'alf the perishin' night talkin' abaht books and pitchers,' he had declared with the grave deliberation of one who had studied a subject exhaustively, 'because you don't want to read books with a bint or take 'er to pitchers. You want to take 'er knickers dahn. Right, mate?'

'Er ... oh, yes, right,' said Douglas.

'Bints respect a bloke 'oo comes straight to the point,' the sailor went on reflectively. 'When I ask a bint to dance I don't mess arahnd; I tell 'er she'd look sweet in me 'ammock—after askin' 'er name, of course: don't want to be crude abaht it. But if you come straight to the point the situation's crystal bleedin' clear to all concerned, you might say. Now it's up to 'er. She can buzz off or she can stick arahnd and join in the fun. Nice, 'ow many of 'em do stick arahnd; 'eart-warming it is, really. And, with any luck, it'll warm somethin' else too! Now, I'm not pretendin' me success is due to the fack that I look like Valentino 'cause I bleedin' well know I don't. No, all I got going for me is a rather chummy manner and the guts to say what's on me mind. This last twelve-month me average 'as been workin' aht abaht one point three aht of five. Can't complain.'

'Very ... creditable,' gulped Douglas, hugely impressed.

'What I always do is 'ave a quick one as soon as I get ashore. And it is a quick one, I can tell you, mate, after a few weeks at sea! I pay for that one. Worth every penny, it is. Puts me at me ease. Then ... London! If me average 'olds out, it'll be seven *filthy* days! Lovely! Might get me face slapped a few times but what the 'ell, eh? That's what I always say.'

'That's what I always say too,' murmured Douglas.

Later, as the train rattled into London's outskirts, the

sailor said, 'You spendin' your leave in London, mate?'

Yes, Douglas replied, he was.

The sailor grinned. 'Feeling like joining forces? We'd be bleedin' irresistible, the navy and the air force—you shoot 'em dahn, I'll torpedo 'em! 'Ow abaht it?'

Yes, he wanted to say. But fear and ignorance answered for him without a moment's hesitation. No, he couldn't join forces much as he would have enjoyed it. He was meeting a girl-friend in London and they would spend the entire ten days together.

'Too bad,' said the sailor, apparently sincere. 'Ten days with the same bint is too long, mate, if you don't mind my sayin'. She'll be gettin' serious. Nothin' worse than that. They're bloody terrors when they get their sights set on a bloke. I've seen it 'appen. 'orrible, it is. Young geyser, gets saddled with a bride; first thing 'e knows there's a nipper on the way; all of a sudden 'e discovers 'e's doing nothin' but tryin' to pay for furniture and washin' machines and encyclopedias ... all on the never-never. Bleedin' tragic, it is, when you consider what the poor sod is missin'!'

As the train neared King's Cross, Douglas tried desperately to think of some way to extricate himself from the imaginary girl-friend—why oh why was he so quick at negative, defeatist invention? He wanted to go with the sailor; he wanted to plunge into life and taste it—and return to Brocklington genuinely, splendidly dissipated!

But at the station the sailor had been out of the compartment even before the train had come to a halt. With a cheery 'chin-chin!' he was gone—to goodness knows how many good-natured conquests. Douglas jumped to his feet and ran to the door. But he didn't call after him. For one thing he still hadn't thought of a good reason for suddenly changing his story; for another, he was scared. Scared but fascinated. He watched the blue-clad figure darting through the crowds, bell-bottoms flapping in eager anticipation of the fun to come.

Glumly Douglas pulled his bag from the rack and walked along the platform towards the ticket collector. Two hours later he was talking to a tall, bright-eyed woman in Lisle Street. She would give Douglas a smashing time. 'Thirty bob. I'll make you feel like you never felt before.'

Here it was: sex at last, and for a relatively modest outlay. A trifle more than two days' pay. Douglas felt his knees wobble with excitement; his teeth began to clatter. He hoped the noise didn't carry.

But later, in the woman's room, with its dented brass bedstead and portrait of Winston Churchill, Douglas's desire for sex had vanished like a puff of exhaust smoke from a Merlin manifold. The woman started to peel off her dress—a purple creation sporting large white buttons; with a generous smile she said he might help her; but no pinching, mind. Douglas stared; there was nothing in the world he wanted to do less than touch her. Her flesh was grey and pasty; half a dozen red spots, three with yellow heads, punctuated her chest above dejected breasts. The ghastly thing was, she tried to be friendly.

'Need a little work to get going, do you? Come on, we'll give it a bit of a wash, shall we?'

The whole business was excruciating. The more the woman talked the more revolting she became. Her fingers probed and stroked and all they accomplished was to make him feel nauseous. Finally she said, 'I give up. I want me money, though. You've had long enough.'

He found the money with trembling fingers and thrust it at her. As he stumbled down the stairs to the street, she called out: 'You really have got your problems, haven't you, ducks?'

It was that remark that haunted Douglas's nights for weeks afterwards. In it seemed to be condensed all the contempt of the female for the inadequate male. It was as if the bright-eyed woman was acting as representative for all her sisters; she spoke for them, and she didn't think much of him.

And Douglas couldn't really blame her.

On the radar screen an oval smudge appeared. It measured slightly less than a centimetre in width, rather more in depth.

The radar operator adjusted his calibrations. He worked rapidly and efficiently; he had done this job many times; he was a professional. He picked up the telephone at his side.

'Fat dog,' he said.

The phrase elicited no amusement or surprise at the other end of the line. 'Fat dog' meant one thing: a large enemy formation.

'Height approximately five thousand metres. Speed about three hundred kilometres ...'

The warning went immediately to the five fighter divisions responsible for the air defence of Germany and the occupied territories. The division alerted the bases under their command. In readiness-rooms, night-fighter crews, already garbed in flying gear, listened to the loudspeaker announcement. The Tommies were on their way. A large formation—as if all enemy formations weren't large these days. Headed toward Kiel. Berlin or Hamburg or Bremen, most likely. But they could be mine-laying. Or they could suddenly turn south. They would certainly turn; they always did; they never flew directly to their targets. But which way would they turn? That was the big question. Which way?

Wally switched on his intercom mike.

'Pilot to crew. It won't be too long to the coast now. Better start keeping an eye open for fighters. You never know, they might be wandering around this far out.'

A moment later Wally felt M-Mother yaw gently; it was the movement of the guns thrusting into the slipstream as the gunners swung their turrets from side to side. From now on the gunners would be keeping up a non-stop look-out for fighters, their arch-enemies. Every few minutes Wally would drop one wing then the other so that the blind spots might be checked. It was a well-rehearsed routine.

Before him and above him the sky was velvety. But still clearing. He could see two aircraft quite distinctly: a Lan-caster with its low-slung tail and a Halifax, purposeful in appearance but far less attractive. In one way it was nice to see other kites: it confirmed that you were heading the right way, but it also proved that the visibility was far too good for comfort.

Horizon to air-speed indicator to compass to altimeter, back to horizon again. Everything normal. Piece of cake.

Wally shifted his oxygen mask a fraction of an inch. It tended to dig a ditch under his left cheekbone if left in the same position too long.

Click. Paul's American-sounding voice: 'Navigator to pilot. Five minutes to the coast.'

'Thank you, navigator.'

'Pilot to crew. We'll be over enemy territory in a few minutes. Any problems, anyone?'

No problems, they told him. Once more into the breach, he thought. Just once more. He glanced to the right; Ger-many was there, invisible in the darkness but vigilant, watching the bombers by radar, calculating forces, wonder-ing what mischief Bomber Command was up to tonight. Already they would be considering Berlin a thoroughly likely candidate for the chop; the route would tell them the op was either for mine-laying or to clobber Hamburg or Bremen or Kiel ... or Berlin.

As the enemy coast drew nearer he became conscious

of the dreadful, fearful noise the aircraft was making. Surely half of Europe could hear it; surely the gunners could pinpoint M-Mother's position by the din. And were the kites in the stream still all heading the same way? They hadn't all heard a command from home to turn around and return, had they? Same little misgivings; they plagued him on the very first op and every one since.

He thought back over the morning. Misgivings, *par excellence*.

By any account that landing was incredible. It might be said that he had been paralysed with ... with what? He thought. It was hard to say. It was even harder to recreate the instant of terror that had so nearly written everyone off. He had thought of himself as a corpse many times; he could picture his body crisp and black, faceless, shrivelled to pygmy size; it was a very real possibility. Why, then, was the same sight so shattering this morning? Perhaps it was the suddenness of it, bursting in upon him like a falling ceiling ...

A manifestation of deep-set fears. Someone had said something to that effect once after dinner.

Oh, hell's bells, why did he have to keep thinking about it?

Horizon to speed to course to height ... Wally was a good pilot, and he was proud of his skill. He enjoyed flying; he had enjoyed almost every flight since his first, in an Avro 504 in the summer of 1933. Five shillings a ride. The ex-RFC pilot had worn jodhpurs and a leather helmet with flaps that miraculously stayed turned up over his ears. The machine exuded a heady smell of Castrol R and fabric dope; its bracing wires sagged and tautened during the taxiing; the whole contraption creaked and squeaked like a rather ancient pram. But it flew, rising from the grass with a noisy dignity, wobbling on the wind, clambering for altitude over the elms at the end of the field. The ground receded; Wally, gripping the edge of the cockpit, looked straight down and the gale from the propeller beat at his hair and the people had become ants and the houses matchboxes and he had never been so deliriously happy in his life. It was all just as he had imagined. He had to savour and store every instant of it; he couldn't let his mind wander; he must watch and see and learn and remember. Later he could drag out every impression, examine it from every angle, and live it again, and again, and again. But if the motor stopped, wouldn't the aircraft simply drop? How sturdy were those thin, fragile-looking wings? Wouldn't a strong wind crumple them like matchsticks and tissue paper? He was learning that the true joy of flight contained a pinch of fear.

Between 1933 and 1939 he had flown a dozen times. He bought a sixpenny notebook. The Log. Every flight lovingly detailed: 'Avro 504. Pilot, Captain McGregor. Took off, Reading, 14 mins. past 3. Landed 31 mins. past 3. Weather clear with scattered clouds. '504, DH Dragon, Gypsy Moth, Avian ...' Then no more five shillings to pay: trim little Tiger Moths in dreary green-and-brown camouflage, with yellow undersurfaces to inform anyone near enough to see that this was a training aircraft—so beware! Keep your distance! Round and round the field at White Horborough: hour after hour of dual: stinging comments from a weatherbeaten face in the rear cockpit: a growing conviction that he had absolutely no talent for piloting (where did one go to convert to gunner or something?). Did Aircraftman Mann intend to pull out of this spin before the aircraft made a large hole in the CO's front garden? Then, astonishingly, the chance to solo! A casual Off-you-go-and-try-not-to-bend-anything. A sedate taxiing, turn into wind. Into the air with uncommon speed: ah, of course, only one bod aboard! Sweet turns—no skidding, no loss of height. Then, one more turn. The field growing in size, throttle back (please don't bounce, please God, don't bounce). Thudscrape. Down. Wheels burbling busily on the uneven ground. The instructor claiming to be surprised to see his pupil back on the ground already. Pupil indignant. What, didn't see that bloody marvellous landing? Even as he said it, Wally knew the answer. Of course the instructor had seen the landing, of course he had seen every moment of the solo ... At No. 5 Flying Training School there were Miles Masters, powerful two-seater trainers with retractable undercarriages and the sophisticated instrumentation of operational aircraft. Then on to Oxfords, twin-engined trainers. (You're for bombers, chum. No Spitfire for you.) Wellingtons at OTU, a Mark 1 Halifax, a Lanc. Finally to Brocklington. No more training; now His Majesty's Government would rather relish being repaid for all the privileges it had bestowed upon the person of Walter Mann, Pilot Officer ... repayment to take the form of assisting HM Government in the destruction of a foe of the aforesaid HM Government ...

'Navigator to pilot. Steer oh-eight-oh.'

'Roger. Oh-eight-oh.'

Any moment now, the coast. Wally said to himself, Paul has us aimed smack at some point on his map, a point, I trust, without flak batteries, a point at which the defences have a chink in them so that we can slip through ...

Something ahead. It looked solid. Yes, it was probably the coast, seventeen thousand feet down ...

Wally adjusted the position of his mask once more. He took a deep breath as the solid-looking piece of the night moved slowly out of sight beneath the nose.

Harry knew he should have left the letter in the crew-room. How many times had he been told? Would he never learn? You weren't supposed to take letters on ops because if you were captured the devilishly clever German intelligence officers could glean all sorts of gen from them. Mind you, it was difficult to imagine how much gen they would dig out of one of Dorothy's letters—unless they happened to be interested in what was on at the pictures in Melbourne.

Now he took it from his pocket once again; he tore the envelope open and took out the sheets of paper. One, two, three, four. A long one this time. Folded so tidily—their very tidiness an accusation against the ghastly untidiness of his life. What a beaut, his life!

It was too dark to read the letter. Good. He had known it would be. He put the sheets back in the envelope, folded it and thrust it into his breast pocket.

Adulterer. Oh, come off it; no need to be harsh. All right, what else would you call it? Harry sighed. What stinking rotten luck. But there *were* people who could look after inconvenient situations like this. He had an idea it was pretty expensive—but not so expensive as having to support a nipper in Leytonbloodystone. Seventy-five pounds was a figure he'd heard during some half-forgotten chat—who had said seventy-five pounds? He couldn't recall. He'd have to find out. Greening could have helped if he'd been a half-decent type ... an MO was there to *help*, wasn't he? ...

'Flak,' said Douglas.

Harry turned and looked over the skipper's helmeted head. In the distance there were flickering lights, little sparklers. Dirty old flak. Same as ever. A searchlight flung its beam into the sky. Nearby another searchlight came into action. The beams crossed; then, inexplicably, the first light went out. The flak came nearer, twinkling lights, fireworks long before Guy Fawkes' night. Abruptly, shockingly, there was a thud nearby. For an instant the bitter smell of explosive touched the nostrils of the crew. The kite jolted, rattled, then flew smoothly on.

'Injun country,' commented the skipper.

It was an expression Paul had once used and for some

107

reason the skipper became fond of it. Injun country was where the bad guys were. Harry pressed his face against the cold perspex window and looked down. Injun country, all the way to Berlin and all the way back. Trust the bloody Jerries to put their capital in an awkward spot.

Harry busied himself for some moments switching fuel-tanks, then he resumed his scanning of the sky. Away to port there was some flak. A long way away—someone must be way off course, Harry thought, unless they're popping away at a Jerry fighter.

The trouble with looking out into the night was that you saw anything your funky old brain instructed you to see. Shadows became shapes, ominous shapes—all of a sudden a cloud was a flight of Ju 88s coming at point-blank range. No wonder rear gunners were wont to fire off incredible amounts of expensive ammunition at absolutely nothing.

A searchlight whipped across the sky; for an instant it caught a Lanc; but it moved too rapidly and the Lanc slipped away.

If I baled out on the way home, Harry thought, I'd spend the rest of the war as a prisoner. By the time it was all over everything would be forgotten and, perhaps, for-given. He smiled wryly as he imagined the scene : engineer clipping on parachute and going forward to escape hatch and skipper asking what precisely he thought he was up to. Engineer replying that he was bailing out in order to escape from pregnant girl-friend and indignant wife; skipper nodding understandingly—permission to bail out ...

S-Sugar took a direct hit.

Phil saw it. He was swinging his turret to the left and was looking out at right-angles to the aircraft's path when the shell struck home.

For an instant S-Sugar was illuminated by a fierce glare beneath her belly. Phil saw the identification letters on her fuselage and he saw the mid-upper gunner turning his turret as he, Phil, was turning his. S-Sugar staggered. At once her wings seemed to have become red hot. They glowed. The immense pressure of hundreds of gallons of burning fuel warped and distended the frail skin. Then fire burst through the trailing edges, gulping at the structure like a foul, hungry monster.

S-Sugar dropped away, turning, trailing a huge plume of fire. She turned as if instinctively trying to head for home.

Everyone yelled at the crew to bale out. Jump, jump, jump! What the hell was delaying them? They couldn't extinguish it, so for God's sake they should get away from it.

'Oh, Christ,' said someone.

At that moment S-Sugar's bombs went off.

The explosion lit the sky, revealing the presence of a dozen bombers in scattered progression. Several small pieces of S-Sugar went spinning away, burning, disintegrating. And then there was a savage, sudden blast; it was darker than before, and there was absolutely nothing left of S-Sugar or her crew.

'Whose kite was it?' the skipper asked.

'Sugar,' Phil told him. 'It was S for Sugar. Ours. I saw the three letters on his side. Clear as day.'

'Fred. Fred Sanderson.'

'At least it was fast.'

'Funny thing, there wasn't all that much flak back there. Just a couple of lousy little guns, I bet.'

'It was a lucky shot.'

'Not for Fred Sanderson.'

'I bet the bastards cheered when they saw poor old Sugar come down.'

'I hope he fell on them.'

'There wasn't much left to fall on anyone.'

The intercom fell silent. Automatically, the airmen began the process of reclassifying Fred Sanderson and his crew.

Poor old Fred. Good type, of course, but got the chop.

M-Mother flew on across the narrow strip of land connecting Germany with Denmark. Soon they would be over water again, Kiel Bay; then they would turn and head inland, toward the German capital. The crew gazed into the night and wondered: wondered whether anyone got out of S-Sugar; wondered whether any of the crew felt anything; wondered about the fate that makes that particular shell travel at exactly the right speed in exactly the right direction with the right setting so that it arrives in that cubic foot of air at precisely the same instant as S-Sugar to set her wings shimmering and glowing and bursting with stinking rotten merciless fire ...

All night-bombing veterans had seen bombers shot down. Often in flames. As a rule, however, no one knew the identity of the stricken aircraft. It was a bang and a confusion of flame and bits tumbling away and then it was all over. Often you couldn't even tell whether it was a bomber or a Jerry fighter or even some new type of flare. But with S-Sugar it had been so unpleasantly different. So *close*. Blast Phil's sharp eyes ... And the flak had been so spasmodic, almost half-hearted, a sort of token shaking of the fist at the passing armada. Such flak had no business scoring a direct hit on a Lanc with an experienced crew, no business at all ...

Ahead there was the glint of water. Below, tranquil countryside. The bombers, twenty miles of them, might have been doing a night-flying exercise over the Southern Counties for all the interest anyone below seemed to be taking. No guns, no searchlights. But the tranquillity fooled none of the experienced crews. Interludes, nothing more. You couldn't fly across Germany for long without *them* throwing explosive things at you. Especially when the sky had become so bloody, bloody clear.

* * *

Drops of condensation formed on the end of Paul's oxygen mask, then dropped on to the charts and promptly froze into small, cake-shaped pellets. He scraped one from a line on the Navigational Observations column of his trip-log; he had been about to make an entry on the line when the drop fell, precisely one eighth of an inch in front of his pencil point. He imagined being an old man with a nose that constantly dripped. Another frigid drop fell; he pressed a gloved finger on it, absorbing it before it had time to freeze. He disliked wearing oxygen. Apart from being awkward, uncomfortable and restricting, it made you an integral part of the aircraft. Just another component, entirely dependent upon the aircraft for survival.

Douglas's voice over the intercom: 'Bomb-aimer to navigator. Looks like Kiel on the right.'

The mid-upper and rear turrets swung restlessly from side to side as the gunners scanned the night sky, eyes narrowed, searching for the fighters. Something! Adrenalin surged into the bloodstream. Teeth pressed down on lips as eyes fought to convert shadows to shapes. No ... a Halli-bag. Relax. Breathe again. Courtesy of M-Mother's oxygen supply. Jesus Christ! A bloke could have a heart attack at this lark. At age twenty.

'Navigator to pilot. Turning in four minutes.'

'Thank you, navigator.'

Everything humming nicely. Piece of cake.

The pounding of rubber on runway ceases; the aircraft becomes alive in my hands. Airborne! At once the flare-path lights disappear. No doubt the control-tower people are thankful that they have succeeded in scrambling twelve Messerschmitts without attracting Mosquitoes.

I push the lever to retract the undercarriage. Somewhere up there in the darkness is a target for me. Tonight I will score.

12

Wally shifted his oxygen mask again. Lord, how he would have loved a cigarette. A week of his life for a cigarette? Yes, a bargain, fair enough. Unfortunately, oxygen masks didn't permit smoking. Besides, he wondered, do I really have a week left to bargain with? Do I even have a day? Yes. Indubitably. He told himself that all he had to do was fly to Berlin, drop his bombs, turn around and fly home. That was all. (Left hand on stick, right hand down to adjust the trim. An automatic movement.) Poor old Sandy had gone for a Burton, therefore, his, Wally's, chances were that much better. Q.E. bloody D. North German coastline down there ahead, ladies and gentlemen; Rostock on the left, population one hundred and something thousand, a major port with splendid petroleum tanks that we keep knocking down and the Jerries keep building up again; notice, if you will, the quite obnoxious anti-aircraft gunners that are indigenous to this part of the Baltic coast ...

'Steer oh-three-five.'
'Oh-three-five.'
'We should intercept in nine minutes.'
I nod. Nine minutes. Five hundred and forty seconds.

Douglas slid through the narrow opening into the nose compartment. It was snug. Lying on his stomach with his head in the plastic aiming bubble, he had the best view in the house. All of Germany spread out before him. Waiting to have things dropped on it from a great height. He plugged in his intercom and oxygen.

At once the girl with the sand on her breast said, 'I'm waiting for you, Douglas. I've been waiting so long. How cruel you are to keep me waiting. Don't you realize that I long to feel your strong arms around me, holding me, squeezing me? Have you no pity, Douglas?' With his fingers on the bomb-selection panel, Douglas wondered what it would be like to feel such a woman against him, flesh to flesh ...

Immediately behind me sits Sergeant Kleeman with his radar; he is perched on a makeshift seat, two metal tubes joined by canvas webbing. Behind Kleeman sits Dorn, the rear gunner, with his twin MG81Zs. Both these men are veterans. Fate has been unkind to them: their pilot, Specht, is laid low with bronchitis; his crew was assigned to me.

Kleeman gives me a change of course.

So now I'm an orphan, technically speaking. I don't know what I feel about it. There's still a numbness. I suppose it is because I have been fearing this for two days already. Dozens of times in those two days I thought of the possibility of my parents being dead, dozens of times I deliberately wondered how I should react. Thus it was no shock. No surprise.

I find myself wondering what the place looks like now. The rooms, the walls, the curtains, the pictures: all the things that were so intensely familiar, all shredded and smashed and pulverized. The cups and saucers and plates: the set with the blue and white lines, and the best set, with the floral design. I used them so many times; now the bits of them mingled with the mortar and dust. Everything soaked with the rain of yesterday and the day before.

Why think of things? My parents are dead. They were people, not things. My mother, short and blue-eyed, with her perennial concern about doing the right and proper

113

thing. My father, plump and greying; a jovial man. He will never be jovial again, never hold his glass of beer or wink knowingly at me when my mother points out some shocking story in the newspaper. My mother will never be shocked again. Are they watching me at this very moment? Do they expect me to avenge them?

'There they are! I've got them!'

Kleeman's voice. He sounds as excited as hell. I imagine his eyes popping as he goggles into his radar.

'Steer oh-seven-five.'

'Oh-seven-five,' *I repeat as I turn the aircraft.*

I look at the compass and set the indicator needle on 075 then I look ahead. Nothing.

'Two minutes to interception,' *says Kleeman.*

'Rear gunner?' *I say,* 'Did you hear? Interception in two minutes.'

'Yes, I heard,' *he replies, a trace of indignation in his voice. Of course he heard. What was I, a novice pilot, doing questioning his combat readiness?*

Guns off safety. Sights calibrated.

I feel very calm. In fact I think I am the calmest man aboard this aircraft. It is as if I am now the veteran and these two are the fledglings.

My right thumb rests lightly on the firing button.

Snug in his electrically heated suit, Len scanned the sky, searching for fighters, paying particular attention to the space beneath and behind M-Mother. The Jerry fighters often chose to come in that way; they would fly beneath a kite and their rear gunner would blast away as they passed.

During his operational career Len had fired his guns perhaps a dozen times in anger. He had no enemy fighters to his official credit; however, he believed that he shot down a Ju 88 near Dortmund in November. The way the thing suddenly twisted away after he fired, and the way it disappeared almost vertically into the darkness, and the sudden flash of light on the ground a minute or so later ... ah, if only he could have confirmed it somehow ...

Len half listened as Paul's voice instructed the skipper to change course yet again. Berlin, first on the left.

Nothing to be seen, not even a glimpse of another bomber. It was enough to make a bloke wonder whether he was really in the right bit of sky. Operational flying was often that way at night, Len had discovered: sometimes there were kites above, below, behind and in front of you; at other times you'd swear there wasn't another kite within fifty miles of you. The truth of it was that the stream of bombers was no solid formation; each aircraft was making its individual way to the target; thus there might be gaps in the stream; there might be fifty aircraft in a mile of sky, none in the next two miles.

Or perhaps just one.

'He's dead ahead.'

Kleeman sounds so sure of himself and his radar set, but I can see nothing ahead. For the fifth time I check to see that the safety is off, yet I am not nervous, my checking and rechecking is done deliberately and quite coolly; this time I feel capable of performing my duty as a fighter pilot.

'How far?'

'Not more than a kilometre or two.'

Should be seeing him any moment now.

'A single aircraft?'

'I think so. Or possibly two very close together.'

My eyes ache with the effort of trying to see what is unseeable. Ahead, the sky seems a little lighter but perhaps it is my eyes playing tricks on me ...

'He's turning.'

*Damn! I want to ask Kleeman which way, but I swallow
the temptation. He's watching his screen; he will tell me
when he is able to tell me. I must wait. I glance from side
to side. God knows, it's possible I might even catch a
glimpse of the Tommy without the radar. It has happened,
they say.*

*The waiting seems interminable. I take my thumb off
the button, to prove to myself that I am capable of patience.*

'Steer one-five-five.'

*I bank sharply. Below there is a glimpse of black water;
there is a faint sheen to it; it looks like oil. The compass
needle jogs around to one-five-five, past it, then back to it
as I correct. For half a minute we fly in silence.*

'He's dead ahead now,' Kleeman informs me.

Thumb back on firing button.

'A single aircraft. Just one.'

*I stare ahead and think of Kleeman's redundancy; I
think about mentioning it to him. I decide not to; he'll
think I am quite mad.*

Kleeman tells me I should be able to see the target now.

'Well, I can't!' I snap back.

*Seconds pass. We rush on through the night sky. I now
start thinking of the sickeningly insignificant things that
might be wrong with Kleeman's radar—a resister, a con-
denser—they might be putting us God knows how far off-
track.*

*'I've still got him here,' says Kleeman. 'He should be
within visual range.' He sounds like a training manual.*

'There he is,' says Dorn.

'What?'

'Starboard.'

*Yes, Dorn is right. 'Well done,' I tell him, as though
he was the man responsible for guiding us through the
night. I throttle back; I don't want to overshoot this one.
What is he? A Lancaster, I think.*

'Stand by for attack,' I tell my crew. Now I sound like a training manual.

For the sixth time I make sure the safety is off. Sight on. Now, what I want to do is to get in close to the Lancaster before the gunners see me. Just a few seconds, that's all I need, so that I can line her up in my sights ...

My thumb caresses the button that controls the two 30-millimetre and two 20-millimetre cannon in the nose, the larger calibre weapons above, the smaller below, all neatly enclosed with their belts of ammunition: 135 rounds for each of the 30-millimetre guns, 350 rounds each for the two 20-millimetre guns.

My left hand is on the throttle levers. I tell Dorn that I am going to attack from behind and then I am going to pass beneath the bomber, giving him a chance to squirt away with his guns.

The Lancaster looks exactly like the silhouette illustrations in the aircraft recognition manuals: low-slung tailplane, elliptical fin and rudders, marked dihedral on mainplanes, four in-line Merlin engines. I was good at aircraft recognition; my only error in one examination was to confuse a Hurricane with an early version of the Messerschmitt 109.

The silhouette moves closer. I can see the turrets swinging from side to side. It's a miracle the gunners haven't spotted me.

Are you watching me, Mutti, Papa?

I press the button.

At once the aircraft bucks with the recoil. The tangy smell of cordite invades the cockpit. I see the fireballs hurtling across the sky at the Lancaster and, even as I fire, the lights flash in the bomber's tail turret. As though I had activated his guns the instant I activated my own.

13

Len had barely time to shout: 'Fighter! Corkscrew port! Corkscrew port!'

As he spoke he fired his Brownings. And as he fired them he died. Two cannon-shells struck his perspex-clad turret. One exploded immediately in front of his face; the second hit him full in the chest.

In that same instant Wally hurled the aircraft into a violent left-hand turn. It was a routine frequently practised over Yorkshire fields, the Spitfires playing attackers. Fighter affiliation. A left-hand turn, a five-second plunge, a sudden straightening out, a climbing right-hand turn, then another plunge to the left. The Lancaster thus followed a corkscrew-like path. All M-Mother's crew knew what to expect when the skipper took evasive action; they had that small advantage over the attacking fighter. The fighter, however, had the far greater advantages of speed, manoeuvrability and fire power.

M-Mother tore downwards. Then, groaning with the torture to her frame, she flattened out and flung herself to the right.

'I see him!' Phil's voice from the mid-upper turret, immediately followed by the busy clatter of his guns.

In the pilot's seat Wally sweated from the sheer physical labour of hurling the big bomber around the sky.

'Rolling to port, gunners. Diving, now.'

Control column hard to the left. Forward. Vicious, abrupt movements. Dust and dirt rose from the floor, hovering momentarily as the floor fell away in yet another stomach-churning dive. At Wally's side, Harry clung grimly to the windscreen handles as M-Mother plummetted, then flattened out. His legs buckled. Eyes wide above his oxygen mask, he looked back through the rear of the canopy. He saw the lights following them across the sky, wobbling directly at them, then, at the last possible moment, speeding by to the left and right. A slim-winged shadow skidded past, turning.

'Climbing starboard now, gunners.'

'I've lost the bugger.'

M-Mother laboured upwards, her Merlins bellowing with the effort of hauling the more than sixty-five thousand pounds of her around like a fighter.

'Rolling to port now. Diving.'

Wally's voice was short. His arms felt leaden; he could feel the dampness of his shirt against his body.

At their stations the crew members listened in fear for the next barrage of fire; each man saw the German fighter in his imagination and it was incredibly speedy and powerfully armed. M-Mother was no match for it. One more burst would surely do the trick and rip the poor old Lanc to pieces …

'Climbing to starboard, gunners.'

Phil's voice, almost complainingly: 'Where the hell's he got to now?'

M-Mother soared, engines howling. Again she rolled, again she dived, again she dragged herself level; nose up, wing over, again and again.

Then Phil said, 'I think we've lost him, skipper.'

'Are you sure?'

'He's nowhere in sight.'

'Did you hit him?'

'God knows. But I can't see him now.'

Relief swept through the metal hull like a fresh wind.

'Nice work, gunners,' said Wally. He steadied the controls. He glanced at the compass and found that their gyrations had turned them almost completely around; they were headed for Norway. 'Resuming course now, crew. Is everyone all right? Any damage? Navigator?'

'OK here, skipper.'

'Bomb-aimer?'

'Everything's all right, thanks, skipper,' Douglas replied.

'Engineer?'

'OK, skip,' said Harry. He rapidly inspected the instruments; no problems. Lucky.

'Wireless op?'

'OK, skip.'

'Mid-upper gunner?'

'Fine, skipper.'

'Rear gunner?'

Silence.

'Len? Len, are you all right?'

No reply.

Charlie said, 'I'll go and have a look, skipper.'

'Roger. Everyone else, keep your eyes peeled. That fighter must still be around here somewhere.'

Charlie squeezed himself out of his seat, disconnecting his intercom and his oxygen after taking a long, deep breath. Leg over the main spar, then into the black, cold tube of the fuselage, swaying and pulsating. He ducked under Phil's turret, still traversing as the little Scot stood guard. No damage to the fuselage, as far as Charlie could see. The Jerry must have been a pretty rotten shot. Ahead was the door to the tail turret. Charlie connected his oxygen and took several deep breaths, then he slid the door open.

He stared for several seconds before shutting it again. He plugged his intercom into the nearest socket.

'Wireless op to pilot,' he said flatly. 'Len's had it.'

'What? Oh Christ; are you sure? Is there nothing you can do for him?'

'No,' said Charlie. 'He hasn't got a head any more.'

Charlie tugged the intercom plug from its socket. Poor

bloody Len. Jesus, no, he shouldn't say 'bloody'. And yet it was the truth. Len was just a hunk of bloody meat. Charlie kept remembering a fox he had once seen after the hounds were finished.

Eyes tightly shut, he clutched at the fuselage wall and fought the waves of nausea. Don't think about it, he kept telling himself, but there was nothing else he could think about. The aircraft jogged in uneven air and he slumped against the side and slid weakly to the floor. He ripped the oxygen mask from his face and vomited in great, agonizing heaves. But his own misery helped quell the memory of the blood-splashed nightmare of a thing that was once a young man named Len. He shivered. It was cold; no heating down by the tail. Across from him was the door. WAY OUT, someone had written. He didn't remember seeing it before; then he remembered; this wasn't George; this was Mother. The skipper had sort of pranged George that very morning. Every bloody thing was going wrong.

He wiped the mess from his mouth and dragged himself to his feet. Sick and dizzy; he felt terrible. He stared at the intercom and oxygen lines. He took moments to realize their significance. He needed them. Come on, Charlie; smarten up; finger out. Oh Christ, where to plug them? Where?

'Where are you, wireless op? Charlie?' The skipper sounded worried. Charlie couldn't reply at once; he fought the heaving of his stomach. Then he managed to say, 'Sorry, skipper. Len, he was such a mess ... god-awful mess ... I got sick ...'

'Charlie, does the turret work?'

The turret? Charlie winced, cursing his stupidity.

The skipper spoke loudly, harshly. 'If the turret still works I want you to operate it. Can you get Len out by yourself?'

'I think so, skipper.'

'Can I help?' Paul asked.

'No. I can do it myself.' Charlie breathed deeply of his oxygen. 'I'll do it now.'

He freed Len's headless, impossibly mangled body of its harness. It was surprisingly easy to drag the body backwards, out of its seat. Len seemed much lighter than he should have been. Did the head make all that much difference?

Blood had frozen over the side window panels creating a macabre, stained-glass effect. Len's oxygen lead was ripped but the source still functioned. So did the intercom.

'Wireless op to skipper. I'm in the turret now.'

'Right, Charlie. You're our rear gunner for a while. Watch out for that Jerry.' Flat, bloody matter-of-fact tone; no time for niceties.

Charlie closed the sliding-door behind him. The air inside the turret was cruelly cold and turbulent; it burst in through the shattered sides. He huddled down, pressing his left hand between his knees as he operated the control stick, confirming the astonishing fact that the turret still worked. Turn to port, to starboard, up, down; everything seemed to be on top line. If only it wasn't so perishingly bloody *freezing!* He thought of Len's electrically heated suit, useless now, torn to bits.

The minutes drifted by. The holes in the turret were far too large to try and stuff. An entire vertical section of the canopy had been blown away, leaving only a short section of framework wobbling in the wind. When Charlie turned the turret to the limit of its starboard traverse, the slipstream was literally scooped into it, a hurricane so fiendishly, agonizingly cold that for a few crazy moments after he straightened the guns again it seemed almost warm. He no longer thought of Len; it no longer mattered to him that the small cubicle in which he sat was spattered with fragments of Len's face and brains and skull. The cold was *really* real. The cold reduced the struggle to elemental proportions: continue to breathe, continue to function, stay in the turret, keep looking for fighters. Nothing else.

Wally's arms still felt curiously electric from the effort of flinging M-Mother around the sky. He licked his lips, dry with fatigue and fright, and he felt the flat rubber taste of his oxygen mask. At least the kite handled well. Nothing vital had been hit. Except Len. Sorry, Len. Sorry as hell. Watch out for the Jerry, gunners. For Christ's sake, keep watching. Spot more power to pull the kite back up to twenty thousand. There. Course? Yes. OK.

First George, now Len. A pulse of fear: was this the way it was starting? Was it all going to lead to what he had seen that morning? A voice in his earphones. Paul's American-sounding voice: target in ten minutes. Always the calm one, Paul. Rather comforting at a time like this. Everyone wetting their trousers, old Paul keeps on doing his sums.

Ten minutes. But what about the Jerry?

The skipper's voice: 'Pilot to crew. We're approaching the target now. Eyes peeled, please.'

I feel the stickiness on my thigh. The pain is minimal, however, a mere pricking. I can still operate the rudder pedals; I still function as a pilot. And I can still see the Lancaster, dead ahead. I keep my eyes glued on him as Kleeman's voice tells what damage we have suffered. Kleeman is hurt; so is Dorn, he tells me. Damn the Lancaster. Damn him. I will get him.

This was where the fighters would be concentrated, around the target. It wouldn't do to let them catch you napping.

Douglas was pleased about the target marking. He sounded like a connoisseur remarking on a succulent morsel of jugged hare. 'Very neat, skipper. See that? Oh, they've done a very nice job, a very nice job indeed.'

Behind M-Mother the sky was tinged with red. Umpteen millions of candlepower twinkled below: flares dropped

123

by the Pathfinders to guide the bombers to the target's centre. Ahead, the first fires were already visible. So were bombers. Bombers lumbering into the target area, their loads of high explosive and phosphorus clutched in their bellies.

'Pilot to crew. Turning on the target now. All set, bomb-aimer?'

'All set, skipper.'

Very chirpy was Douglas. Apparently oblivious of the danger of flying straight and level over one of the world's most energetically defended cities. Busy as hell, was Douglas. Lining things up in his box of tricks. Calculating height and drift and speed. While everyone else just wanted to get it over with as rapidly as possible. And wanted to get to hell out of it. But this was the point of it all, the training, the planning, the organizing, the incredible expense; this was the reason for their being in the air at this time, at this place.

Wally gripped the control column with both hands. He steered along the path of markers, ignoring the dazzle of lights on either side. High Street into the centre of Berlin: just follow the bright lights. The kite bucked as flak burst near by. Fragments of the shell pattered like hail. Small fragments, thank God.

'Left-left a bit, skipper.'

Douglas's voice. Wally imagined him, lying full-length in the nose, eyes glued to his box of tricks. Douglas was a good bomb-aimer; too good for the nerves, a few times. One hideous August night over Dortmund he had insisted on three bomb-runs before he was satisfied and finally pressed the tit.

'Left-left a bit more, skipper.'

Now there were dozens of aircraft around M-Mother. And they were far too visible for comfort. The diarrheal truth: if they were visible to M-Mother's bods, then M-Mother was visible to them—and to the fighters. Wally had the same feeling about bomb-runs as about visits to the dentist; the same vulnerability, the same helplessness; there wasn't anything you could do, except take it and hope it might not be quite as bad as it might easily turn out to be.

'Steady.'

There could be no evasive action during the bomb-run. The aircraft had to travel straight and true while the bomb-aimer lined up his target. Flak had to be ignored. Bombs had to be dropped according to plan otherwise the whole exercise became a gargantuan waste of time and effort and money and courage and life.

'That's it. Very nice, skipper. Hold it there.'

One squadron commander was known to secrete motion-picture cameras beneath pilots' seats, recording on film the movement of turn and bank indicators during bomb-runs. If a pilot's nerves let him down, causing him to fly an evasive course during his bomb-run, the squadron com-mander would know about it—and soon the entire squad-ron would know about it too.

'Drifting to the right a bit ... yes ... left-left ... a bit more. Good.'

Beside him, Harry was a snouted, leather-and-rubber silhouette, eyes fixed on the target ahead, gloved hands poised to dart to the throttle levers if demanded. Harry. Harry's pregnant girl-friend. Good God, he hadn't told Harry of the results of his visit to Greening, the MO. Such as they were. He'd completely forgotten. A searchlight traversed the sky from left to right and back again, a motion reminiscent of a windscreen wiper. Flak-blasts nudged M-Mother, like rude passers-by in Oxford Street. Lord, this was hardly the time to tell Harry to tell his girl-friend to take very hot baths with mustard and consume lots of castor oil—or was it castor-oil baths and consume lots of very hot mustard?

'Still off to the right a bit, skipper. OK, that's better. Hold it.'

Nearly there. Ordeal almost over. Far away to the left something, someone, went down in flames, a writhing, agonized path, the shortest distance to oblivion. A fighter, please Lord, make it a fighter.

'Hold it there. Steady ...'

Like a photographer: smile, please; watch the birdie. Come on, Doug; drop the bloody bombs; who gives a damn whether they hit anything or not? ... Every gunner in Berlin, popping off at us ... law of averages states clearly and definitely that any one Lancaster flying straight and level over Berlin for more than fifteen seconds is bound to get it, good and proper.

'Steady ...'

Wally became conscious of the pain in his shoulders; he was leaning forward, straining against his harness, as if trying to break through it and escape. I won't go round again, he thought; if Doug fucks up this run, I won't go round again. I'll refuse ...

'Steady ...' Voice a tone higher, nearing the climax of the ritual now ... 'Hold it ... hold it ... Good.' Pause. The moment of decision: to drop or not to drop.

Flat voice: 'Bombs gone.' It was done.

Relieved of her burden, M-Mother rose, swaying as she accustomed herself to her new state of lightness. Wally's hands moved to retrim her—and at the same moment he heard the voice in his earphones. It was a strained, muffled voice. It made no sense, in spite of an impellingly urgent tone. Wally started to reply, but he didn't have time. Phil's voice bellowed:

'Fighter! Corkscrew! Corkscrew!'

M-Mother shuddered. The full force of the fighter's cannon and machine-guns caught her amidships, bursting through her fragile skin, exploding within her, filling her with flying, screaming, searing metal ...

126

14

A perfect attack. I see the flashing of exploding shells all
along the big bomber's fuselage. She staggers. I know I
have done her terrible damage. But suddenly I am too
close. Quickly I throw the Me into a tight turn; we hurtle
past the Lanc, almost brushing her sides. The mid-upper
gunner blazes away; I see his tracers sailing above and
behind as we turn.

'Good, good. Well done.'

Kleeman's voice is weak but he has courage; I feel very
fond of him at this moment. I hope I can get him back to
base to be patched up by the medics. In the excitement I
have forgotten my own wound.

I turn back and swoop up beneath the Lancaster for
another attack. It's still flying. I'm almost glad. I want to
hit it again; I want to see my shells exploding along its
body, mortal wounds to pay it back for my parents and for
Dorn and Kleeman and, yes, for me too. I wonder how
seriously I am hurt. There's still no pain. Perhaps it's nothing more than a splinter; even a minor wound can bleed
profusely.

I fire again; flickering, darting, my shells speed across
the sky—but already the bomber is tumbling on to one
wing. I hit him as he falls. Something breaks away. Already
I am past him, turning violently. I mustn't lose sight of
him; I want to see him crash; and I want Kleeman to see
him crash.

M-Mother fell out of the sky.

Torn, battered, she hurtled down toward the burning city, her pilot slumped over the controls. The aircraft's speed mounted with every foot. The indicator jerked past three hundred and twenty-five, three hundred and fifty.

There was no time for terror. Harry, clutching at the window handle and the panel for support, knew he had to drag the skipper off the stick and then pull it back. It was *clear-cut—and there wasn't an instant to lose. If he didn't pull the stick back in time the kite would just go straight into the ground and be blown into a million bits. The crew with it. But now the aircraft's speed fought with him, tried to pin him, to immobilize him. His arm was leaden as he grabbed at the skipper's arm. Painfully he pulled himself toward the pilot's seat. But something stopped him. He couldn't move. It was as though he was tied.

And he was.

His oxygen lead was stretched to its limit, an absurd fetter, a stupid little component that could kill everyone. He tore the helmet from his head.

Now the streets of Berlin had become terrifyingly distinct. M-Mother needed height in which to pull out of a dive, but soon there would be no height left.

Harry heaved at the skipper's shoulder, shoving him against the fuselage wall, wrestling his hands and feet from the controls. He grabbed the wheel and pulled. And pulled. Nothing happened. The almost-solid mass of speeding air paralysed the elevator surfaces.

Maximum diving-speed of the Avro Lancaster Mark 1: 360 m.p.h.

Harry didn't know what speed M-Mother was doing. He didn't look at the dial; he simply pulled. He jammed his feet against the instrument panel. And pulled. Every fibre of his being he exerted on this one task. He strained until his arms threatened to tear out of their sockets.

'You bitch, you bitch ...!'

Briefly a searchlight flooded the cockpit with dazzling whiteness; and was gone. A web of streets; water glinting redly; a string of fires, like windswept plants.

Dimly he was aware of someone at his side, more hands hauling with desperate strength.

Then the column moved. Manpower won the fight. Outside, the control surfaces deflected the screaming air. M-Mother began the agonizing business of pulling out. She flexed under the fearful stresses. She shrieked in every corner of her frame. She had to collapse. She had to fall apart in the air. Her wings had to buckle and rip away. They had to.

But they didn't.

Harry saw the darkened buildings rushing at him. Then, as M-Mother flattened out, he felt himself being thrust into the floor; his insides stretched and sagged; he couldn't breathe. The buildings changed direction; they showed their sides to him, then they streaked away below. To the right, a light flak gun fired a long burst that went sailing through the night, chasing them ineffectually; a long string of coloured balls of fire; you could almost count them as they wobbled by ...

'You beaut ... you bloody beaut ...'

Now Harry couldn't stop talking to M-Mother. She was a beaut. She was marvellous. She'd pulled out. He was alive. The kite was the right side up and still flying and there was Berlin, sombre and grubby-looking, zipping along just a few feet below. Streets, houses, lamp-posts, a bus, shops, a railway station ... a church with a tall spire; at a distance it seemed to move quite slowly then, suddenly, it accelerated and dashed at him at insane speed to nip away, a blur on the left ...

Douglas was yelling in his ear.

'Too low! You're too low. Pull up! You'll hit something!'

Christ, yes, he was right. Harry nodded. Up. Pull back on the stick.

M-Mother wallowed, one wing dragging. She began to skid, turning flatly. But at least the ground dropped away a bit; the buildings slowed down to a run.

Keep the wings level, Harry told himself. Keep the bloody wings level or she'll side-slip straight in. Christ yes, that's exactly what she'll do.

Douglas was behind the seat trying to see what was wrong with the skipper, reaching over and around to pull him back into his seat. But his seat was half occupied by Harry.

'Is he dead?' Harry yelled. Hopeless. Douglas couldn't hear a word.

He wished Douglas could somehow get the skipper out of the seat; it was bad enough trying to fly the kite without having to sit almost sideways; he could barely reach the rudder pedal with his left foot.

He glanced quickly at the air-speed indicator: two hundred and forty. And slowing. Hold her at about two hundred, Harry told himself. Two hundred. Jesus.

Douglas was yelling in his ear again. Something about first-aid and trying to stop the bleeding. Harry nodded. Go ahead, cobber; what the hell are you asking me for?

Dazed, Paul picked himself up from the floor. He held on to the navigation table and he wondered why the table was at such a strange angle; it was bent up like the lid of a used tin can. There was a smell of burnt explosive.

Then he realized there was no sound in his earphones. What had happened? Had everyone baled out? For an instant panic jarred through him; then he saw the reason for the silence: the intercom lead had pulled from its socket.

Charlie's radio equipment was a shambles. It looked as though a large mailed fist had smashed down on it and spread it all over the navigation compartment—or what was left of the navigation compartment.

Paul looked down at himself, fearful of seeing something missing—a hand or an arm or a leg. Didn't people say a guy could be badly hit and then not notice he'd lost anything until he shook hands or took a walk or something? Relieved, he observed that he still possessed two arms and hands and legs and feet. No sign of blood.

What the hell was Harry doing, bare-headed, in the skipper's seat? And Douglas, yelling and gesticulating ...

Then Douglas came aft and now he was yelling and gesticulating again, this time at Paul. Douglas took Paul's intercom jack and connected it with the nearest socket in the wall.

'The skipper's hurt,' he said. 'I've got to get something to stop the bleeding.'

He pushed past, back into the dark tube that was M-Mother's body. Paul tried to move forward to help Douglas get by but his feet skidded beneath him. He fell and his hands were in hot oil. The stuff was running all over the cockpit floor. Boiling oil, he thought inconsequentially.

The fighter struck again.

Shells burst against the fuselage with sharp hollow sounds: it sounded like someone hitting a galvanized steel roof with a stick. M-Mother tottered under the multiple impacts. Something smashed into the instrument panel tearing away a gauge and a section of metal frame. Beside Harry, a perspex panel crinkled into opacity.

The Me turned away.

Wally saw the building quite distinctly. It was an important-looking building, a town hall or something. It had a turret on top; an architectural afterthought. The building dashed by; and for an instant it looked as if M-Mother's port wing-tip was going to slice the turret off.

Consciousness returned slowly, reluctantly. There was a brief interview with a girl who was covered with plaster dust and there was a party and none of the guests would speak to him or even acknowledge his existence. Wind howled along a narrow, seemingly endless corridor. It was hard to make progress against the wind; even bent double it was almost beyond him to put one foot before the other.

The din of the wind became the din of the engines. He tried to think. Had he seen a building? Or had he imagined it? Why was he looking out along the wing? Think. Puzzle it out. He became aware of the fact that his face was squashed against a window. A cold window. He moved his head so that the cold and the pain mingled. It's going to happen, he thought, without emotion. I'm going to get the chop just as I was told I would. So there really are signs and they really do mean something. It was an item of truth to be accepted and considered and stored away. But not for long. He told himself that he should have gone sick or something, anything to get out of this trip. It wasn't fair on the others. Poor sods.

He tried to move but something was pinning him against the fuselage wall. He closed his eyes again, wondering dully whether he really had seen a building with a turret on top. It didn't seem to matter very much. Then a hand was on his shoulder. 'Skipper? Skipper? Can you hear me?' An urgent, anxious voice. Wally started to shake his head to make the voice go away but the action caused an explosion of pain. Ah, it hurt so. But he was awake. His eyes focussed on the window and on the wing. For an instant he was terrified; the ground was so close, he thought the kite was hitting the deck. The facts flooded in: Harry was flying; it was indeed Harry that was pinning him against the wall.

He, Wally, was wounded or something. He'd been asleep. Somehow or other the kite had come down from twenty thousand feet to zero feet. And somehow it had survived the fighter attacks. Yes, he remembered the fighter attacks now. He was the skipper. He had to command. He moved his hand to his mask-switch.

'Harry,' he said, 'would you please get to hell out of my chair?'

Douglas saw the dark shape of the Messerschmitt, breaking away from its attack. A moment later he saw the flames. Deep within the fuselage, behind the main spar. His reaction was instantaneous. Fire had to be killed at once. There could be no delay. Kill it—or it would kill you.

He grabbed a fire extinguisher from its rack and hurled himself over the spar. He fired the extinguisher in desperate haste, aiming the liquid at the flames, kicking them as if they were snapping animals. Even as he did so he saw the flames spread to the fuselage walls, eating through the very structure of the aircraft. He yelled for the others to come. He needed help. He couldn't handle this alone.

The smoke spun around him, stinging, choking, driven by the fury of the air bursting in through M-Mother's sides. He kicked at a blazing metal box; it burst apart and he sprayed the valves and the wires. But the fire leapt about, maddeningly agile.

Someone had to come. At once!

The flames were all he could see through the smoke. Now they were behind him. In a moment they would eat through the fuselage; the kite would come apart in the air. He attacked the flames at his right, then at his left. A nightmare of savage flickerings and glowings.

Then the extinguisher was empty. He dropped it. No time to think about it. (But, oh Lord, why didn't someone come? ...)

A thick flying-suit would smother them. Quickly. Hardly feel the heat through all that padding. There. Squash. Flatten. Press hard. Harder. Squeeze out all the oxygen, every last bit of it. Choke the fire. Strangle it. Ah ... hot now but in a moment it would be dead. Then a moment's coolness. Next one. Arm along bulkhead. Neatly flattens foot-long fire in single motion. Smooth action. Getting better at this. Poor old sleeve, though, blackish and smelling a little odd. Now, an awkward one. A brute. Right in a corner. Kneel down to get at it. Knee it to death. Knees down, Mother Brown. Give us the knees and we'll finish the job ... More, how many more of the little blighters? None of you will get away, you know. Each of you is doomed. I'm getting to you, one by one. Trousers glowing a bit. Smother it against a bulkhead. Push hard. Painful, but the fire gets squashed. Over and over again. Smarts ... hurts like the devil ... flame smells ... sight blurry ...

He bellowed. It hurt, it hurt ... oh, so cruelly. On one knee he beat at the last glowing remnant of the fire with his bare hand; his glove had burnt away ... his mind seemed clogged with the smoke ...

It took moments for Douglas to realize that now he had beaten out the fire in the aircraft he had to beat out the fire that was consuming him ...

15

Harry and Paul crouched beside the pilot's seat, like visitors at a bloody hospital.

'I'm all right,' Wally said, slowly, distinctly, taking the feel of the controls and watching the ground hurtling along, hideously close. 'My head aches like hell but I can see straight. What's the damage to my head?'

It seemed a curious question but it was necessary.

He felt them take off his helmet and touch his skull; then the earphones were pressed against his ears. Paul's voice said:

'Something gashed you, Wally. The bleeding seems to be stopping; it's a messy-looking thing but it doesn't look too deep. Are you sure you're all right?'

A nod. A signal for them to replace his helmet; he had to wear it in order to communicate with them. Then they told him of the damage, the oil, the radar, the wireless; they told him the Me was still lurking behind them.

Phil said, 'He's a bit higher than us, skipper. I think he's having trouble seeing us against the ground. So keep low. Glad to hear you're all right now.'

Phil, Paul, Harry, himself. What of Douglas and Charlie and Len? No, Len was dead. Think hard. Charlie was in the rear turret. Or was he? Doug? Went aft, according to Paul. He said he'd go and check. Nod ... OK. Engines? Miraculously untouched. Their steady, healthy roar was a hymn of hope.

Paul was calling the rear turret again. Nothing. Poor old Charlie. The fighter must have got him. And Douglas, where the hell was Douglas? Well, he'd worry about them in a moment. Right now, the fighter was more important.

But could he fly the kite all the way to England? Could he land it when they got there? Perhaps the kite was falling to pieces at this very moment. It was possible; she had been badly hit.

But that was something else to put aside for the moment; among the batch of things to worry about later.

Phil's voice came over the intercom : 'The silly bugger's still looking for us. He's going around in circles.'

Wally wet his lips. The trouble was, the fighter had them on radar. They couldn't give him the slip; eventually, inevitably, he'd be down on M-Mother like a ton of bricks.

'He's quite a long way back now,' Phil reported. 'Bastard.'

'Keep an eye on him.'

He watched the countryside, a grey and bleak pattern, unwinding and slipping out of sight in rapid, monotonous motion. The course was due west. Paul was working out a new course. Wally wondered whether they would ever need it.

The hot oil had run into the fuselage well; it was disappearing through cracks in the floor. Harry said it was hydraulic fluid, which boded ill for the successful operation of the flaps and undercarriage. Something else to worry about—later.

Paul announced the new course; then he said he was going aft.

I think they must have crashed. Kleeman's radar is deceiving us; we're chasing a flock of geese or something. I swing the aircraft into another turn to the left as I hear him tell me that we have overtaken the target again. I tell him I think the Lancaster has crashed. He disagrees: his box of electronic tricks doesn't lie.

I don't like flying this low at night. For one thing, I am inexperienced—and I don't pretend to be otherwise; men like Veit—even Kleeman—have flown more hours at night than I have flown in total. Poor Kleeman. Poor Dorn; we think he is dead.

A new vector. My head aches from staring into darkness, trying to judge my height and trying to see the Lancaster.

This one won't get away.

It's been incredibly lucky. I hit him again and again. I saw the hits. No mistaking them. I thought he had gone when he dived over the target; I couldn't imagine how he could pull out of that dive. I wanted to see him crash. Instead I saw him recover. Then more hits. Flashes all along the body of the thing. I saw flames inside the fuselage. But I suppose someone managed to put the flames out. Someone. A member of the crew. Strange, I hadn't thought of the men within the machine. I was attacking a Lancaster and when I saw my shells bursting in its fuselage I still thought of it solely in terms of damage to a machine. But the Lancaster has a sizable crew: seven, I think. Perhaps I have already killed several men aboard. The rear gunner, almost certainly. I saw shells exploding inside the turret; surely no man could survive that. Then the other hits, all along the body; the other occupants could hardly have escaped unscathed.

I have killed a man. At least, I think I have.

The fact has no significance for me at the moment. I think about it and I don't care. Odd. I expected to care deeply.

Paul recoiled at the sight. It was so unbelievably bloody foul. Douglas was there on the floor, *burning* ... and the flames that were eating at him were, at the same time, illuminating the aircraft's interior: the black, charred body of M-Mother, her metal melted into weird forms through

137

which howled a two-hundred-mile-an-hour gale. It was nightmarish ... and through Paul darted the instinctive reaction: run ... get away from this horror! For an instant he hesitated, then he threw himself at Douglas, beating at the flames, strangling them, destroying them. It was rapidly done. And then it was dark inside the aircraft again, dark and full of beaten smoke and noise and stench and rotten, tortured metal. The empty extinguisher rolled against Paul's leg. Suddenly it was obvious what had happened. God, why hadn't Douglas called for help? Wasn't there even time for him to get another extinguisher? He shook his head; he felt tears pricking his eyes; he didn't know whether they were caused by the wind and smoke or Douglas's condition. Anger jarred him; he wanted to shout out at the stinking pointlessness of it all. Little Douglas.

You poor bastard, he whispered. I don't know whether you're alive or dead. But what a mess you are ... and how you stink.

He moved the limp and strangely shrivelled body back to the rest bunk. The wind was a little less ferocious here. Clumsily, apologetically, he fumbled with the first-aid kit and administered a shot of morphine. He bundled up Douglas as best he could. Then he found an intercom jack that still worked and he told the others what had happened. Poor Doug, they said. Morphine, they said. Wrap him up, they said. Phil was cackling about the smoke and the smell of fire as if it was news, as if it hadn't already eaten poor Doug. Oh Christ ... Paul kept shaking his head. It was so rotten, so god-awful rotten.

But now there was nothing else he could do for Doug; it was time to find out about Charlie. He had to do it; someone had to.

Crouched, he stumbled back along the fuselage. It swayed and creaked and reverberated amid the engines' din. It was bitterly cold; the winds screamed and whirled in lunatic fury into every corner and crevice. He ran his hand along the fuselage wall; it trembled like a frightened animal under his touch. Ahead of him was blackness. Then, without warning, he tripped; he fell; and his hands touched a cold stickiness on the floor; his knees rammed into something solid and substantial. Len. Oh God, it was Len. Len who no longer had a head.

This was Hell. Deafening, vibrating Hell. Paul scrambled to his knees and stared at the turret door. There was a dead-man's handle; you pulled it to bring the turret fore-and-aft if the gunner was wounded or dead. If Charlie is dead, he said to himself, I'm going to leave him there.

He took a deep breath of frigid air then he pulled the handle and slid the door open.

Charlie beamed. He started talking but Paul couldn't hear a word; he had to persuade Charlie to plug into an intercom jack. Then the story bubbled out. He had tried to shout a warning about the fighter but he couldn't speak; his jaw was frozen. And the turret jammed; it wouldn't turn; the guns wouldn't fire; to top it all the intercom had gone dead.

'Thank Christ you've come down where it's warmer,' he said. 'Oo, mate, it was cold in there!'

M-Mother continued to nose her way bluntly across the German countryside.

At the controls, Wally tried to ignore his headache; there were important things to think about. The crew. Charlie was looking after Doug. Paul had worked out a heading that would take them to a point on the coast near the German-Dutch border; now he was taking a fix on Polaris. Just checking, he said. Good old Paul. Phil was manning the mid-upper and keeping an eye on the Messerschmitt that still lurked behind M-Mother, like a footpad waiting for a dark corner. The kite was flying well; engines buzzing nicely; Harry was keeping an eye on things in that department.

Far to the left, a glow. Another raid, perhaps. Magdeburg? Potsdam? Wally wondered briefly about the chances of mingling with the bomber stream; it would be an infinitely safer way of getting home than trying it alone: the anonymity of sheer numbers; the proverbial needle in the haystack. But you couldn't expect to join up with a bomber stream if you didn't know what route they were flying. No; M-Mother had lost her own stream; she would have to make it back alone.

The countryside kept unrolling like some endless gloomyhued painting. There was light enough to see fields and farmhouses, roads, a village. No colours though. No people around; no glimmers of light. And, so far, no flak. By chance, M-Mother had found a peaceable part of the Third Reich over which to journey.

He glanced out into the greyness to port. Thin slivers of light probed the sky; tiny sparkles flickered momentarily and were gone. So harmless-looking, from a distance.

He rubbed his eyes. He felt suddenly weary. The fuselage drummed pleasantly against his left shoulder. How delightful to settle on the floor and let one's eyelids droop and slowly drift off to sleep ... He snapped awake. No! He had to concentrate. He had to make decisions. It was up to him to get the kite home. Like it or not, he was the skipper.

He didn't like.

A small village appeared in the windscreen; it burst out of the darkness at enormous speed; then it was gone.

Paul's necessarily rough-and-ready navigational calculations put the aircraft on a course passing between Bremen and Hanover. Wally hoped to miss both cities by the biggest margin possible; both cities had formidable anti-aircraft defences.

He had almost forgotten about the fighter.

Then Phil's voice shrilled in his earphones. 'Break to port! Fighter! Break to port!'

Wally sucked air, then his teeth clamped as he swung the aircraft to the left. His every sense anticipated the bullets smashing, slicing, searing through metal and flesh, red-hot steel thrusting its way into fuel ...

Phil's guns clattered as something hit M-Mother on the port side, causing her to lurch as she turned. The grey countryside streamed by the wing-tip. Harry's hands were on the throttles, waiting for Wally to call for more power. The control column swung to the right. A nod; yes, more power!

'Now where is he?'

Wally straightened the aircraft and glanced at Harry, his face tense and apprehensive. We're done for, he said silently. Don't you realize that, you stupid Australian oaf.

Sorry, Harry; sorry.

Phil reported, 'Ah, there he is. Keeping his distance. Come on, laddie, come on over here and I'll give you some more of the same. I hit you, didn't I?' He had forgotten he was talking to M-Mother's crew. 'Come on over here; don't be shy. We'll give you a warm welcome.'

His mocking tone grated on Wally's nerves.

'Mid-upper gunner, just tell us what he's doing.'

'Sorry, skipper. He's keeping his distance. But he's coming alongside. To port. See?'

Yes, there he was: long, slender fuselage, twin tails, twin engines: Messerschmitt 110. About five hundred yards away. A silhouette out of range of the Brownings.

Harry growled, 'What the hell's he waiting for?'

Wally asked, 'Did he hit us? Anyone have any damage to report?'

'OK back here,' said Phil.

Wally edged M-Mother back on to the right course. The Me followed.

'Friendly little bastard,' said Charlie.

Wally watched the fighter. It was behaving like an escort; its higher speed was causing it problems; it would pull ahead then have to turn to fall back in step with the slower bomber.

Wally wondered about the man in the Messerschmitt's cockpit. It seemed likely that the man would kill him, waiting for an opportune moment, then turning and blasting away with his cannons and machine-guns until M-Mother crashed. It was as simple as that. Phil, good gunner though he was, could offer relatively feeble defence; his twin Brownings were no match for the fighter's arsenal. Therefore, the fighter would win. The fighter should, in fact, have won already. Only prodigious quantities of good luck had kept M-Mother in the air until now. Surely the supply of available good luck was running low. For Len and Doug it had already run out.

Wally looked at the Messerschmitt. You want more than a probable, don't you, he thought. You won't be satisfied until we hit the deck and you see us hit the deck. You shouldn't have any trouble getting confirmation of us, lots of people around will probably see us crash. Perhaps we'll crash in the middle of a town. You've fired a lot of lead at us; frustrating for you that we're still aloft ...

Harry nudged him.

Silently he nodded toward the port-inner temperature gauge.

The needle was soaring.

'Glycol leak,' said Harry flatly. 'See the white flame? Engine'll be red hot in a little while. We're losing power from her already.'

'What's up?' said Charlie from the depths of the fuselage.

Wally's temper flared. 'For God's sake, let's have some intercom discipline!'

'Sorry,' said Charlie, contrite.

Wally asked if there was anything that could be done from the cockpit; Harry shook his head. No use throttling back? No. Eventually it would heat up and burn? Harry nodded. All right. No sweat. A Lanc could fly perfectly well on three engines; many had limped home on two. The dud engine had to be stopped and its prop feathered so that the drag would be minimized. A slower ride home, that was all.

He realized that he was telling himself all the things he should be telling the crew.

For a short period I was horribly nauseous. I thought I would disgrace myself and vomit in my own aircraft. With the nausea came a pathetic weakness. I hardly had the strength to operate the controls. It seemed to me that I was probably bleeding to death. I imagined the blood pouring out of the wound in my thigh, draining my body until I lost consciousness. I remember thinking of Kleeman. The poor fellow is stuck in his seat immediately behind me, badly wounded. Even if he were fit, it would be physically impossible for him to move Dorn's body to get out through the hatch. The only way Kleeman will get out of this air-craft is through the hatch—and he can accomplish that only if someone removes Dorn's body for him—and that only if I get back to base in one piece. The designers of the 110 paid scant attention to the survival of radar operators.

Kleeman doesn't know I am wounded ... I haven't told him. He is probably wondering what we are waiting for. Why don't we attack?

In a moment we will attack. The nausea is fading; I feel some of my strength returning. The Lancaster is a durable monster. And the gunner is an excellent shot. A marks-man to respect. For several minutes now we have been fly-ing in a sort of long-range formation. In a way we are like two boxers, each waiting for the other to make the first

143

move. No, *hardly correct: only one of us is required to make the first move. If I do nothing the Lancaster will simply continue flying towards England.*

'He's changing course,' reports Kleeman in a croaking voice.

I thank my dutiful radar operator. Surely one more burst will finish the job. At this altitude the end will be mercifully quick. Veit told me of a Halifax he shot down near Schwerin; at treetop level the bomber was trying to sneak back to the coast and home. Veit said he set both starboard engines on fire and, with the rear gunner shooting all the time, the Halifax suddenly tipped on to one side. A wing hit the ground; instantly the thing became two balls of fire that went rolling across the field, through some bushes and across a road. A horrible, yet fascinating sight, Veit said. The next morning Veit drove out to the field to examine the wreckage—some of it still smouldering. The local burgomaster insisted on being photographed with his hand on Veit's shoulder and with the remains of the Halifax in the background, as though the two of them had shot the bomber down.

My thigh is beginning to feel stiff; that same feeling one has after the first tennis match of the season. I wonder whether I will ever play tennis again. What I should do, of course, is turn at once for home. If I am repairable, they will repair me. The best of everything for our gallant flyers.

'Are we going to attack?' Kleeman finally asks the question.

I nod. 'Yes, but I am having trouble with my gunsight. I'll have it fixed in a couple of minutes.'

He says no more. I must wait a little longer until my strength returns completely. I am keeping my eye on the Lancaster. How will I attack him? From directly behind? Or shall I try a lateral approach, raking the side of him as I turn on him? But the mid-upper gunner of that Lancaster *is unquestionably a much better shot than I am. And, at the moment, I imagine he is rather brighter. What I would prefer to do is approach from below. I am sure I could finish him in a few seconds. But he is too damned low. I can't go beneath him without running a distressingly good chance of flying straight into something on the ground.*

Which is just what he would like.

'Flak!'

The yellow and red dots wobbled their seemingly leisurely way up through the night, then suddenly accelerated and sped by.

The Lancaster hurtled over the source of the flak. In the greyness below could be glimpsed the dull glint of steel barrels, sandbags, a few scattered huts, a vehicle or two.

M-Mother shuddered from a blow in the starboard wing. She tipped to one side then dragged herself back to level flight.

'Everyone all right?'

Everyone was. Phil asked whether it was Paul doing the shooting from the front turret.

'Yes,' said Paul. 'I wonder if I hit anything.'

'You missed me,' said Phil. 'But only just.'

'Where's the fighter?'

'Still with us,' said Phil. 'Just tooling along.'

'Too bad the flak didn't knock him down,' growled Charlie.

Wally asked about the hit; did anyone see what was hit and how badly? Everyone agreed it was the wing that had been hit; no one could see the extent of the damage.

He glanced through the thick perspex of the canopy. The port inner's propeller blades stood stiff and still, sentries standing guard over a wounded engine. A third of a mile away, the Messerschmitt flew a gently undulating, parallel course. Wally's eyes narrowed. Was the German pilot a sadist who derived pleasure from watching his victims for long periods before killing them? An inhuman swine in a black flying-suit? A Prussian with duelling-scars?

A small town appeared to starboard. Paul came forward, peering at the place until it slipped away beneath the wing. It had a river coming in from the north. Otherwise undistinguished. No flak, no lights. The town expressed no displeasure at M-Mother's passing. Paul studied his charts, frowned, shook his head, shrugged.

Harry said he was transferring fuel. The act cheered Wally quite unreasonably. It was an act of confidence. It stated that M-Mother was in the business of getting back to England; it thumbed a nose at the Jerry. Then, almost instantly, he was unreasonably depressed. Bloody silly, he thought; we're all going potty, bothering about transferring fuel, with an Me on our tail.

He readjusted the trim. The kite was working well on three engines; and the controls seemed undamaged. Lucky. Still, hadn't the crew always been lucky? Even in disaster they were lucky. Lucky as hell.

But I'm going to get the chop tonight, Wally said to himself. This all-important life of mine is going to come to a messy end. Oh Jesus, I hope it doesn't hurt too much.

16

M-Mother sped on across Germany, a black monster shaking windows and doors with its din, opening uncounted eyes, frightened eyes ... that softened as the din swept away into the distance and became a faint drumming before silence rolled in on its path. Sighs of relief. Was it ours or theirs? Some people said you could tell by the noise of the engines. What good did that do you anyway? What could you do except hope it wouldn't drop anything on you —or fall on you? You couldn't do anything. Uncounted prayers were said, thanking the dear Lord and the Blessed Virgin for protection that night from the evil purposes of the enemy.

I look at my watch. Its luminous hands tell me I have been airborne almost an hour. My wound is hurting now: a dull throbbing that extends up the entire right side of my body. It could be some type of paralysis that is just beginning to take effect.

The Lancaster is back to treetop level. He sways smoothly as he dashes for the coast. A handsome bird, the Lancaster. And I just keep following him like a faithful servant. But I daren't fly as low as he flies. I'm simply not that good. I know it. And I am sure Kleeman knows it, too.

There is one thing to be said for the pain: it is making me more alert. My mind seems to be functioning almost completely again. Physically I am weakened, but only a little. It doesn't require great strength to push a joystick and press a trigger.

Kleeman hasn't spoken for some minutes.

We pass over a lake; at the one end stands a fine house. Is it full of sleeping children? I hope the noise of us didn't scare them too much.

Soon the Lancaster is sure to come a little higher. Then I will pull the throttles to maximum power and as soon as I am within range I will open fire and I will keep on firing until he goes down.

Then, Kleeman, old friend, we can go home and take Dorn with us.

It was unnerving, knowing the bastard was behind you but being unable to see him.

Phil reported: 'He's dead behind us, skipper. Bit higher than us.'

'Keep your eyes on him.' Bit higher ... almost directly behind ... In all probability he was going to sweep down suddenly. 'Phil, if he comes at us, I'm going to turn to port. OK? But you've got to tell me when to break.'

Phil said OK, he understood.

Wally switched off his mike. He hoped he sounded capable and confident. He felt neither. He felt bloody awful; his head ached savagely; his limbs seemed made of putty; they would surely stretch and twist and crack if exerted.

Paul was at his side, chatting about what a strange guy the Messerschmitt pilot must be, like a relative who won't go home after the party. He said he couldn't figure out what the bastard was up to; could Wally? Wally shook his head. He wished Paul would shut up.

In the peculiarly human way of reassessing dangers as they become more familiar, the crew members of M-Mother found themselves being less frightened of the Messerschmitt the longer it stayed. They began to accept the presence of the twin-engined fighter as part of the scheme of things. Night fighters usually came hurtling out of the darkness

148

to clobber you with cannon and machine-gun and disappear before you could see them; but here was one in full view, being almost chummy. And this was no momentary phenomenon; the Me had pottered about for an incredibly long time. It was something to tell the lads in the Mess, something to add to the folklore of wartime flight: the right sort of tale: danger and whimsy in more or less equal proportions: The Tale of the Lonesome Me.

As M-Mother flew on, minute after minute, hope grew in the men who travelled within her. They had survived four attacks by the Messerschmitt. Or was it five? Or six? They were still flying. They had lost a couple of the lads but losing crewmates was something they were prepared for, indeed every man had fully expected it to happen ever since the tour began. Situation: three engines going, skipper back in the pilot's seat—and if anyone could get this thing back to base, it was he. Every minute that passed meant they were that much closer to the coast. And after the coast, the sea. Mind you, the coast was no picnic. Guns a-plenty along the bloody coast, chum. You held your breath as you went over. All kinds of unpleasantness was almost sure to be chucked up at you. But once you were past, there was the sea ... and home ...

Paul busied himself with his charts and his pencils. The result of his labours was a new course: three-ten.

'We should reach the coast in about thirty-five minutes.'

Wally nodded. He glanced at Paul, who winked. A private joke; but what was it?

For several miles they flew along a railway line; a station abruptly materialized and then was gone. Paul asked if there was a name on it.

Suddenly more flak. Light criss-crossed the night in fiery arcs. It was concentrated stuff that raked through treetops in a furious attempt to hit the fleeing bomber. It lasted for perhaps fifteen seconds, then M-Mother was out of sight of the gunners.

Wally breathed again. 'Any damage?'

Charlie reported that something had come through the fuselage on the port side and gone out through the starboard side. 'But there are so many bloody holes already I don't think it made any difference, skipper.'

All we ask, Mother dear, is that you hold together long enough to get us back to Brocklington. He asked Harry about the engines. Harry said OK, so far.

The Me kept following.

If only he could close his eyes. If only he didn't have to watch the ground streaming along a few feet below ... if only he didn't have to keep adjusting the kite's trim to compensate for the missing engine ... if only he didn't have to keep sounding vigorous and hopeful. The sounding vigorous and hopeful was perhaps the hardest of all. But it was vital. You had to inspire confidence at all times. At all times. No matter what the circumstances. Indeed, if the circumstances were hopeless that was the time to sound most hopeful.

Phil said, 'I hit him, skipper, when he attacked us before. I bet he's badly hurt and he's just waiting for more fighters to come so that he can go home.'

It wasn't a pleasant thought.

Wally sighed. Doggedly gripping the control column with both hands, he stared ahead. The pain in his head seemed audible; he could hear it as well as feel it. A roaring, a thundering, battering at his skull, pressing against his eyes. He daren't relax, even for an instant. Stare ahead. Watch the ground. Keep translating objects into sizes and sizes into relative distances: lightning calculations: the only way to stay alive at this lunatic altitude.

More flak. Streams of bright dots, jogging along in a merry, innocent-looking way, curving away behind.

'Everyone all right?'

Everyone was.

Wally pulled back on the control column and M-Mother swept over a low hill, down the other side, following the contours of the ground like a telegraph line. Dangerous, but at a safer height the flak would surely have clobbered them by now: to offer gunners a relatively slow-moving target was a sure way to get the chop. Low down, the Lancaster was a blurring image in the darkness, nipping behind trees, disappearing into the night before proper aim could be taken. We hope, Wally thought.

Paul sat on the jump seat, torn map and pencil in his hands. The pencil had a freshly sharpened point, Wally noticed. Paul wrote something and held it up for Wally to see.

ARE YOU OK?

Wally nodded, unreasonably irked that Paul should ask the question.

Paul noted his reaction; he wrote:

I JUST ASKED.

Wally smiled; he felt like a sulky child tickled into merriment. Fool! He told himself not to be such a bloody fool in future. What future? He leant to one side. Paul was telling him he thought the kite was straying too close to Bremen. He suggested a sharp turn to port, a south-westerly course for three minutes followed by a turn to starboard; in ten minutes they would resume their original course.

Wally announced: 'Pilot to crew. We're turning in a few moments to avoid flak. Phil, let me know what the Messerschmitt does. OK, here we go!'

He turned suddenly, hoping to be out of sight before the Me woke up to what was happening. For a terror-stilled instant he thought he had misjudged the turn. M-Mother's broad wing thrust down at the speeding earth. The trees—great clutching things—were too close. Wally abruptly remembered the Lanc at Brocklington last summer. Something went horribly wrong with a landing. Inexplicably the pilot turned as he came in over the road; wing down, he began to cross the airfield in a north-easterly direction. His turn steepened. A wing tip brushed a tree and seven lives terminated rapidly in a sickening welter of shattered metal and exploding fuel.

The Merlins bellowed; valiantly they dragged M-Mother out of the turn.

Phil, delightfully unconscious of the danger of the turn, was burbling happily over the intercom. 'You caught him napping, skipper! He's still on the same course as before. Oh, bloody nice work!' A moment later: 'Ugh, hell! He's turning too. Damn.'

Christ, the work, the sheer bloody manual labour of hauling the aircraft back to level flight. Wally had no thoughts for the Messerschmitt or the flak or the crew or even of getting home. Life consisted solely of surviving the next few moments, of wrestling with the controls, making them obey his shaky strength. How ridiculously weak he was! His arms felt like matchsticks. His body felt empty, frail, in imminent danger of collapsing.

Her wings finally came level with the ground. Wally found his arms and hands shaking violently from their efforts. He had to press hard against the control column to squash the shaking. I mustn't pass out, he thought. I mustn't. I've got to stay conscious, I've got to keep my wits about me. I've got to.

Phil's voice again, serious now: 'Skipper, he's staying right behind us. I don't know but he's got that look as if he could be lining us up for another attack.'

Oh God no.

So utterly, bloody defenceless ... cannon-shells ripping through the fuselage, chopping the crew down, smashing through the armour-plate, thudding into his back ... Don't ... don't do it ... chemically treated water in his throat and great hands on his head and shoulders, thrusting him down undeterred by his strugglings ... lungs stretching ... panic boiling along every nerve ... then a moment's respite but hardly sufficient time in which to draw a decent breath ... hands on him again ... down, down ... and Mr Powell ticking them off for monkeying around in the pool ... because Mr Powell didn't see bullies and victims, only distur- bers of the school peace. Fifty lines each: Forbes Major and Williams and Morley and Mann. For monkeying around.

'Pilot to mid-upper. When you tell me to break I'm going to port. OK? Same as before.'

'Roger, skipper.'

Probably no need to remind Phil; he wouldn't have for- gotten instructions of only a few minutes earlier. Phil was a top-notch type. So was Len. So was Doug. So was every- body.

'He's still staying dead behind us, skipper.'

Paul stood slightly to the rear of the pilot's seat, one hand bracing him against the armour-plating. A slender snake of a river came rushing into view. Paul leant forward, torch on, searching his chart; his head bounced up to look over Wally's head to port.

I hope you know where the hell we are, Wally thought.

'Heading two-eight-five.'

Wally turned the aircraft, speeding low over a farm, a road, a small forest. A village appeared, a neat cluster of tiny buildings, formed by two roads into a cross ...

Phil, harsh and urgent: 'He's coming in, skipper! Get ready to break! Hold it ... now!'

17

Through a chink in the black-out curtain over his bedroom window a twelve-year-old boy named Ernst Stähler saw the great Lancaster rush into view over the village; it was so low he thought it was crashing; it turned on to one wing which seemed to brush the rooftops. Then he saw the Messerschmitt. Above the thunder of the engines he heard gunfire. Specks of light flashed between the two aircraft. Something hit the roof of Ernst's house as the Lancaster straightened out. Then the Messerschmitt rushed by in pursuit. Ernst immediately ran down the stairs to the ground floor, across the kitchen, pitch-black but for the soft dying glow of the stove, and out into the street.

Just in time to see the bomber's right outer engine catch fire.

Eyes wide, he watched, expecting the bomber to crash at once. But it stayed in the air, the burning engine a flickering light becoming smaller and smaller until it vanished, leaving only the throb of the engines. Soon that sound dissolved.

Ernst turned and looked the way the aircraft had come. He waited a minute or two but no more planes appeared. The street was quiet again. And cold. Ernst suddenly realized he was wearing only pyjamas. He went back into the house. In three minutes he was asleep again.

Harry's finger stayed on the engine extinguisher button. Now the starboard outer propeller was milling to a halt. But the flames kept licking back from the nacelle, angry ugly tongues waiting for their moment to multiply and gobble up M-Mother.

The aircraft shuddered as cannon-shells and bullets slammed into her. Like a beast in agony, she rolled desperately to the right and left; but there was no escape; her pursuer was agile and meant to kill; he stayed on her tail pumping out streams of missiles.

M-Mother fought back. Tracer poured from her turret amidships. As though connected by a leash of fire, the bomber and the fighter rushed low across the farmland. The bomber was crippled, staggering, barely able to stay in the air. A section of cowling broke away and spun back past the Messerschmitt. A piece of the starboard wing followed. M-Mother, it seemed, was breaking up in the air.

Wally delayed no longer. 'Pilot to crew. I'm climbing. Prepare to abandon aircraft. Repeat. Prepare to abandon aircraft.' Frantic afterthought: 'But for Christ's sake, wait till I tell you. Don't jump yet. Wait for the word!'

This was it. End of tour. End of everything. Wally wondered whether anyone was alive to hear his word to jump. He glanced quickly back. Ah, Harry and Paul were there ...

Mercifully the shooting had stopped.

He was afraid someone might jump too soon, while the aircraft was still too low. 'Keep your helmets on. I'll tell you as soon as we're high enough for you to jump.'

Sweat pouring down his face and body; arms dead with fatigue, he dragged back on the control column. Full power on the two good engines ... she would climb ... but slowly, sluggishly ... poor old weary warrior with only half her power to keep her going, her sides slashed and torn ....

Within M-Mother's fuselage, apprehensive fingers reached for parachute packs, the packs that had been lugged out to the aircraft so many, many times, stowed away, then dragged out on landing and lugged back to the Parachute

Section and the WAAFs' tender care. Now the packs were being clipped on to rings jutting out from the harness webbing. Helplessness jarred the courage of every man. He could do nothing, absolutely nothing, until the kite reached a decent altitude. And she could barely stagger upwards. She would blow up any second now; no one would get out alive.

Wally was hardly conscious of Harry's fumbling efforts to slip the skipper's parachute in position on his chest. A comradely gesture, part of an oft-practised routine; but quite pointless. Wally knew he would never get out in time. Even if he managed to coax Mother up to jump-height, there'd be no chance for him. The crew might make it but the moment he released his hold on the controls, Mother would tumble. She would hit the deck before he could get out of his seat ...

The altimeter read one hundred and fifty feet. M-Mother continued her agonizingly slow ascent. The crew waited. They knew what to do when—if—the kite reached jump-height. There had been scores of idle days at Brocklington when the Squadron Commander ordered the air crews to don their flying-gear and get aboard their aircraft and then see how rapidly they could leave the various escape hatches. Common-sense practices, he called them. Bloody binds, the crews had called them.

The crew of M-Mother stared through the windows at the flames fluttering around the starboard outer nacelle. They looked at the flames as patients might look at fatal growths. There simply wasn't going to be time.

Deep within the dark fuselage, Charlie clipped Douglas's parachute pack in position. As he worked he kept telling Douglas that he was going to be all right; they would jump together; Charlie would pull Douglas's rip-cord and push him away to fall free. But was there really any point? Wasn't he already so far gone that nothing could save him anyway? As for jumping together, it was a lot of nonsense; it was impossible; Charlie knew it. But, damn it, it was better than doing nothing. He took Douglas's dreadful body and pulled it gently toward the hatch, across the fuselage that trembled with the efforts of M-Mother's two good engines. Any moment now, there would be one hell of a bang and the kite would fall apart and that would be that. Charlie sighed. Flying was bleeding dangerous; he had known that when he volunteered, hadn't he?

In the cockpit Harry finished disengaging Wally's harness. Wally nodded his thanks in a stiff, oddly formal way. Then he indicated the front of the aircraft. Harry was to make ready to jump. Harry said OK; there was nothing else he could do. He took a last look back then he ducked beneath the instrument panel and squeezed through the access. He turned the escape-hatch handle; the hatch bucked, pounded by the air outside. Through the transparent nose Harry could see the ground hideously close. Christ, the kite wasn't climbing at all! They'd never get high enough in time! Not a hope! He didn't feel fear, just a dull resentment at the futile order of things; one long bloody futility ending in the biggest futility of all, trying to beat the game when your number is up. This was it, the chop ... 'Regret to inform you that your husband, Sergeant Harold Whittaker, RAAF ... got himself killed in action—but don't feel too badly about it because he was playing around with other women, had one in the family way, as a matter of fact ... no loss, lady ...'

M-Mother's second escape hatch was over the navigation station. It was the hatch through which Paul and Charlie were to exit. Paul tried to open it; the lock had been bent out of shape and wouldn't turn. He had to smash it free with the empty extinguisher. At once the hatch fell in, admitting a torrent of frigid air. Where the hell was Charlie? Paul stared into the blackness of the fuselage. He

157.

called Charlie on the intercom but there was no reply.

The aircraft shuddered as though it was fighting head-winds of fantastic velocity.

Paul waited at the hatchway, gripping its edges, ready to hurl himself through. In an oddly detached instant, he realized that he was frightened in the same liquid-legged way as he had been, aged fifteen, with Mrs Lambert: elderly, thirty-seven-year-old Mrs Lambert of the hennaed hair and heroic chest to whose house he delivered groceries and who had seduced him while her 240-pound steelworker husband snored off a hangover upstairs.

The kite wasn't climbing, for Christ's sake!

He glanced quickly into the cockpit. Wally was there, alone.

He loosened his helmet. He would pull it off the instant he heard the bale-out order. He'd be through the hatch in a flash. He had a chance. He did. He did like hell. The kite wasn't climbing, therefore there wasn't going to be any bale-out order.

Oh God, Mrs Lambert.

His fingers tightened on the hatch. He wanted to live. Damn, damn it, he wanted to live! And he felt like screaming at the idiocy heaped upon idiocy that led to his being here, trapped in a burning bomber about to be blown into small pieces. Was it all planned, right from the moment of his first breath? If so, it was a stupid, pointless, stinkingly rotten plan ...

Wally's voice, strained and apologetic: 'She won't go any higher. I'm sorry, chaps. I can't make her go any higher. Sorry ...'

Why was Wally apologizing? It wasn't his fault. It wasn't anyone's fault. No one was blaming him, for Christ's sake ...

Then Wally said, 'Crash land ... I've got to ... No choice ...'

Perhaps one chance in fifty, Paul thought. That's about what I have. He turned to go aft; in doing so he glanced at the starboard wing. His imagination painted the picture before he saw it: flames, beaten into savage ferocity by the slipstream, engulfing the wing, reaching angrily at the fuselage ...

But there were no flames.

He stared. No flames. Stupidly, he looked back at the port wing, as if the fire might have moved there. No flames. No bloody flames at all; the fire had gone out.

He told Wally.

'What?'

'The fire's gone out!'

Charlie scrambled out from behind the main spar to see; Harry appeared in the nose access like a startled rabbit peeping out of its warren. Everyone started talking at once.

They agreed that the extinguisher, bless its little metallic heart, had effectively doused the source of the fire, but some fuel or oil had continued to burn until consumed; what they had seen, therefore, must have been a conflagration without substance: a burning-brandy-on-the-Christmas-pudding type of fire ... Harry said he'd once heard of a Wimpey with its port engine on fire. The crew called Mayday for all they were worth and on the ground there were fire engines and ambulances and chaps in asbestos suits and other aircraft were diverted to godforsaken places all over the country—and while the Wimpey was wobbling in to land, the fire went out. Just like that. Terribly embarrassing, Harry said.

Wally retrimmed the aircraft as he levelled out just above the treetops once more. She would fly on two engines. More or less. Actually, she could even stagger along on one, but she needed two to maintain an altitude. On one engine she became not much better than a glider, slowly but surely returning to earth ...

The Messerschmitt! Wally blinked. Good God, what was he thinking of! Was he losing his mind, *forgetting* a Jerry fighter on his tail?

'Phil! Mid-upper gunner! Where's the Me?' No reply. 'Answer, please, Phil! Phil!'

My ammunition is gone. First the 30-millimetre guns then the 20-millimetre. I keep pressing the button, frantically pressing, as if expecting sheer fury to rearm the guns.

A minute ago I thought it of no consequence anyway: the Lanc was on fire; all I had to do was stay back and watch and eventually it would crash. But it didn't. It's still flying, still heading for England, on two engines. And now the fire is out ...

No one deserves such luck, good or bad.

What now? I keep following, watching the bomber.

I won't let him get away. Of that I am absolutely sure. Somehow I will bring him down. How? Shall I fly straight into him? That method is sure. It has certain disadvantages. Obvious disadvantages.

'Are you out of ammunition?' Kleeman asks in a flat voice.

I shake my head. A jam, I tell him. I'll have it cleared soon.

Kleeman doesn't reply.

Aft of the main spar the fuselage was a howling nightmare. Hurricanes tore through the jagged, shuddering holes in the walls, to be whipped into vortices within the structure.

Charlie stared aghast at the great gashes in her. The kite was a bloody strainer. You could see the ground through a huge hole in the floor: a hideously unreal sight.

Everything vibrated insanely: the two remaining engines couldn't be synchronized.

Charlie had to step to the extreme right of the fuselage to avoid the hole. He was as scared as he had ever been. He was scared that the kite might break up as his weight passed into the tail section that seemed to be held on by nothing more than a few shreds of metal. Black, burnt metal. It looked like cinders.

He reached Phil's turret. The Scot's legs jutted down into the fuselage, feet in stirrups. Phil hadn't answered ... but his intercom might easily be damaged. Charlie touched his legs, tugged at his trousers to attract his attention. But Phil didn't respond. He couldn't. He was dead. Dead in his shattered turret.

18

Paul scribbled. Stared. Scribbled. Then: 'Fourteen minutes to the coast.'

Crisp, businesslike. All the assurance of a railway announcer. We *will* arrive ... not we *may* ... if we're as lucky as bloody hell.

But the Me isn't going to let us get to the coast, Wally thought. One more bullet in the right place and M-Mother will become one of those exploded views they have in *Flight* and *The Aeroplane* ... and perhaps she doesn't even need the one bullet ...

I wonder, he thought, if I should try and put her down somewhere, just plonk her down and hope for the best ...

Charlie was in the useless mid-upper turret, keeping watch on the executioner.

A straight ribbon of grey appeared and swept across the windscreen, angling from right to left, then vanishing. An arterial road—*Autobahn*, in German. It seemed to spark a great deal of interest in Paul; he was on his feet, head bouncing from charts to windows and back again. Wally asked him where they were.

'Just about there,' Paul said, his finger indicating a spot slightly to the left of Bremen. He glanced at Wally. 'We could make it,' he said.

Wally nodded. If the Me wasn't behind. If the kite wasn't damaged. If. If. If. If. Countless ifs.

Poor Phil. The longer the kite stayed aloft the greater the casualties. The lads were being knocked off, one by one. And Phil's turret U/S. Their luck deserted them when they lost G-George. No, *they* didn't lose George; *he* did. Their smart, bloody skipper. Christ, the vibrating ...

Paul said, 'How's the head, buddy?'

'The head's OK,' said Wally. He referred to it as he might have referred to a part of the aircraft.

Germany was endless: field after field emerging out of the night in dismal, monotonous procession.

When Wally closed his eyes for an instant a storm of light specks came rushing at him, like impenetrable flak. Don't let me pass out, he pleaded; I've got to stay alert. A lake, its water shimmering icily, appeared and was gone. Wally caught a glimpse of a man standing on its bank, legs astride, hands on hips, Mussolini-like. He wanted to look a moment longer at the man, a fellow human being, a groundling, possibly the last he would ever see. But there were trees at the far end of the lake, trees to be missed by the narrowest of margins. It was as though a cannonball, coarse iron and immensely heavy, occupied his skull. It was a hangover multiplied by ten.

He told the crew—the three of them—to jettison anything that wasn't absolutely essential. And so they began the unsavoury business of disembowelling M-Mother; her radio and radar went first, empty extinguishers, useless seats, dead lamps, anything that could be removed. As they worked the crew regarded M-Mother's torn and trembling frame anxiously. Already she had taken far more than any aircraft could sensibly be expected to take. Only a stubborn streak was keeping her aloft; she had guts; good old Mother. It was tempting to ascribe commendable human attributes to her but the fact was that at any moment a longeron might finally give and the others would follow and so M-Mother would disintegrate. And then there wouldn't be a snowball's chance in hell for anyone.

Thus the occupants of M-Mother passed the long minutes in conjecture. They wondered how much damage was concealed by the fire-blackened wing surface. They wondered how seriously the structural integrity of the fuselage was affected by the great holes in the floor and sides. They wondered about the skipper. They wondered about the Jerry.

And M-Mother continued to make agonizing headway.

Quite equably I consider the idea of deliberately crashing into the Lancaster.

I wonder where we are. I could call base; they would tell me; they would give me a course back home. But my job is to destroy the Lancaster. That is really what matters. If I call base they will doubtless direct another fighter here to finish the job for me. To hell with that. This Lancaster is mine. He has become the most important thing in my life.

He changes course, a few degrees to port.

I ask Kleeman how he is. No reply. I snatch a glance backwards. Kleeman's head lolls over his radar set. Is he dead?

A new thought occurs to me: Is it possible to startle the Lanc pilot into crashing? He is desperately low—and surely, with only two engines, he is too underpowered to manoeuvre violently. Could I, then, sweep in so close that he turns too sharply to avoid me? At that height he can afford no mistakes.

Neither can I.

I would dearly love a cigarette.

Very well, then ... I have a package, in my tunic pocket. I can undo the zipper of my flying-suit with one hand, guide the aircraft with the other. There. And my lighter.

This is the first time I have smoked during a flight. Strictly against regulations, of course—and normally I obey regulations. Actually, in these dismal old 110s it's a thoroughly sensible regulation; often there are gasoline
164

fumes floating about in the cabin. But tonight it is worth the risk of accidental fire. (Mind you, if I do succeed in getting back from this mission I shall make sure that the stub of the cigarette is disposed of before I land.)

I can see the reflected glow of my cigarette in the cockpit canopy window panels. I enjoy it enormously; without question the most enjoyable smoke of my entire life. I sit with the dials of the instrument panel before me, the canopy sweeping up and over me, the fields and trees rushing below, an enemy Lancaster flying just ahead. Aside from the pain in my thigh, I am strangely content. There is a rightness about this; perhaps it is the simplicity of it all that appeals to me. I have decided to do something and there is no question in my mind; I will do it. I might die in the attempt. It is very possible. I accept the fact. I am undismayed by it.

My God, this chase is becoming almost leisurely! Here I am, sitting smoking a cigarette, completely lacking in any sense of urgency! Fantastic ...

Suddenly I am frightened. It is the fear of a little boy too far from home, a little boy who doesn't know which way to turn. A little boy afraid of making the wrong move.

It is like looking at a picture of myself, aged ten.

I am wounded. I am out of ammunition. I should turn and head for base. Even if I destroy this Lancaster, it won't make any difference to the war; it won't change the course of history. Therefore, I ask myself, why? I don't know. Is it my parents' death? Vengeance? I must be honest: No. I think the reason is within me. Deep within me. My fingers tighten on the stick.

19

'Jesus Christ, look out!'

Paul's arm thrust out at the shape in the window.

Wally swung the control column to the left as the Messerschmitt came darting out through the dimness ahead: a sudden, deadly shape with great bulbous engines and a glint of window and slender body; curving nose with radar antlers ...

Gone.

'The crazy bastard!'

'I don't know how the hell he missed us,' said Harry.

Wally called Charlie. 'Can you see him? What the hell is he doing now?'

'Turning, skipper. Going around in a big circle.'

Wally snapped, 'Why weren't you watching him? He nearly clobbered us.'

Charlie stammered, 'I'm sorry, skipper. I was looking all over for him. I couldn't see him. I was going to call you ... when he came in from the side.'

'Watch him.'

'I am, skipper. He's turning.'

'Harry, you man the front turret.'

Wally ran his tongue over his lips. It wouldn't be so bloody nerve-wracking if only he could turn and watch for himself; but at this height he daren't take his eyes off the ground for an instant.

At his side, Paul had his head against the roof, trying to see the Messerschmitt.

Charlie: 'He's coming up behind again, skipper. No; now he's turning again. You should be able to see him now, on the starboard side ...'

Wally flung a glance to the right. Yes, there he was, banking, black-and-white crosses clearly visible on his wing-tips. He was swinging in from the side. He suddenly became huge. Then he had vanished.

'He's bloody barmy!'

Wally stared. He didn't know how the Messerschmitt had missed.

Charlie said: 'He's turning, skipper. Same as before.'

Then Paul said, 'He didn't shoot.'

'What?'

'He didn't shoot.'

'My God, you're right!'

He simply hadn't noticed: no gunfire from the Me. No gunfire could mean only one thing, surely: no ammunition.

'I guess he can see we're kind of knocked about,' said Paul. 'Maybe he thinks one good blast of slipstream from him and we'll fall apart.'

He's not too far wrong, Wally thought.

Harry was of the opinion that the Me pilot had gone completely off his rocker; Charlie seemed indignant. The Me wasn't playing the game. If you were out of ammo you went home; everyone knew that.

'Cut the chatter,' Wally said. 'Where is he, Charlie?'

'Still turning. I think he's coming in again.'

Wally sucked in air. This time he'll hit us, he thought. And even if it isn't this time it'll be the time after that. He's going to keep on getting closer until we hit the deck or he hits us ...

It would almost be a relief. Not to have to fight any more, just to let it happen.

'Charlie, you're the look-out. You've got to tell me when to turn. I can't do anything very spectacular with only two engines but I can at least turn when he's almost on us.'

Charlie said, 'He's a good way off. He's straightening. He's coming around again. Heading for us. OK. Now get ready ... ready ... Break!'

M-Mother lumbered to the left. The fighter quickly changed direction and roared directly over the bomber's tail. Harry whirled the nose turret and fired a long, pointless burst; the tracer sped away in gently curving lines.

Wally saw the Messerschmitt flash over the cockpit, swinging away to the right. Arms trembling, he hauled M-Mother back on course. Oh God, how close was he that time? Those bloody propellers couldn't have missed the canopy by more than an inch or two!

The dark shape of the fighter slid away into the night, its agility mocking the Lanc.

'He gets closer each time,' said Paul. He sounded curiously disinterested, as though remarking on a fact completely without significance to his well-being.

Charlie reported, 'Coming around again, skipper. Same as before. Daft bugger. I don't think he gives a damn whether he hits us or not.'

True, how true. Wally nodded. The Me pilot didn't care; obviously he had accepted the loss of his own life as the likely price of destroying the bomber.

'Here he comes, skipper. Get set to break to the right this time. OK? The right. He's getting closer. Just a sec ... right, now!'

Once again the ritual. A flat, clumsy turn by the bomber, lunges by the fighter. Seemingly unavoidable collision ... a miss by some miracle or other ... the bomber, shuddering, turning back on its forlorn course for home. Three more times the fighter darted at it like some ferocious insect. Each time the bomber took the only evasive action it could: sluggish turns to the left and right: turns that were hardly more than gestures. Bathed in sweat from the exertions of manhandling the controls, Wally wondered groggily whether he shouldn't simply fly M-Mother straight and level and let the Messerschmitt do his beat-ups. Eventually there

168

would be a collision—but there was going to be one anyway, whether he tried to evade or not.

Someone was at his side, half standing in the cramped space, one arm on the armoured back of the seat. It was Paul. He was pointing to starboard.

'He's taking a rest.'

What? Ah yes, so he was, riding along, a lanky silhouette.

'I'm watching him,' Charlie reported.

'Roger. He's trying to put the wind up us.'

Trying. He marvelled at the tone of his voice. Calmness personified. He didn't sound like a man in the final stages of mental and physical disintegration.

'Is everyone all right?'

Everyone. The entire crew: three voices. All absurdly relaxed, now that the Messerschmitt wasn't actually blasting them to bits. Why hadn't they run into any other Jerry fighters?

Paul was busy with his maps again. Retrim once more, hand on shivering lever. The bloody vibration ... enough to drive you round the bend. Now, a minute's comparative peace ... except for the steam engines in the head ...

He inhaled deeply. It was painful but it seemed to give him strength. He glanced again to the right; the Me still flew alongside.

It can't be too easy for you either, Wally said silently to the German pilot. A collision isn't going to do you any more good that it will me. So why not be a good fellow and give up? Go home and rest. This is the last time I'm coming over here, so it won't make any difference if you shoot me down or not ...

The crew was still working as a unit; there was still an organization and there was still morale because there was still hope. The boys had been through a hell of a lot but they knew there wasn't much longer to go until they reached the coast.

They still have confidence in me, Wally thought. They believe I can somehow or other get this kite home no matter what the damage. I've driven them home so often they think I will always be able to do it.

He wondered how long it would be before he died. A minute? An hour? A skipper had to dole out confidence in large portions. Even if the skipper had no confidence he had to find some somewhere; he had to dig deep and dredge it up and hand it over ...

Paul had a new course. A few degrees to the north. 'We should hit the coast in about five minutes.'

Five minutes! A lifetime! What chance did they have of surviving five minutes?

'Roger, navigator, thank you. Where do we hit it?'

'A little south of Emden,' said Paul, 'I hope.'

Wally nodded. A lot of flak around Emden—but perhaps their zero-feet altitude might surprise the gunners ...

Paul scratched his chin and stared ahead, the conscientious artisan about to witness the quality of his labours. He grinned at Wally.

'We're doing all right, buddy.'

Wally nodded. Briskly. An of-course-we're-doing-all-right nod; it went without saying.

'I hope those bastards haven't eaten all the bacon and eggs by the time we get back.'

'They'll keep some for us,' said Wally. 'Or there'll be trouble.'

Wearily he began the task of retrimming M-Mother; she was wandering to the right, trembling, as if from fright. But no, M-Mother wasn't frightened; she had all the courage in the world; only the humans aboard her could feel fright ...

Harry swung the turret to the left and right as far as it would go. He depressed the twin Brownings, then pointed

170

them at the stars. He scowled at the Messerschmitt and told it to come a bit nearer and he'd knock the pilot's head off.

Harry was cautiously optimistic. In spite of everything the Jerry had done, George was still flying. No, not George. Mother. Sorry, Mother.

If he shot down the Me, he'd probably get a DFM. There weren't too many flight engineers with DFMs for shooting down Messerschmitt 110s. In fact, he didn't know of any.

Paul announced a shift in course. The skipper thanked him.

A cool one, the skipper. Harry respected the skipper. He respected his manner of conducting himself, his observance of the niceties even when he obviously felt like death warmed up and when things were far from bright around him. Roger and thanks. The right wing just fell off, skipper. Roger. We're about to hit the sea nose-first. Roger; thank you. Here are your angel's wings. Thanks so much ...

Harry thought how pleasant it would be to win a gong. Wouldn't the family be impressed! Harry, scrawny little Harry! Arch and Hilda's boy! A flaming hero! Valiant, son-nephew-cousin-uncle, defender of our island Mother Country ...

He frowned. Hold it, there was the little matter of Rose, wasn't there? He'd rather conveniently forgotten about her. But it was unlikely she would return the favour. Not bloody likely, not while she was carrying his child.

Carrying his child! What a hell of an expression! Wasn't there a pleasanter way of putting it?

Wretchedly he stared at the Brownings' muzzles. You could say she had a pie in the oven or she was in the family way; but it all meant the same appalling thing.

He stared into the darkness, towards home.

It didn't mean anything, he told his wife. I want you to know that. I didn't love her or anything like that. It just happened. I'm really sorry. I didn't mean it to happen. I love you, he added.

It seemed important to say those things, to put them into words even if the words could not be heard by Dorothy—or even by him. If he got the chop, well, at least he would have set the situation straight in his own mind.

Paul said they should be seeing the coast any minute now.

Harry's teeth scraped along his lower lip. Crossing the coastline could be a nasty business: one bloody gun after another for miles and miles. And all those gunners could have been told about the solitary Lanc, low down. Nasty. It could be very nasty, Harry thought.

'Harry.'

'Here, skip.' Silly damn thing to say. Where else would he be?

'You might get a chance to shoot a bit. We're close to the coast.'

'OK, skip. I'm ready.' Like a bloody boy scout.

He flicked off his microphone and squinted into the night. It would be nice to see something. A big, fat ammo-dump perhaps; a nice well-aimed squirt from the twin Brownings —and everything would go up in a bleeding wizard bang. Hero Whittaker.

No, on second thoughts, it wasn't such a good idea. The kite was too close to the ground for comfort. Twerp Whittaker.

If we get past the coastal flak we'll be all right, Harry thought. As long as the engines keep going. As long as the kite doesn't shake herself to pieces. As long as the skipper stays awake. As long as that crazy bugger in the Messerschmitt ...

Not very cheering, listing all the as-long-as's.

Ah! Flak! His heart jolted. Dots of light came swinging up toward M-Mother from the right.

Lights swerving across the sky, brilliant against the darkness, wobbling past at colossal speed. More streams of lights hurtling up from other points, cascading past M-Mother like illuminated showers.

Harry blazed away with the Brownings, his turret swinging from left to right, his tracers seemingly mingling with the oncoming missiles, flurries of lights skidding, falling in every direction ...

Then it was over. M-Mother had disappeared from the gunners' view.

Harry sighed with relief.

The skipper said, 'Everyone all right?'

'OK here,' said Paul.

'I'm all right, skip,' said Harry.

Charlie tried to answer but his mouth was full of blood.

My nerves are letting me down. I am shaking so violently that I can hardly control the aircraft. I have to clench my jaw until it hurts. In a moment it will be better; my nerves will calm themselves.

I was so incredibly close to death; how I avoided hitting the Lancaster I shall never know. I was so close that I saw the pilot quite clearly. He must have thought he was about to die. He must be wondering how my propellers missed the canopy.

The Lancaster is in pitiful condition; I didn't realize just how badly I had damaged it until I flew close enough to see. Two engines are out; the fuselage and wings are full of holes. I don't know how it is holding together.

The pilot must be good. I respect him for his skill and his courage. God knows what it must be like trying to fly at treetop level with an aircraft in that condition. It's sad that I have to try and kill him, because in a very small way I am beginning to know him. He is a person; perhaps I would like him if I met him. But now we will never meet; I have to kill him and he knows it.

I see Otto, smiling in his sardonic way as he expounds on his favourite theme: the human animal's sexual compulsion to kill its own species—and its incredible justification of such killings. Otto was able to apply a sort of bizarre logic to his arguments; unless you were very careful you would find yourself agreeing step by step that you donned uniform for one basic reason only: to prove your manhood by becoming a killer, figuratively speaking slaughtering someone and dragging the body home to dump before the eyes of some female whose body you wished to possess. Otto could be very glib and very amusing.

But I reject the idea that I am trying to kill because of some deep-rooted instinct. I am not compelled to. I am trying to destroy this aircraft because it is my duty to do so.

Charlie saw Paul bending over him. He saw the Canadian plug in his intercom jack; he saw him frown at the blood on his hands.

'You stopped one, buddy.' Paul sounded like a Yank. 'But you're going to be OK. No sweat. Does it hurt much?'

But Paul's voice had already become dim in Charlie's ears. He felt the numbness spreading over his body, limb by limb, muscle by muscle. It would have been nice to see the nippers again ... and Sally. Poor old Sal ... What about the house? Would the pension be enough...? Would it...? He should have made arrangements....

Things had been good for a long time for Charlie. But he'd known all along it wouldn't last ... he'd known ...

'Skipper. Paul. Charlie's dead.'

'Oh God ...' He shook his head. The whole crew, one by one. If anyone should have made it, it should have been Charlie. Dear old Charlie with his wife and brood of kids and his cockney voice and his balding head. What was the sense of it all? Why? Why?

He saw the glint of water ahead.

20

M-Mother had become a mockery of an aeroplane, a metal scarecrow; she had no business being in the air, yet she wobbled on, two engines bellowing discordantly, straining to maintain her precarious balance in the air. As an aircraft, M-Mother had been reduced to the most basic of proportions. She was capable of staying in the air; nothing more; she could barely manoeuvre; she had no reserve of power; she could no longer defend herself; she could send no messages; she could receive none; she couldn't even return to earth without destroying herself because her undercarriage and flaps were no longer operable. She flew badly because her body and wings were torn, the surfaces broken, fouling the airflow on which she depended aloft. The remnants of her crew huddled together in the cockpit area as if seeking mutual protection and moving as far as possible from the death and destruction aft.

Behind M-Mother flew the fighter, impotent because its nose-guns were empty and because its rear gunner was dead and because there wasn't room in the aircraft to permit manhandling the gunner's body from his seat and taking his place; besides, there was no longer anyone to attempt to take his place. Two hundred rounds remained in the twin MG81Zs. Two hundred rounds that would make short work of the Lancaster. But two hundred rounds that were utterly unreachable.

Of the ten men aboard the two machines, five were dead, one was close to death. Blood mingled with hydraulic fluid; flesh clung to aluminium-alloy stressed skins.

Thus on a March night in the Year of Our Lord One Thousand Nine Hundred and Forty-Four, an Avro Lancaster Mark 1 and a Messerschmitt bf110 G4-R3 crossed the coastline of northern Europe at a point close to the joining of Germany and The Netherlands.

Paul identified Delfzijl on the port side.

They were over water. No one had fired a shot.

A small vessel of tug-boat size swung into view, then vanished beneath the port wing. Wally watched the water speeding beneath him. It was black, empty, a vast, constantly moving mass. The waves, angry-looking things, churned endlessly, capturing fragments of light from the sky, tossing them, swallowing them.

In spite of everything, the kite had made it to the sea, but she was shuddering, groaning; she might pack it in at any moment. Then they'd be in the drink. Airmen who had survived ditchings said that contact with the water was like driving into a brick wall at forty miles an hour. You stood an excellent chance of being knocked unconscious by the impact—and it was a bad time to be unconscious because as soon as the aircraft stopped smashing and splashing through the water it was desirable to get out. Hurriedly. M-Mother's crew wore Mae Wests; and aft in the fuselage there was a dinghy. Had it survived the attacks? It seemed unlikely.

Now, a new worry.

'Pilot to engineer. Harry, she's pulling to the right more and more.'

Harry nodded, frowning; frowned at pressure gauges, frowned at temperature dials, manifolds, oil ... Head shaking; lousy, bloody things could be telling lies. Starboard inner not delivering full power but nothing actually wrong, according to the lousy, bloody instruments.

'Is it going to keep going?'

'I don't know, skipper.'

176

Curt, snapping voice in reply. 'We've got a bloody long way to go across the sea.'

Unimpressed Australian voice: 'I know that, but I still don't know if she's going to keep going or not.'

Wally nodded. Fair enough. Harry said he would keep an eye on the motor.

Suddenly Paul's voice yelled over the intercom: 'Wally, he's close! Right under our tail!'

Wally shoved M-Mother into a turn to the right; simultaneously the Jerry fighter snapped into a left turn.

'The crazy bastard,' said Paul from the astrodome.

Wally dragged M-Mother back on to course. There was little life left in her now; her response to the controls was lethargic, as if she knew there was no point in going on, as if she knew the result would be just the same whether she gave in now or half an hour hence.

Wally knew just how she felt.

I nearly hit the Lancaster. And quite accidentally. God, I must be weaker than I thought. The plain fact of the matter is that I drifted for a moment or two into unconsciousness. I fell asleep. I came to only a few metres from the Lancaster's tail.

Abruptly I realize something. The Lancaster didn't fire at me. Not a shot. It's an important realization. It startles me into alertness.

I edge the aircraft toward the Lancaster's starboard side. I present a beautiful target for the mid-upper gunner—as poor Kleeman and Dorn discovered. But this time there is no reaction from the bomber. The turret doesn't even move.

What a target the Lancaster is now!

I glance over my shoulder. Ah, if only one of you were still alive we could finally finish off this one ...

An idea occurs to me. It's a mad one, a gamble—with

*the highest stakes you and I are able to offer, Herr Lan-
caster. But it might work. It might ...*

'He's staying pretty close,' Paul reported.

Wally didn't reply; he was concentrating on correcting
the trim, trying again to counteract the effects of unsyn-
chronized engines.

Paul's voice crackled urgently: 'He's moving in. Get
ready to break to the right.'

Wally grabbed the controls with both hands. He doubted
his ability to move the thing; it seemed to get heavier and
more awkward with every passing minute. His head
throbbed mercilessly.

'He's coming directly behind us. A bit higher.'

Wally couldn't see the Messerschmitt but he could imagine
it, black and sleek, hovering over the stricken Lanc like a
bird of prey.

'Hey, that's bloody odd.'

'What is it?'

'He's putting his wheels and flaps down.'

Wally glanced at Harry who turned to gawk back
through the observation blister.

Paul said, 'You'd better get ready to break, skip. He looks
as if he's going to do whatever it is he ... break now!'

The Lancaster slewed roughly, engines screeching; the
Messerschmitt bounced as it hit the slipstream. It turned,
its wing slicing at the bomber's tail like some great scythe.

'He's trying to knock our tail off!'

There were seconds of complete silence over M-Mother's
intercom. The airmen were stunned; the sly bastard, he
was going to try to get in close and smash their fin and
rudder away with his wing. He could do it, too, if he was
good enough. And there was a slim chance he might get
away with it. Rudders were fragile things; a wing could
go clean through a rudder and probably not get much more

178

than a dent or two for its trouble. As for Mother, she'd go straight in. Not the faintest hope of holding her; no pilot could hold her; not Gibson, not Fauquier, not Lindbergh, not Wally ...

Wally heaved Mother back on to course. His arms burned with fatigue; he wondered if he was going to pass out.

It would solve a lot of problems, he thought.

'Pilot to engineer. We'll have to keep dodging him, Paul. You'll have to tell me when to break. It's up to you.'

'He's straightening out dead behind us. About a hundred feet above us. Still got his wheels down. Coming at us again, skip. Get ready to turn the other way. To port. All right? Port this time? OK? Now!'

Suddenly the ocean sloped. The wing darted at the speeding sea. Another wing, the Messerschmitt's, slashed across the Lancaster's path: then it was gone.

Paul's voice, toneless: 'You crazy bloody bastard, you crazy son of a bitch.'

The Messerschmitt was turning again, steeply.

This is terribly difficult, far more difficult than I had supposed. But I perhaps can excuse myself; I have had very little experience in trying to knock tails off Lancasters.

The pilot of the Lancaster knows what I am trying to do. And he is using every last morsel of skill to fight me. He stays hideously low, making the slipstream from his propellers a dreadful threat. A false move on my part and his slipstream could put me in the sea.

My thigh still aches. I think, however, that the bleeding must have stopped. I feel better, a little stronger, I think. I feel as though I could live a long and healthy life. I could. I think it's extremely unlikely that I will. The fact doesn't distress me. I accept it—even though I hope fervently that I might be able to get back to base. How much of a chance do I have? I wonder. Perhaps one in ten. More likely one

*in fifteen or twenty. Consider the altitude. It's going to
require a great deal of luck to knock off the Lancaster's
tail and get away in good enough shape to fly back.*

But surely to God I deserve some luck tonight.

*Where are we? How far to England? My father visited
England many times when he was young. He has relatives
there; a cousin or uncle or something. No; he had. Perhaps
my late father's cousin or uncle is in this Lancaster. I have
never met an Englishman; I don't know that I have ever
seen one, except for the pilot; and all I saw of him was his
helmet.*

*The Lancaster is changing course a few degrees, still
doggedly heading home on his two engines.*

*My mathematics teacher was a man named Ulrich. He
had doleful eyes and a long jaw. A pervert, they said.*

*Why on earth am I thinking of Ulrich? What possible
connection is there between Ulrich and this? Poor wretch.
They found him with a fifteen-year-old boy in the wood
just beyond the school fields. It was a scorching day in early
July. A sick, frightened man and a fifteen-year-old boy. A
boy who was never discovered. At fifteen a boy is lonely and
confused; a learner not a conqueror; no match for women.*

*Where is Ulrich? In the Army, probably. Perhaps he has
expunged his sins with feats of manly courage. The pain in
my thigh intensifies.*

The sky has the hard beauty of dark glass.

When the Messerschmitt swooped again, Paul fired the
Very pistol at it.

The flare missed—but it must have startled the German
pilot for he swerved violently and turned away.

M-Mother's three-man crew laughed uproariously at this
minor triumph. Even Wally, who couldn't see the incident,
had laughed as he imagined it. He laughed so much that
tears blurred his vision; he had to wipe his eyes while his
180

shoulders still pumped with mirth. Harry awarded Paul a DFM—Distinguished Flare Marksman.

It hurt a man's ribs, to laugh suddenly, unrestrainedly, after so much tension.

During the next few minutes, Paul fired off the remaining flares. He succeeded in getting one close to the fighter's port propeller; the others went far astray, balls of sparkling light spinning aimlessly, illuminating the dark, tossing sea, before being consumed by it.

Harry said, 'He's coming in again, skipper. Hundred and fifty yards. Up a bit higher than last time. He's scared of the flares.'

Again the ocean tilted as the Messerschmitt dived. The ritual was repeated: the heavy, ponderous bomber swerving away as the fighter's wing swung past the tall tail unit. It was a slow-motion version of the antics of butterflies over the surface of a pond. Again and again it seemed one or other or both the aircraft must hit the water; by inches they kept missing the clutching waves, to part then merge again ... Paul checked the compass; M-Mother was headed almost due north. He turned to speak to Wally.

God, he thought, the poor bastard's had it.

Utter exhaustion was etched into every line of the pilot's face. He was ashen, his eyes dull.

Paul touched his arm and indicated the T-marker: at right-angles to the course the aircraft was actually on. The error was obvious, glaring. On this course they would head into the lonely frozen waters off Norway; their fuel would soon be consumed and they would have to ditch.

Wally stared at the compass. For a moment it seemed that his brain wasn't registering the evidence of his eyes. He simply looked at the compass. Then he frowned; without a word he turned M-Mother back on to the correct heading. When it was done he stared through the windscreen as before.

Paul leant back against the shuddering fuselage wall. A few feet away the sea churned as it sped away behind. How much longer? Over an hour, he calculated. Seventy minutes at least. Would the kite hold together that long? At the moment it felt as though it wouldn't last seven minutes.

Beyond the scarred perspex panels of the cockpit canopy the great wing flexed and trembled: an expanse of bent and fractured metal that by some miraculous balancing of forces still kept the whole dismal contraption in the air.

He told Wally: 'He's a hundred yards back. Still staying back.'

Harry said, 'The temperature's slowly going up on the starboard inner, skip.'

Wally's voice was flat, apparently devoid of interest. 'Is there anything you can do about it?'

'No. It's the oil pressure. Leak, I suppose.'

'Could it be the gauges?'

'No, it's not the gauges.'

'Navigator, how long before we get to the coast?'

'At least an hour.'

'Roger. Engineer, do you think the engine will hold out that long?'

'I doubt it. But you never know.'

'You think it's unlikely?'

'Bloody unlikely. But it's possible, I suppose.'

Paul watched the Messerschmitt, a thin shape in the darkness. It seemed likely the trip would end in a ditching. If the dinghy wasn't full of holes, and if they got out in time, it might be all right. The dinghy radio would be able to crank out a signal for the air-sea-rescue boys to home on ... Even if the kite held together and if the engines kept going long enough would Wally be able to drag her over the cliffs? Would Wally himself last long enough? The poor sod was so tired, he just didn't care any more.

Fear was a sickly weight in his stomach. He kept thinking of the fuselage flooded by bubbling, rushing water, splashing over the seats and controls, through the passage-ways, rising far too rapidly to permit anyone to make it to the exits ...

Wally said, 'Is there anything else we can jettison?'

And good old stout-hearted British Wally, wounded, in pain and the final stages of exhaustion, asked the question just as he might have asked if there was another record to put on the phonograph.

'I don't think so, skipper.'

Paul ducked down from the astrodome; he could look forward into the cockpit, back into the darkened fuselage. There was nothing else to be thrown overboard; everything that was removable had already gone. He watched Wally; his helmeted head was visible over the armour plating; he was trimming and re-trimming, trying to get this bucket of bolts home.

Back in 1942, some genius at the Air Ministry had decided that heavy bombers didn't need second pilots; one pilot and one flight engineer were sufficient.

I wish that guy was here right now, Paul thought.

'There are the parachutes,' he told Wally. 'They're not much use if we can't get high enough to use them.'

'No, we'll hang on to the 'chutes,' Wally replied.

Surely it was all academic anyway. God, you could feel the kite expiring, shivering herself to death.

Then a thought occurred to him. He didn't wait to think it over. He switched on his mike and said:

'Skipper, would about four hundred and fifty pounds make a big difference?'

Wally said, 'Four hundred and fifty? Yes, of course. Why?'

'Then why don't we jettison the three dead bodies in the back?'

He saw Wally half turn his head.

'What did you say?'

You heard, Paul thought. He said:

'Len and Phil and Charlie are dead. Between them they weigh about four hundred and fifty pounds, probably more. We can save that weight by jettisoning them, if you think it's worthwhile.'

'Jettisoning' seemed the wrong word. But Paul couldn't think of a more suitable one. He said:

'I know it's a hell of a thing to do. But it doesn't make any difference to them now, does it?'

He sounded callous, metallic, North American.

Wally said, 'We'll wait a bit.'

'Wait?' said Paul. 'OK. You're the skipper.'

He stuck his head back in the astrodome, resenting the fact that he was the one who had had to make the suggestion, resenting even more the fact that it had not been acted upon.

Oh Christ, what did it matter now?

Where the hell had the Messerschmitt got to?

21

The pain is unendurable. And yet I endure it. I keep thinking the pain will tear me apart physically or it will cause
me to lose consciousness entirely. A few moments ago the
sound of my engines became strangely distant, somehow
unrelated to the fact that I am sitting here in the cockpit,
guiding my aircraft in endless pursuit.

I have to keep reminding myself that the Lancaster is real
and that I am chasing it; it is not a dream. Or nightmare.

I stare at the Lancaster as though enough staring will
send it into the sea. I can see it hitting the water in a huge
burst of spray, wings cracking, breaking back ...

I bellow with pain. I can just hear my voice above the
engine noise. I sound like a creature at the zoo. Me, in my
speeding, metal cage. Species: Homo Sapiens, circa 1944.
Extra-wild specimen bent upon destruction of similar
creature because similar creature bent on destruction of
him ...

The pain diminishes. I light another cigarette. I think
how curious it is that the cigarette smoke remains almost
motionless in the cabin in spite of the speed and force of
the wind just a short distance away beyond the windscreen.

Perhaps my mind is going. Why not? Ah, but I know
if I can get that Lancaster I shall be at peace. He means that
much to me.

The cigarette is delicious. I wonder whether, in the
Lancaster, they can see the glow in my cockpit.

My fuel is well below the half-way mark. I suspect that
the instrument is optimistic; if I want to reach base I should

185

*probably turn around now. No; it's unthinkable. First
comes Herr Lancaster. Then I will permit myself to think
of the problems of getting back to base. If I am capable of
thinking of anything by that time.*

'Temperature's still going up, skipper. But slowly.'

'Thank you, engineer.'

In a way it would have been a relief to hear Harry say
the temperature had reached the critical point and that the
engine was about to go. Then there would have been no
choice but to ditch. No more trying to coax this disintegrating pile of machinery through the air. No more trimming
and re-trimming. No more juggling with the throttles to
squeeze a fraction more power out of the good engine so
that the other one could take it a little easier.

And no more wondering about the rights or wrongs of
dumping Charlie and Phil and Len overboard.

Approximately forty minutes to land.

Assuming the compass was working correctly.

His arms throbbed with the agony of holding M-Mother.
She wanted to turn because of the unequal power from the
two Merlins; he had to dissuade her, drag her back on
course.

Wally knew he was going to die that night. He knew it
without doubt. He had seen himself die; he had attempted
to ignore the warnings but now he knew that he had been
foolhardy. He had abandoned hope for himself; but the
others? What could he do to help them live? He couldn't
answer the question. He could think of nothing except trying to reach England.

Harry's voice came over the intercom: 'She's holding
pretty well; she sort of goes up a bit then stops, then goes
up again.'

'Thanks, engineer.'

'Is she going to last?' Paul asked.

'She might,' Harry replied with all the grave deliberation due a professional opinion. 'Then again she might not.'

'I could have told you that,' said Paul.

Wally glanced back. Harry was busy with his dials; Paul stood half out of sight beneath the astrodome. He lolled against the fuselage wall in an attitude that seemed to say that he was tired of the whole business and if he was to die he might as well be comfortable while it happened. An Englishman would surely stand more rigidly, defensively. Americans and Canadians seemed to think they were the equals of everybody and everything—including death.

He adjusted the trim again. M-Mother responded sullenly, one wing still dipping as though it was heavier than the other. She was maintaining her height and speed. Just. Any lessening of the power would mean a forlorn flopping into the sea. No skill could keep her aloft without sufficient power.

Would four hundred and fifty pounds make any difference?

Harry's voice crackled in his earphones. 'Better ease up a bit on the port outer, skipper. It's beginning to get a bit warm. It's overworking.'

Wally flung a glance to the left, past the rigid propeller of the inboard engine, to M-Mother's last wholly sound source of power. He'd been working it too hard, trying to make it compensate for all the other engines. Now it was letting him know that it had to be treated more reasonably if it was to keep working.

Wally wanted to argue with it: I can't lessen your output by more than a fraction because the starboard inner is getting dangerously hot. You see the difficulty, don't you? Between the two of you, you have to deliver enough power to keep us at a constant altitude. I can't let up even a fraction or I'll be in the drink!

He adjusted the throttles: a shade less power from the

port outer, a shade more from the starboard inner. If he did it quietly, carefully, perhaps the starboard inner wouldn't notice ...

Now M-Mother had to be trimmed again, her flying surfaces minutely adjusted to balance the forces of lift and drag.

It was a hell of a thing to ask.

'Paul, are you absolutely sure they are dead?'

Paul said, 'Len and Phil and Charlie are dead, skipper. I don't know about Douglas.'

'There's no question about Len or Phil or Charlie?'

'Jesus, no! You don't think ...' Then his voice was quieter. 'There's no question.'

'Very well.' It was necessary to be absolutely clear about it; there could be no misunderstanding. 'Len and Phil and Charlie then. Just the three. Douglas must stay. Can you manage it alone?'

'Yes.'

'OK,' said Wally. He took a deep breath. He stared through the scratched windscreen. Without thinking, he re-trimmed the aircraft. Still on course. Still aloft, incredibly.

Well, he'd never have to explain his actions to the CO. He'd never have to tell Ann.

He kept staring ahead, toward an invisible England.

A few minutes later Paul's voice crackled in his earphones: 'They're overboard.'

Overboard. He acknowledged.

'I'm coming forward,' Paul said. 'I'll get another fix. Harry, can you stay in the dome a bit longer?'

'I've got to keep an eye on the motors,' said Harry.

'Just a few minutes.'

'OK,' said Harry.

Wally looked at the control column. He tried to tell himself he noticed a difference in the way she handled. But

188

there was no difference. He asked himself what he had expected—a great bombs-gone leap? They had lost four hundred and fifty pounds, not eighteen thousand. He adjusted the throttles a fraction of an inch; perhaps those few pounds would make the difference between the engines continuing to function and not continuing to function. It seemed important that the bodies hadn't been discarded without effect.

But the vibration was worsening. Under his right hand the throttle levers trembled violently, savagely, as if determined to shake themselves free. The whole aircraft was a mass of tiny movements, shudders transferring themselves from component to component, intensifying, multiplying.

I know how you feel, he told M-Mother. Too bloody tired to go on. We both just want to flop down. I understand. I sympathize. But keep going a bit longer. Please.

Christ!

He kicked at the rudder pedals and swung the control column as the sea came rushing up at him, a huge tumbling mass, ridiculously angled, awesome in its proximity. The waves snapped at the Lanc, anxious to snare her. A wingtip sliced the crest of a wave. M-Mother righted herself, trembling anew.

22

The mind worked slowly, painstakingly. It weighed each fact, considered it with extraordinary care as if it were entirely new, entirely novel to the human experience. It worked slowly because a barrage of unrelated pictures and impressions kept interfering with the deductive process. Pictures contained people; the people said long-forgotten things. Bobby Dawson saying that the park gates were locked at eight o'clock and the only other way out was over the walls, but the walls had fragments of broken glass embedded in the cement on top of them. Ted Layton saying that a girl had drowned and that her body was a funny purple colour. Tony French saying that W. G. Grace was the best cricketer who had ever lived or ever would live, ever. Fred Jones saying that girls had things called periods which made them bleed once every month. Aunt Mary talking about the nasty piece of work from London who carried on with Pauline Evans for a fortnight and then took himself off, never to be seen again. The man at Dunphy's asking how much butter this week. The man at Scouts chilling them with the dread consequences of not keeping your toe-nails clipped. The prostitute saying that he really did have his problems, didn't he?

The mind worked slowly but finally it reached a conclusion. It told Douglas that he was dying. He was halfway between life and death. That was why he kept seeing all those people again and hearing them say those things they said years ago. He attempted to deny the fact that he was dying. He attempted to shake his head. He attempted to speak. But those were the actions of life. They were beyond him now. He tumbled slowly, surrounded by waves of grey, and sounds, rhythmic and persistent.

Now terror swept over him. He was a sinner. All his life he had been obsessed by foul thoughts; he had been unable to control them. Now for the reckoning. No excuses would do; he was to be punished just as he had been warned from the pulpit time and time again; the miserable, worthless sinner was to receive his just deserts. And how righteously frightful they would surely be. Fire to purify the unworthy soul; fire to sear away the filth; fire to punish, punish, punish ...

Harry doubted the engines would last; they were heating dangerously.

Paul wanted to say: Can't you think of something bright, something hopeful to say? How about squirting the fire extinguishers at the engines? Wouldn't that cool the goddam things down?

He heard Wally's flat, impossibly weary voice say: 'Pilot to crew, if we have to ditch I won't be able to give you much warning. If either motor packs up it won't be long before we hit the drink. OK, everyone?'

Paul frowned. Did Wally think he was addressing six other men? Poor bastard. He thought of the burnt shell that was M-Mother's body. What would happen the instant she hit the water? Would she break up immediately? And then, straight down?

'There's a hand-crank radio in the dinghy,' Wally was saying, 'so that will help the air-sea-rescue lads get a fix on us.'

He sounded less than convincing. Paul wanted to tell him not to try cheering up the men any more; there weren't any left.

He looked at the starboard engine. Keep going, friend,

he thought, keep going a bit longer. I don't want to get the chop on this trip ... He pressed his face against the freezing perspex surface. He could see the Messerschmitt. The vulture. Waiting patiently for its victim to flop into the sea and die. Under Paul's hand a metal rib trembled like the enfeebled limb of an old, old man. The aircraft was becoming a loose, wobbling thing, sagging and stretching under its own weight. A moment ago it seemed to have reached the limit of its endurance; now it was still staggering through the air and its condition was worse. At least the boys in S-Sugar went quickly, cleanly; no dragged-out death ritual for them ...

If I get back from this one, thought Paul, I'll paint. Good stuff. No more commercial junk.

'How are the temperatures, Harry?'

'Still going up, skip. Slowly still, thank God.'

Bad news half-mixed with semi-good news. The engine temperatures still rose—but they rose less rapidly than they might. The wound wasn't quite as fatal as might have been expected ...

Paul glanced at Wally—he looked dead; his face was drained of life; he kept staring ahead as though what he saw wasn't registering. But his hands kept moving, adjusting, trimming, persuading M-Mother to fly some more ...

He leant across and shouted in Wally's ear.

'OK, buddy?'

Wally's head moved in a sharp, curt nod.

'Anything I can do?'

Wally shook his head.

Paul yelled, 'We'll make it!' Nod. 'You'll see the coast in a couple of minutes!' Another nod. 'Listen, you old bastard, I'll buy you the biggest whiskey you ever saw if you can get this bucket of bolts back home!' A tiny smile, quickly gone. 'You're doing just fine!'

So much for morale-boosting. Paul could think of no

other words of encouragement. He watched the grey sea rushing out of the shadows ahead, blurring with its speed as it scampered away behind. He remembered Charlie and Len and Phil.

Harry was saying the Jerry was nuts.

'I don't think so,' said Wally. His voice was dull but oddly assured. 'He's simply set out to do something and he won't let go until it's done.'

Moisture specked the perspex windscreen and was beaten by the wind into fiercely straight rivulets angling away to the side and vanishing.

'Poor old bitch,' said Harry. 'She's had it.'

Don't say that, Wally thought. She might hear. She might be offended.

Harry said, 'Shall I stay here in case you want me to work the throttles?'

'Yes, please, engineer.'

'I'll keep an eye on our friend,' said Paul.

Wally was conscious of the fact that his mouth was slightly open; he could feel the cool air passing between his lips. He was too tired to close his mouth. Any minute now ... a black line through the shadows, growing bigger and broader, soon it would fill the entire windscreen ... it didn't matter where they crossed the coastline; England positively groaned under the weight of airfields.

All M-Mother had to do was stay in the air.

There was a voice in his earphones. He had to press them hard against his head. The voice was Harry's. Saying that the port outer was now way past the danger mark and it was bloody well going to go any second now.

'Thanks, engineer.'

Thanks a hell of a lot. A heavy glance to the left, half expecting the outer engine to be glowing or sprouting flames. But it looked harmless enough. Don't listen to

193

Harry, he told it. Ignore him; he doesn't know a bloody thing about engines.

I am cold. Incredibly, unbelievably cold. Surely my blood is congealing in my veins. The cold seems to come from within me; it has nothing to do with the temperature in the cabin. Am I dying? Perhaps. Yet I still have control over my limbs; I can still fly this aircraft. I can still see; I can think.

I push myself hard against the back of my seat. Wedged this way, I can overcome the trembling of my body to some extent. Now my shoulders pulsate rather than tremble. I press my head back against the padded rest; my body is semi-arched; every muscle is taut; it is a peculiarly comfortable position. I can actually forget about my body for what seem like quite long periods. I am able to concentrate all my remaining powers of observation and logic upon the Lancaster. My prey.

My heart pounds. There is a variation in the shadows ahead. The coast? I swallow the bitter taste of fear. No, it's not the coast, not yet. A brief reprieve. A few more moments in which to gather the scattered remnants of my courage. I dread the sight of the coast. I will do it. Much will depend on how neatly I hit the Lancaster, how much of an obstacle his tail unit turns out to be. I imagine my wing should slice through it like a knife through butter. Afterwards, I will turn for home—if I am still able. I wonder dully whether I have sufficient fuel.

It feels as if the inside of me has turned to ice. Brittle ice. If I move it will shatter; it will tear and slash at me with its sharp, broken edges. God, the pain is coming back. It rises and spreads from my thigh along each vein. It travels quite slowly, as if relishing each moment of new infliction. Searing heat combines with deathly cold and I yell and scream and bellow every foul word I know. My tortured

194

mind invents new obscenities. I shout about God's excrement, about the phallus of Christ. I hear my voice above the engines' roar. The words intermingle into a single insane explosion of invective. Then, mercifully, the pain ebbs. At once I am contrite. I reason: Very soon I am liable to be called upon to explain those incredibly foul remarks; wouldn't it, therefore, be a sensible idea to apologize right now? Yes. I am sorry; I regret, please forgive. And at the same instant another corner of my brain is asking why I should ask for forgiveness. Didn't the pain compel me to blaspheme? Therefore, isn't the pain to blame? And doesn't God send the pain . . .?

I can't see the Lancaster! Where is he?

Ah, there. I almost lost him.

Something ahead.

A dark, solid-looking line.

The coast!

Involuntarily, my hands react, swinging the aircraft away, out to sea. I have to straighten out and place the aircraft back on course. I imagine swarms of British night-fighters buzzing towards me, hastening to protect their big brother. But nothing so far. All is tranquil. I adjust the throttle setting and the trim and I prepare myself.

Wally saw the streak of land through the shadows. No mistaking it this time: land, without a doubt, and friendly land at that!

He switched his mike on.

'England,' he said simply.

At his side, Paul's face was one huge grin. Harry loudly asked the engines to please keep going a bit longer.

'Nice work, buddy,' said Paul.

You found it, Wally thought, but he was too tired to say it.

He looked at the Messerschmitt. It was flying across their

path, slightly higher, wings angled as it performed a shallow turn. For a long moment it looked as though the Jerry was heading for home. Then he turned sharply.

Paul was pointing at him. Wally nodded.

'What the hell's he up to now?' Paul talked conversationally, as though discussing an interesting specimen at the zoo.

Wally gazed at the coastline. It was taking form, revealing its depth, its rugged line. Hope began to flicker within him. Good God, they had almost made it! There it was: England! Right there! So beautifully close you could get out and swim to it!

So that was where he was going to die.

Oh Christ, it was time to tell the crew to get ready to jump. Time to start climbing. Time to be left alone.

'He's coming up fast behind us, skipper.'

Who? He had to think. God, yes, the Jerry! Perhaps it was another Messerschmitt, not the one that had chased them all the way from Berlin. Not the one with empty ammunition trays. Perhaps this one was at this moment lining up behind M-Mother, taking careful aim, finger on trigger ...

'Christ, skipper, he's coming right at us!'

23

The bomber is in the centre of my window panel. First as a silhouette against the water, then, as the distance between us is gobbled up, I see him in detail. I see the shattered tail turret, the great rents in the fuselage, the blackened wing, the bits of torn metal, thrashing violently in the slipstream. And faces. Behind broken perspex I see the pink blobs of faces framed in helmets of dark brown. A hand presses mask to mouth; above the mask eyes are wide with fear. I can almost hear him, voice shrill, shouting a warning to his crew-mates. Directly beneath the turret is a large letter M in dull red. The left central bar of the M has almost vanished; one of my shells must have entered the fuselage at that point; there is a long, curving scar along which, on both sides, the paint has been neatly sliced away. Further forward the fuselage ribs stare nakedly at me: a V-shaped section of metal skin has vanished. Strangely, the ribs seem undamaged. How could the shells destroy the skin without damaging the ribs? In the cockpit there are two figures: one, the pilot; he sits hunched forward in his seat; I see the light-toned harness-straps over his shoulders. At his side, another man, holding on to a bulkhead; he turns to look at me and his head sags to one side as though in utter despair.

Extraordinary, the clarity of the impressions. That fragment of time is extended far beyond its true span. There seems to be time to be a spectator, to inspect the enemy with professional interest; in incredibly leisurely fashion my eyes travel the length of the bomber's fuselage. I am impressed by what my guns have accomplished; I am impressed by

197

the fact that the Lancaster is still in the air ...

And then I am upon the enemy. I am hurtling directly into his top turret. The bomber makes no attempt to evade me; it simply staggers on through the air, an old crippled bird vainly trying to reach home.

I know precisely what I must do. But I don't. A touch of rudder ... pressure on the stick ... simple actions ... But I don't.

I can do it. I have the courage. The determination. But I don't.

Oh God!

Ahead, the English coast looms out of the darkness. I am perilously low; my propellers barely clear the water. Why don't I simply shove the stick forward? An instant; no more; a mere instant, then eternal peace. But that requires courage. I have none; I have proved that fact conclusively. The brain orders but the body refuses.

My mouth is open. Still I keep gulping down air.

The cliffs become huge in front of me.

A cripple pushed off balance, M-Mother wobbled in the fighter's prop-wash, one wing sagging towards the water. She crabbed to the left, a clumsy, ugly motion, a skidding with wing and tail surfaces working at odds. Her wing-tip stabbed at the water; spray spattered the blue and red of her roundels. Hands thrust at control column, feet at rudder pedals, more hands on throttle levers, dragging her, coaxing her, persuading her to pull herself together for one last bloody effort.

Oh, Christ, but he was tired. Oh Christ, but that was a near thing. Oh Christ, how many near things did that make it? Oh Christ, oh Christ ... Arms of solid lead, eyelids of iron, head crystallizing into a million fragments of separate agony, each striking in turn, every sinew tugged and tightened and stretched to breaking-point. As M-Mother's wings came level, Wally felt tears smarting his eyes. He blinked. He felt a tear on his face.

'You know, that was a goddam near thing.'

Paul sounded indignant, no longer afraid.

Wally nodded. Yes, it was near. But one lost one's capacity for appreciation of near things.

And then they were over England, M-Mother's tattered wings swaying heavily as she cleared the cliff-top by thirty feet. The ground swept away in a gentle descent from the cliff-edge. A house jumped out of the gloom. An English house. A road angled across their path. A road going from somewhere in England to somewhere else in England.

Wally glanced at the port inner. Its propeller stood stiffly. The engine had lost its glycol; it couldn't cool itself; it would run itself to destruction. But it would run long enough to clamber to a decent altitude.

Harry was at his side one hand on the armour-plate at Wally's back, the other on the throttle bank.

'I want you to start the port inner.'

Harry stared. 'The port inner?'

Christ, no time to talk about it, to consider the pros and cons, the ins and outs of it.

'Yes, the port inner. Start it! Pilot to crew.' Crew? What crew? 'I think I can get the kite up to a half-decent altitude. Be ready to jump. And I don't want any bloody arguments, do you understand?'

Paul said, 'You can't jump. You know damn well the kite will spin in the moment you let go of the stick.'

'I said I didn't want any arguments, Paul.'

'I'm not arguing. I'm stating a goddam fact.'

'I'll be all right.'

'Like hell you will.'

Harry yelled, 'Skip, the Jerry again!'

Wally's hands tightened on the controls. Not again, Christ, not again. Desperation was two taloned hands clutching, thrusting at his chest, trying to tear him apart.

'Where is he?'

'Behind us. Bit above us.'

Stay there, for God's sake, stay there. It seemed as if he was being shredded, fibre by fibre. Feebly he wondered whether he would go berserk before he was killed. He could feel his insides palpitating. He watched the grey, indistinct landscape unrolling before him. The same landscape. The same everywhere. Endless countryside, endless journey. What the hell did it all mean? Why should all the myriad events that make up a life lead finally to a seat in a doomed bomber? What was the point of it? He kept thinking: These are the last few moments of my life. I tried to tell myself I didn't believe it but now I know it's true. It's ending just as I was told it would end.

'Starting port inner, skip.'

'OK, start it.'

Harry leant forward, gazing across the cockpit toward the silent Merlin outside; he pressed the starter button. The propeller jerked, stopped, moved again, then suddenly dissolved in a blur. M-Mother swung to the right, but now she was controlled by something close to normal power; she had to obey.

Wally said, 'Get ready to bale out.'

Paul said, 'What about Doug?'

Doug! God, he'd forgotten all about Doug! Damn Doug!

'I'll try and land as soon as you jump.'

'OK,' said Paul. 'I'll ride along with you.'

Ride along ... What the hell was that? Some line out of a Western? Oh Lord, he was too tired to argue ...

'Jerry's dead behind us.'

'How far?'

'Fifty yards or so.'

Swine, thought Wally. Swine, swine, swine.

200

Then Paul shouted, 'That's Nettleford! I'm bloody sure it's Nettleford!'

Wally glanced down. A cluster of houses and a narrow river curving through them.

'Jeez, we're almost dead on,' said Paul delightedly.

It seemed an odd time to be pleased about an exercise in navigation. Wally wet his lips. Perhaps he hadn't heard correctly. Perhaps everyone was going round the bend. Bonkers. Was it any wonder? They were all coming apart at the seams just as poor old M-Mother was. But in a few moments it would be all over. For him, anyway. For the others, there was a fragment of a chance.

'Just follow the river, skipper. Recognize it?'

Turn left at the gasworks.

Paul sounded positively gleeful. 'We'll hit Brocklington in a couple of minutes!'

Literally.

Altimeter: two hundred and fifty feet. Too low. Come on, you lazy bitch. Up them stairs. Sorry! Apologies! Not bitch. Didn't mean it. But please climb. Please. For the lads.

M-Mother shuddered insanely as she staggered upward, her structure protesting, groaning for mercy, for rest, for sweet oblivion.

Paul's voice over the intercom, reporting on the Jerry, sounding like a commentator at a baseball game.

'Still there, buddy. Dead behind. I'm watching him.'

It was then that he had the idea. A ridiculous idea. Lunatic. The sort of idea to be expected from a brain paralysed with fear and fatigue. He told Harry to get into the front turret.

The Australian hesitated an instant, as if suddenly fearful of being sacrificed to save the others. Then he disappeared into the nose. His voice came over the intercom: he was in the turret.

Wally nodded, dimly realizing a second later that Harry

wasn't there to see the nod.

It was an effort to speak. He asked Paul about the Jerry.

'He's straightening up ... Coming in again!'

Tongue over dry lips. 'Get ready,' he told Harry.

He prayed. Please, God, oh please, God, don't let me down. I'll do anything. But please, please ...

'Now!'

Leaden, pain-numbed arms threw M-Mother into a right-hand turn. She groaned, protesting, the dying beast jarred into action yet again. Engines screeching, temperatures soaring, steel expanding, lubricants disintegrating. She roared across the Messerschmitt's path. Wing crossed wing; sword crossing sword. Then the Messerschmitt was past. He had overtaken Mother.

Eyes glazed, Wally jammed the controls to the left.

Mother staggered. Her port wing dropped, flailing the air in a single motion like a paddle slapping at water. Shuddering, she straightened.

Oh Jesus, don't stall! ...

He shoved the nose forward.

'Now!' he bellowed. 'Now!'

Harry fired. He kept his finger on the trigger. The reek of exploding cordite swept back into the cockpit as the fireballs scudded across the night.

Up ... slightly to the left ... Now the Jerry was directly ahead, beginning to turn, tracer dots dancing around it. Then its wing angled down. Something broke away from one engine, fluttered back, disappeared beneath M-Mother's nose.

Harry kept firing.

He kept firing even after the Messerschmitt's starboard engine exploded and its aileron broke free; even after the fighter reared up in its dying agony, trailing flame almost vertically.

*   *   *

I clutch the control column to my stomach. Aircraft slowing. Beginning to shake. Convulsive shudders. Everything rattling, shaking as the speed slows to nothing. Incredibly, the flames from the engine burn upwards for a moment, smothering the propeller. Then, clattering, we tumble. I sit, watching. Control column still pulled back into my body; I am holding on to it as if believing it will protect me. The flames from the starboard engine illuminate the cockpit; the dashboard dials still gaze at me as usual; they should be shouting warnings, winking lights, blaring buzzers. The cockpit is filling with smoke. Bitter-smelling, bitter-tasting stuff. I start to bellow with terror, then I stop. I make no effort to stop; I simply cease to bellow. Perhaps my brain works for me, deciding without my help that it's useless to waste the last few seconds of a life in a lot of pointless bellowing. I feel the dreadful lurchings of the aircraft as it picks up speed, diving, then wobbles off to one side in a drunken sort of attempt to level out. Amazing how light it is now; the flames are snapping at the cockpit windows, melting, scarring the perspex. I am not frightened now. I know I am going to die in a moment but I am not frightened. My mind works well. I am aware of what is happening and in a dull sort of way I feel a certain pride in my ability to accept the situation. I think of my parents again; I see their faces; but I can't recreate their voices. Will I see them in another life? If so it will be soon. I hope there is another life. I hope I am worthy of it. Probably not, probably ... Angled hideously, the earth rushes at me. Right wing down. It will hit first. I see a line of small buildings. Houses. Pavement. A street lamp. A man. He hurls himself down, burying his face in his arms. A fence. A flimsy thing. Through the flames I see the wing hit it ... smash through it. A building. Instinctively I wrench at the control column. The aircraft responds angrily. Grass, neatly trimmed, blurs past me. The building skids by to the left.

Missed. Then my bones crack; the harness bites deeply into me. The aircraft jars; the wing disappears as it hits a tree. Instantly the ground revolves. Something huge and burning breaks away, spilling fire. An engine. The other wing slashes into the ground, crumpling, collapsing. The noise is fantastic. The snapping of a million twigs amplified a million times. Everything is breaking up around me. The aircraft disintegrates as it plunges across the grass. It suddenly rolls; the world is upside down. And now the upside-down world is full of fire. At once I am a madman. Awful, searing heat consumes the last vestiges of my sanity. I see my left glove burning. The fire quickly eats its way up my sleeve. Flesh blackening, bubbling, raw nerves exposed. Bones. Quickly blackened. I try to shield my face but now everything is burning. I scream out, for mercy from God knows whom. I paw at the flames and my hands are flames. Hands touching grass. Grass untouched by fire until my burning hands touch it.

But now there is no pain. No noise, no sight.

I can rest on the grass.

24

The port inner seized—then vomited great waves of flame. Behind the motionless propeller the nacelle was lost in brightness, dancing, whirling brightness that was eating through the structure so that in a moment the wing would fold like paper.

Wally hurled the control column forward. Not an instant to lose. Get the thing on the ground; it was the only hope. Beside him, Harry was frantically pressing the extinguisher buttons. Pointless gesture; no chemical was going to put this fire out.

'Crash landing!'

Too bloody bad he couldn't have dragged her high enough for the others to get out. Too bloody bad. Now everyone was for it. Now it was all coming true.

His hands pulled back on the column as the dull grey ground swung into view. No time to pick and choose a place to land. Just wallop her down on the nearest bit of *terra firma* and hope for the best ...

'You'll make it, buddy ... you'll make it.'

Paul's voice. Words to encourage Wally or Paul? The last communication. Should have wished the crew good luck or something. The crew? The two of them. Anyway, by now, if they had any sense, they would have ripped off their helmets. Good luck, anywaywaywaywayway. Oh Christ, I'm sorry, sorry, Mother, sorry, Father, sorry, Ann, sorry, Owen. For past sins. For thoughts, Unworthiness. Jesus, let it be fast. Make my life just end ... without pain. Can't land there. Houses. A street of them. Horizontal bee-

hive. God, why houses *there?* The wing will fold and we'll
she'll be smothered in plaster and yet she'll smile even
go into someone's drawing-room and we'll kill a girl and
though the years have been stolen from her. A field.
Gasometer, speeding by, top level with kite's wing-tip. Fire
confusing my vision. Am I seeing reflections or the real
thing? Don't know what the hell is ahead. Can't fly around
to look. No time. Not a bit of time left. Hand out. Reach,
touch, grasp the throttle levers. Christ, they're hot! Pull
'em back!

Suddenly the din of the engines ceased. The vibration
ceased. Dumbly, M-Mother sank toward the blurring grass,
the blurring blackness.

Wally gripped the control column as a drowning man
grips a rope. He stared ahead, breathing in shudders, his
brows curling in anticipation of terror. In a second he would
see it: the thing that would kill him. A house, a wall, a
tree. It would come looming up out of the blackness and
there would be nothing he could do. He'd been lucky in
the past but now that luck was all used up. Supply
exhausted.

SweetJesusOhGodAnnbreastshandswarmthsunwater ...

He dragged the control column back into his lap. Nose
up until the last possible instant.

Tears filled his eyes, sparkling, reflecting the berserk
flames.

OhGodChristMother ...

M-Mother's belly hit the ground. A rending, snarling,
grinding clatter. She half bounced. A huge fist hammered
at her, once, twice, again and again, great merciless blows.
Crushing her brave body. Ripping everything from its
moorings. A hideous confusion of noise and movements.
Part of the canopy fell in, struck Wally a glancing blow.
Cold air. Slapping him in the face.

And then, impossibly, it was still.

Wally blinked. Dazed, he realized nothing was moving. Controls motionless. The aircraft was at rest. It had landed. More or less. It had brought them back. It had brought them back. It had brought them back. It had ...

'Skipper! Let's get the hell out!'

'Help me with him!'

Dim, far-away sounds. Voices. A hand grabbed his shoulder. Another fumbled with his harness. Dragging him bodily. It hurt. It hurt like hell. Bumping him against things in the aircraft.

'Quickly, for Christ's sake!'

Cold wind again. He stumbled. Fingers opened. He fell. He felt the dampness of grass. He opened his eyes. He saw his hand outstretched against the grass. A very dirty hand. Oil and grime.

'It's OK. I don't think she's going to burn.'

'Is he hurt?'

'Christ, I don't know. Skipper?'

'Wally? Hey, buddy.'

Yes, yes, yes, yes, I hear you. But I'm examining my hand.

'The bloody wing came right off.'

'Wally?'

He said, 'Hullo, Paul.'

'OK?'

A nod.

'You got us down, buddy. Great job.'

'Lucky.'

'Lucky like hell. It was bloody marvellous driving.'

'Too right,' said Harry's voice.

I am alive, Wally thought. I don't understand why. I *knew* I was going to die. There was no question about it. So why am I alive?

Someone was ringing a bell. There was the sound of a motor.

'We were on fire. How is it that there's no fire?'

Paul pointed. 'You took the port wing right off when you hit the tractor.'

'The what?'

'The tractor.'

'I didn't see it. I didn't even know the port wing had come off.' He smiled. What a hell of a pilot: didn't even know his port wing was missing.

He looked at the port wing and the tractor burning away in a peculiarly deliberate manner; the petroleum-fed flames bulging like fat men.

M-Mother lay awkwardly, lopsidedly, the stub of her port wing sticking out in a mess of broken cables and shredded metal, her starboard wing spreading its dejected expanse over the grass. Part of the tail had collapsed; it hung sadly, twisted backwards after having been dragged along the ground, still connected to the fuselage by wires and buckled tubes.

'Poor old kite.'

'Kenesky's going to be pretty pissed off about it.'

It was an incredibly funny thought. He laughed until he passed out.

25

'It was a damn good show,' said Pinkerton, looming over the bed and beaming in approved hospital manner. 'Getting that kite back, really a damn good show. I got some of the details from Paul and Harry Whittaker. Four of your crew gone, two engines dead, turrets out of action, really I can't tell you how impressed I am.'

'I suppose Doug Griffith is dead.'

Pinkerton nodded. ' 'Fraid so. He died before you landed, according to the MO. Couldn't have done anything for him anyway, he said. The poor chap was too far gone.'

'We threw the bodies of three men overboard.'

'I know. It wasn't a very pleasant thing to do, Wally, but you were right to do it.' He nodded. 'It was the right decision.'

'I hope their parents and wives think so.'

'Don't worry yourself about it.'

Wally stared at the flat white ceiling. The trouble was, he didn't worry about it. He felt no guilt; he felt nothing. Len and Phil and Charlie and Doug were shadowy figures from an incredibly distant past.

'Sergeant Griffith should get a VC for putting out that fire with his bare hands.'

'We'll talk about that later, Wally.'

'And Harry Whittaker shot down a night fighter, did you know that?'

'Yes, it crashed near the village, in the school grounds.' Owen smiled. 'I think it's your kill rather than his.'

'No. He should get a DSO or something.'

'A sergeant can't get a DSO,' said Pinkerton.

'Why the hell not?'

'It's a decoration for officers only; you know that.'

'Is it? That seems unfair.' He found himself looking at the ribbons beneath Pinkerton's wings. DSO and DFC. Hero's badges. You really had to do your stuff to win a DSO. DFCs were different; you could get one for keeping your bowel movements regular. But a DSO was something special.

'The only puzzle,' he said, 'is why the hell I'm alive.'

'You were lucky,' said Pinkerton. 'Damned lucky. The MO says it's nothing serious. Mild concussion, something like that.'

Wally smiled. 'What the hell does he know?' He wriggled his toes in the luxury of the warm bed. It was bloody good to be alive. Bloody good.

Pinkerton grinned too. 'I'd better be on my way,' he said, rising.

'It was nice of you to drop in,' said Wally. 'I mean it.'

'My pleasure.'

'Are the other lads all right? Paul? Harry?'

'Yes, they're OK. As a matter of fact, they want to come and see you but I persuaded them to wait a little while. I knew you'd want to see me first.'

'How right you were. Immediately on waking, I thought, When shall I see my Flight Commander?'

Pinkerton chuckled. 'Oh, and by the way, there's someone else who wants to see you for some strange reason.'

And then Ann was in his arms and her cheeks streamed with tears and she was saying that she hadn't cried until now and she was sorry she couldn't stop crying but, oh God, she was so glad he was alive. 'I thought you were dead, Wally. I did. I thought you were dead but you came back to me, my darling, you came back ...'

She buried her face in his shoulder and he patted her hair

210

and his eyes blurred. The bed will be drenched, he thought. He blinked the dampness away. Ann was talking but her words were muffled by his pyjamas. Gently he turned her head.

'You didn't come back ... All the other aircraft came back except Sugar and yours. And no one knew what had happened. We waited and we waited. Nothing. God, I just turned to ice, Wally. I didn't cry. I couldn't. There were no tears in me. I just didn't feel anything; it was as if I had just frozen. I spoke, I worked but I felt nothing. And then you came in—but we didn't know whether it was you or Sugar or who it was and I hardly dared hope it was you. And then you crashed and I saw flames go shooting up and I thought of you inside and ...'

Wally held her face in his hands.

'You had a worse time than I did.'

She shook her head and turned and kissed his hand. 'No, no, I shouldn't even talk about it. Oh God, I'm so terribly sorry about poor Doug and Charlie and the others. But I'm glad it's them and not you. Is that a terrible thing to say, Wally? I'm sorry if it is but it's the truth. I mean it. The only thing that matters is that you're alive. I love you so much, my darling, and I'm so incredibly grateful that you came back. I didn't sleep. I couldn't. I was too happy. I had some lunch, though.' Her pinkish eyes blinked at him. 'What am I talking about?'

'I don't know but please don't stop.'

She kissed him, twenty-four times, all over his face and neck.

'Oh God, I didn't hurt you, did I?'

'No, do I look hurt?'

'No, but your bandage ...' She looked at it, touched it gently. 'The MO told me it wasn't much.'

'Just a skull fracture.'

'What? Oh, Wally, don't joke about it. God, I'm lucky.

I don't deserve to be so lucky. I've done nothing to deserve it. But I don't care. Lord, now I'm crying again.' She dabbed at his pyjama jacket and then looked up at his bandage again and her tears intensified. Slowly they dried up. 'Sorry.'

'You're sweet and I love you.'

'Oh Wally, I'm so glad ... No, I said that before. But I am glad. And grateful. You know,' she said, 'I was so frightened about this trip. I know you'll say it was hindsight but I had a *feeling* about it.'

'No,' he said. 'I wouldn't call it hindsight.'

The GPO took half the evening to put the call through and then Rose's old twerp of a dad answered it and spent about two bobs' worth asking about the weather in Yorkshire. Finally he said he would get Rose.

'Hullo,' she said. 'How are you?'

She sounded awkward; Harry guessed old man Horner was still within earshot. Nosy bastard.

'I'm OK,' said Harry. 'What about you?'

'I'm all right,' said Rose. Then she added: 'All right.'

Harry straightened. 'You mean, *all right*?'

'Yes.'

'You mean, nothing more to worry about?'

'That's right.'

'Bloody good.' Harry turned and grinned at a bespectacled sergeant with long eyelashes who was waiting to use the phone. 'You're a clever girl, Rosie. How did it happen? Well, it doesn't matter; it *did* happen; that's all that matters, isn't it?'

'Yes; that's right. Yesterday; last night, actually.'

Happily, Harry wondered if it coincided with Doug's last call of 'Bombs gone'.

He said, 'Good girl. Well listen, I've done my last trip. My tour's over now. I'll tell you all about it. I'm getting some leave soon; I don't know just when, but soon. I'll come down to London and see you, shall I? All right? Good-oh!'

They said their goodbyes with affection. Harry told her he would see her soon and he was looking forward to giving her a big hug; Rose told him to take care. He said he certainly would—and she giggled and said she didn't mean that at all and he was a saucy thing.

Back to the bar, a whistle on his lips. He would have another beer then it would be off to bed for a good night's kip. He needed a good sleep. But he felt so happy he wondered whether he would be able to sleep. Perhaps a couple of whiskeys would do the trick, calm him right down. Did the bar have any whiskey? Still immensely pleased with life, he raised his right arm to beckon the bartender.

Then he remembered the letter. It was still there, in his right-hand breast pocket.

Dorothy.

She was sweet too. Wasn't she? Of course she was— although it was hard to remember her exactly. He didn't want to hurt her. Not Dorothy. No reason to. Well, what she didn't know wouldn't hurt her. Hell, if Dorothy was near, would he even *think* of other women? Of course not.

He paid for his drink and took it to a quiet corner and sat down. He had to read the letter. It was a duty. It was going to make him feel a bit of a louse but he had to do it. And he had to reply. That very evening. A penance. It would cleanse his soul. Or something.

He settled himself and cleared his throat as if he intended to read it aloud. He found the letter behind a squashed packet of Senior Service. He brushed the cigarette tobacco fragments away and opened it.

'My dear Harry …'

Rather formal tonight, aren't we, old girl?

'I hope this letter finds you well.'

Standard Mark One opening. Always hoped the same thing.

'By now you must be near the end of your tour of operations. I hope you are still all right every time I read of raids in the newspapers.'

He blinked ponderously. Reading Dorothy's writing wasn't easy after half a dozen pints.

'Now this is going to be difficult for me to tell you about, Harry. All I can do is come right out and say it.'

Harry blinked again.

'I have met someone. He's an American and his name is Ralph Lucas and he is a lieutenant in the US Marines. I have to be honest about it, Harry, and tell you that it's not just a casual friendship. We have committed adultery together.'

Stunned, Harry thought: It's bloody difficult to commit it apart.

He put the letter down and stared at a New Zealand sergeant with a ginger moustache and black eyebrows.

Dorothy? Dorothy and some Yank? Lieutenant Ralph Bloody Lucas of the US Bloody Marines? Impossible. Out of the bloody question. *His* Dorothy?

She wrote: 'I don't know how you will react to this news.'

He shook his head. He didn't know either. He held the letter up as if to confirm its existence. He shook his head again. Surely the whole thing was a mistake. It had to be a mistake. These things happened to *other* people.

Please, Dorothy, say it's a mistake.

But Dorothy said only that Ralph was a wonderful fellow and that she wanted Harry to try to understand.

I don't understand, Harry said silently. I don't understand at all.

It was so appallingly unfair, it was the unfairest thing that had ever happened to anyone at any time in all of history. Unthinkingly, Harry began asking himself questions, rather theatrical questions: Was there no decency left in the world? Was there nothing left to believe in? His face twisted; images replaced words. He clenched his fists. He wanted to hit out, smash at them because he could see them, the two of them, their bodies shiny with obscene sweat; arms, a dozen of them, with writhing, exploring fingers. Dorothy and the Yank. The bloody Yank. The bastard. The handsome, rich bastard. Why did he have to pick on Dorothy, his Dorothy? Weren't there enough girls in America, for God's sake?'

'You're in Wally Mann's crew, aren't you?'

Harry looked up. A sergeant pilot, in best blues, hand in pocket, mug of beer in the other, smiling.

'I hear you bent my kite a bit.'

'What?'

The pilot sat down. 'I'm Kenesky,' he said. 'That was my kite you fellows pranged. I just got back from leave and heard about it. I'm glad you made it, though. It sounds as though it was a dicey trip. You're lucky to be alive.'

Harry nodded absently. 'Yes,' he muttered, 'lucky as hell.'

Faces, pink and smooth and eager for anything extra-curricular, turned to a score of windows as the two lorries rumbled across the quadrangle, around behind the chemy lab, past the assembly hall, then, bumpingly, out to the centre of the sports field. There the lorries stopped. From the first, half a dozen airmen emerged, adjusting forage caps, tugging down on denim blouses. A sergeant stepped from the cab; ordered the airmen to get that nasty mess off the grass and into the back of the second lorry and quick about it. It didn't take long. The nasty mess had little substance; it fell apart as you touched it; it crumbled; it filled the air with tiny black fragments of itself. Hardly worth shovelling the stuff into the lorry; a good stiff breeze would blow it all away in no time flat. Only the wing-tips and the tail section with their black-outlined-in-white crosses and swastikas remained unconsumed. But they were tossed unceremoniously into the back of the second lorry where they lay in a bed of ash; and when the lorry drove off they bounded and the elevators and ailerons jerked: the muscular spasms of a dying eagle.

Sawley, unshaven, his threadbare dressing-gown pulled tightly around him, sat in the corner by the window and sketched Paul. It took an hour. It was a gem: vital and jagged and brittle like life itself.

Then he told Paul to keep the sketch—and not to stare with his mouth hanging open; he wasn't giving him the ruddy Mona Lisa, he said, just a charcoal.

Confused, delighted, Paul stammered his thanks. 'I'll always treasure this, Mr Sawley,' he said. 'It will always hang in my house.'

Sawley nodded. 'I'm glad,' he grunted. 'I'm glad it gives you some pleasure.' He eased himself to his feet and walked stiffly across the studio, his slippers flapping on the uncarpeted floor. He rummaged through a stack of boards and canvases; then he found what he was looking for: a flat package wrapped in brown paper and tied with string.

'Your work, Paul.'

Paul's heart pounded. 'Yes, I remember bringing it.' So Sawley hadn't tossed the stuff aside and forgotten it, after all; he'd considered it worth keeping.

'I wanted another opinion,' Sawley said. 'So I sent your things to some people. People with opinions I respect.' He puffed on his briar, looking out at the village through the window. 'They agreed with me.'

Paul waited. He was more frightened than ever he had been aboard M-Mother. He felt his hands moistening.

Sawley said, 'You can draw, lad. And you've got a good eye.' He paused for an agonizingly long moment. 'Aye, but that's all, you see. We don't see anything original in your work. Nothing to make us sit up and take notice. We think you're a good enough craftsman, but not an artist. Of course, it's only our opinion.'

It didn't take long to utter the words. Paul absorbed them; he managed a thin smile. 'I think I really knew it all along,' he said.

Sawley relit his pipe. 'Bring some more of your work the next time you come, lad. We'll have a look at it and have a talk about it.' He nodded as he spoke, in the mechanical way of the very old.

Paul thanked him and said, yes, he would indeed bring some more work the next time. But he was lying; he knew there would never be a next time.

He dreamt it was all imagination, all happening during the instant of collision. He was still strapped in the pilot's seat, his hands still gripping the controls. Ahead, filling the windscreen, a colossal tractor. Already the aircraft's nose had hit it and had disintegrated into a billion fragments. His body was rocketing forward, seat and harness anchors ripping from the floor, metal and flesh about to fuse in the awful heat of utter annihilation ... and in this scintilla of time his brain created the day-dream: The Miraculous Wheels-Up Landing Complete With Fortuitous Breaking-Away of Burning Wing ...

He awoke, biting into the loose flesh of his wrist. He opened his eyes. Green and puke walls. HM Government shade. Heart pumping out the message that it was only a dream and that he was definitely, indisputably, incredibly alive.

He thought, I do believe I'll ask Ann to marry me today. But it was Pinkerton whose head appeared in the doorway. How was Wally? Better? Good show, good show. Treating him well, were they? Good show, good show. He came in, smiling his smile that was always unexpectedly attractive.

'You've been recommended for a DSO,' he announced.

Wally stared. 'I don't want a DSO,' he said. 'I didn't do anything to deserve one.'

'We think you did,' said Pinkerton.

Wally shook his head. 'No. Doug Griffith deserves a VC. He earned it. He did something brave. All I did was try to survive.'

Pinkerton still smiled. 'You did much more than that. You forget: we were there to see the whole thing. And most impressive it was, shooting down a Jerry right over the field. Almost in the Mess, actually. I was quite relieved when it finished up in the playing-field, I can assure you. Quite a show. We all went dashing over there to look at Jerry and then you came walloping down by the wood ...'

Wally was suddenly chilled. 'Owen,' he said, 'did you see the Jerry immediately after the crash?'

'Yes, why?'

'Did you see the pilot?'

'The pilot? Yes ... but ...'

'He was out of the aircraft, wasn't he, Owen? Burnt to a crisp ... lying on his back ... arms reaching out ...'

Pinkerton frowned. 'You mustn't upset yourself.'

'I'm not upset. But I'm right, aren't I, about the pilot?'

'Well, yes, substantially. Who told you?'

Wally sank back into the pillow. 'I'm not sure,' he said, 'I'm not sure at all.'